End Times

End Times

A Novel

Rio Youers

iUniverse, Inc.
New York Lincoln Shanghai

End Times

iUniverse books may be ordered through booksellers or by contacting:

iUniverse
2021 Pine Lake Road, Suite 100
Lincoln, NE 68512
www.iuniverse.com
1-800-Authors (1-800-288-4677)

Because of the dynamic nature of the Internet, any Web addresses or links contained in this book may have changed since publication and may no longer be valid.

This is a work of fiction. All of the characters, names, incidents, places, organizations, and dialogue in this novel are either the products of the author's imagination or are used fictitiously.

ISBN: 978-0-595-43786-3 (pbk)
ISBN: 978-0-595-69420-4 (cloth)
ISBN: 978-0-595-88116-1 (ebk)

Printed in the United States of America

For Emily

Lotancila

1

You have noticed that everything an Indian does is in a circle, and that is because the Power of the World always works in circles, and everything tries to be round: The sky is round, and I have heard that the earth is round like a ball, and so are all the stars. The wind, in its greatest power, whirls. Birds make their nests in circles, for theirs is the same religion as ours ...

Even the seasons form a great circle in their changing, and always come back again to where they were. The life of a man is a circle from childhood to childhood, and so it is in everything where power moves.

—Nicholas Black Elk, Oglala Sioux

To deliberate is to pursue with intent and consideration, so it is defined, though mention of torment—even pain—is grossly lacking in the definition. Deliberation: to deliberate; without haste, slow. *v.* Consider, debate.

Wherever you are, I'll be there.

I look at my hands, at my aching thumbs and the lines on my palms, where my future has been drawn with some uncertainty, where my past has been etched into the skin like an engraving of despair. Every scar and every line; my hands are like pages—like mouths that want to scream.

Wherever you go, I'll be waiting.

The Girdle of Venus is the curve of her hip, caught in a moment of candescence as she turns to me, as inviting as a flower unfurled. The angle where fate-line touches heart-line is so surely her way of smiling. I recall how each drop of rain on her naked skin was an emerald, and touching her I was a king and shimmering.

Winter rain. It caught one thousand colours, reflecting the world onto which it fell. Prismatic rain, drawing ochre and ruby, the rich hints of the season passed, and the jade of the laughing conifers. It was a cartoon downpour, falling slow and lazy.

Should I even begin, knowing as I do that I may lose you along the way? Such is the ruin of truth when it reaches beyond what we can accept. Tag it fiction and be done (I am a journalist by profession; the cynical might venture that fiction is all I know). Can I degrade myself, my emotions, by appearing here as a character in a story—no more real than Uriah Heep or Holden Caulfield? I want this as much as I want sympathy, but some things, I have learned, run a set course regardless of intervention.

There is a condition in my choosing to continue, one of integrity; I have to be honest to myself, if not to you. What would the following be without honesty, but at best unnecessary and at worst utter humiliation? I will not—I cannot—censor this account. Besides, it is not in my nature to be half-hearted, as you will learn. What you read is what happened, exactly how it happened. It could unsettle you. It could blow your mind. And so, at the risk of losing you along the way, I deliberate.

Cold sweat. Hands aching. Do you want to know about Mia Floats Softly? Should I begin with her, or with the fall of Ursa Major—how I believed heaven to be fragile beneath the feet of angels? Should I tell you about the Legend of White Buffalo Calf Woman? And will you believe me when I tell you about the girl in the woods, who smiled as she burned?

This is going to be more difficult than I thought.

The darkness began long before the telephone call, but it is with this unfinished communication that I will begin. He had a familiar voice, but I couldn't put a face to it. My call display read **PRIVATE NUMBER**, and this was all I could look at as I heard his desperate words, punctuated by the shrill rush of an inhaler. My mind raced. I knew several people with asthma but—

A familiar voice, his warning started but not finished. I heard one final, frantic whoosh on the inhaler and the line went dead, and I was left trembling, listening to the pounding of my heart and, at the other end of the line, nothing but nothing.

*   *   *

'Scott Hennessey?'

'You got me.' I always clamp the handset between my ear and my shoulder; it hurts if I hold it in my hand too long. I looked at the words **PRIVATE NUMBER** on my call display and inquired: 'Who is this?'

'You know who I am. My name would mean nothing to you, I'm sure, but if you were to see me … you'd remember.'

There was no suggestion of enmity in his voice, no threat in his words, though something in their delivery forewarned me. My mouth suddenly became dry.

'I know you?'

'Yes, Scott. Yes you do.'

His breathing was deep winter: wind and ice. As I considered my retort I heard his inhaler for the first time. In the next moment deep winter became the sigh of July.

'I'm sorry, I—'

'Old wounds, Scott. Does time really heal? I used to think so, but every now and then you get those painful little reminders, and it all comes flooding back.'

'Are you from the Centre?'

A second whirr from the inhaler took the wheeze out of his voice. 'Do you mean the Institution? No, Scott. Think back.'

'Listen …' I had no idea what to say. Confusion smiled at me, and my eyes remained fixed on the call display: **PRIVATE NUMBER**. Even when I closed my eyes its afterimage was there, as solid and bright as Vegas. I stuttered something, both aware and afraid of the memories (*think back*). My heart started to beat a little quicker, and then he was talking again. The unhealthy wheeze crept into his voice, more with every word.

'You're doing well for yourself, Scott. That's good. I read your articles in the *Post* when I can, even that indulgent Local Life column you pen under the name of Sarah Shaw. Tell me … is it hard to make a deadline when you don't have any fingers?'

'Who is this?'

'Old wounds. Wouldn't it be heavenly to forget—to forget everything? But she's back: the girl in the woods, and if I can find you … so can she.'

He took another gasp on the inhaler, and there followed a silence during which I was touched by memories. They were half-grasped, like shadows flickering in the dull peace at the back of my mind. I knew they were glimpses of events from my past, and I knew they were bad.

He spoke again. His voice was a sibilant chain of sounds I could barely distinguish, rattling desperately, as if he knew that time were running out.

'What did we do, Scott? What did we *do* to that girl?'

I didn't want to hear what he had to say; I wanted him off of my cloud. My thumb twitched an inch from cutting the connection.

'I don't know what you're talking about,' I breathed.

'She's back, Scott, and she's taking us out one by one. She's already got to the others, and now she's got to me. You're next, Scott. Take—'

He was breathing in gasps. It sounded like air slowly being let out of a balloon. I heard his inhaler puff and pull again—twice, three times.

'I don't know what you're talking about.' But I looked at my deformed hands and thought I *did* know. There were fragments of memory—glimpses of fire, and a naked girl. The shadows at the back of my mind flickered and danced, mocking me. My phantom fingers screwed my hands into fists.

'She killed my fucking wife. I *know* it was her, I—'

'You're crazy,' I said, listening to him wheeze and groan, almost feeling his pain as I tried to push those shadows back where they belonged. 'Do me a favour: hang up and don't bother me again.'

'Do *me* a favour and listen. It could save your life. Get away from here, Scott. Get as far away as you can, and don't come—'

He said no more. I stood with the handset between my shoulder and my ear, listening to a maddening rhonchus as he struggled to breathe, my mind a patchwork of images: memories and faces, all out of focus. I heard the rush of his inhaler one more time, cut short when, blissfully, the line went dead. I suppose he hung up on the verge of some asthmatic collapse, but I couldn't help imagining a slender female arm, blazing, reaching over his shoulder from behind … burning fingers cutting the connection.

I was left with a constant tone filling my head: the sound of nobody there. I thought it was the sweetest sound I had ever heard.

PRIVATE NUMBER didn't call back to finish his warning. I never heard from him again, but would see a photograph of him following his death three months later. The *Post* revelled in the story, and I was able to view some of the photographs deemed too disturbing for publication (X-shots, we call them). As I stared into his dead eyes—recognising him, remembering him—I heard his wheezy words again: *She's already got to the others, and now she's got to me. You're next, Scott.* But by then it was too late; she already had me. Completely.

I let the handset fall into the cradle and stood silently for a moment, hoping the broken pieces of memory would fade into that dull niche in my mind. I put one hand my thumping heart and the other on my thumping head. I have no fingers on either hand; only the thumbs remain. I cut off my fingers with a Japanese sushi knife between the spring of 1990 and the summer of 1993.

We'll get to that later.

*   *   *

The Great Bear: Ursa Major, a distinctive constellation shooting its seven brightest stars into the belly of the night, a pattern known in Europe as the Plough. The Pointers (Alpha and Beta Ursa Major) make up the outside line of its bowl and are thus named because they point towards the polestar, commonly known, of course, as the North Star. There is a double star visible at the apex of the Plough's handle. This is called Mizar, the first ocular double star to be discovered.

On clear winter nights, if you cast your gaze up and to the left of the Great Bear, you can see its little cousin Ursa Minor, the Little Bear. The polestar is also a feature in this constellation, pin-pointing the end of its handle.

The zodiacal constellations march their route along the ecliptic (the yearly track of the sun across the sky). I recall that the sun was in Libra the first time it happened. Libra, meaning 'balance' in Latin. The irony here is that I never needed balance more than at this time. I watched them fall, one after the other. From the Scales on, the essence of myth burning from the sky.

Now take the Andromeda Galaxy, a part of the impressive Andromeda constellation. More than two million light years away, it neighbours our Milky Way, but is the most faraway *anything* that can be seen with the naked eye. To the southeast of this wonder we have the winged horse Pegasus, flying in the heavens with its three brightest stars forming a square (the Great Square of Pegasus) with Alpha Andromedae. Another of the Greek myths immortalised in the stars is Orion the Hunter, standing with his club held ready, my favourite of all the constellations. His belt is three bright stars in a perfect line, his sword a dot-to-dot of three more stars—not quite as bright—hanging south of the belt and encompassed beautifully by one of the more perceptible nebulas in the night sky.

The constellations. Eighty-eight of them on the celestial sphere, and I could make them disappear—every last star. No smoke, no mirrors. Nothing up my sleeve.

According to the ISDD (Institute for the Study of Drug Dependence), only one percent of heroin users start with heroin. There is no prevalent pattern in the transition to addict. Everybody is different, no two reasons are the same, though it would be fair to state that a high percentage start with softer drugs—Class B gear like marijuana or speed, before experimenting with LSD and ecstasy. This is where most users draw the line. The next step up (or down, if we're to be completely honest) is cocaine. At approximately fifty pounds a gram, it is not economically viable for a majority of weekend superstars. A small percentage become addicted, and an even smaller percentage—those with a compulsive disposition, it would appear—make the final leap and shoot heroin into their veins.

But only one percent begin with heroin, and *I* was one of the one percent; I was straight on that horse.

I'm compulsive, and always have been. I get this 'all or nothing' attitude from my father—a gambler who would throw money on anything, on any odds. *Money's not important, Scottie,* he would tell me after my mother's constant remonstrations, and even at an early age I wondered why, if it wasn't important, he kept trying to win the stuff. Terminal illness couldn't even stop him; he was diagnosed with bone cancer at the age of fifty-five, and as it raged through his skeleton like termites through Grandma's furniture, he kept gambling. You'd have thought he would have spent his final months doing something different, something special. Not a chance. Indeed, these were the last words he said to me: *Take this money, Paul* (the cancer had done a number on his mind; he would often call me Paul, or Dennis, sometimes Stuart.). *Put it to win on Kalamazoo in the three-forty at Aintree. Don't forget to take the price—we'll split the winnings.* I looked in the newspaper and saw that there was indeed a horse called Kalamazoo running in the three-forty at Aintree. It appeared my father's deterioration did not stretch to forgetting the names of horses. Respecting his dying wish, I placed the wager and Kalamazoo inched home at fourteens. I spent his half of the winnings on a wreath fashioned into a finishing post. It looked pretty good, and somewhat apt, lying on top of his coffin.

That was my father: a hopeless obsessive. I understood long before he died that this was his nature, just as it is the nature of some to be charitable, or dangerous, or to fill their veins with jack.

All or nothing. That's me, as well—a regular chip.

Not that I blame my decline on my father, or on any genetic inheritance. I take full responsibility for my actions. I was eighteen years old the first time I made the stars disappear. I was a fresher at St. Chad's, Durham, old enough and intelligent enough to know what I was doing. At the time I'm sure I had a reason to shoot up, but I just can't remember what it was. There are a lot of things I don't remember and this frightens me. I'm only thirty years old, after all.

Whatever the reason, I did it, and my addictive nature compelled me to keep doing it, and keep doing it, and keep doing it. I kissed the sky, as Jimi sings in that old song, and the sky responded:

Ursa Major slipped beyond the horizon like a bear on ice. The Scales tipped and Orion fell. One of his stars—Betelgeuse, I think—exploded like fireworks, and I could only stand there, looking at the sky, locked to the spot with my breath caught in my throat and my eyes flashing, thinking that heaven was collapsing. The angels wore boots and they clomped and stomped and heaven—the very ground—was falling beneath them.

Stars spinning. Stars burning. Stars shifting and falling: heroin raced through my veins like electricity through wire, sparking vivid little spasms and jolts that made my mind smoke like an old fuse box with too much juice to handle. This was no hallucination. I had a perfect sense of connection; I knew where I was and what I was doing. The stars were moving, *disappearing*. It was great to watch.

I lasted only three weeks at Chad's as a heroin addict; when I should have been studying and attending lectures I was stealing car stereos and picking pockets, doing whatever was needed to feed my habit. My decline was obvious, as was the reason for my decline, and to the great shame of my mother—who had been so proud when Durham accepted me—I was sent down: a euphemism that means I was told to hit the road, Jack, and don't you come back no more.

And I hit the road. I went *down*. Chasing my addiction, I lived on the city streets for over a year. This was a period of unendurable torment; when I wasn't thinking about my next fix I was contemplating suicide, and only discouraged from this act by the promise of my next fix. I had no pride, no *soul*. Believe me; it doesn't get much worse than having your asshole popped by some slobbering old fag with his dick in an empty Golden Wonder packet. I feel a deep and reverberating sadness that I allowed myself to regress to this state. I feel no humiliation, however, and felt none at the time. This may surprise you, but when you decline into such disrepair you are really too forlorn to feel anything. Humiliation is one of many emotions enveloped by the terrible haze of desperation.

I was 'saved' on December 24th 1989. I went through the throes of turkey and became clean again. I had hands to hold, and I grasped them like a man at the edge of some sheer precipice will grasp the one thing that keeps him from falling. I will detail these three and a half years later, but for now I will tell you that, as well as losing my fingers during this period, I also lost my mind. I admitted myself into a renowned psychiatric institution (known simply as the Centre) in the summer of 1993, where I was brainwashed, drugged, beaten, and sexually abused. This is where I met Sebastian Cross, my best friend, a wheelchair-bound victim of domestic, social, and verbal abuse. Together we agreed, returning side by side to society in the summer of '95, that our time at the Centre had been a cleansing experience, educational, motivational, and enough of a headfuck to destroy most people. But I wasn't most people. I wanted out of that hellhole and my compulsive nature urged me once again.

All or nothing, remember?

After leaving the Centre, it occurred to me that I possessed a degree of intelligence. I had (in a previous life, it seemed) been accepted by one of the country's leading universities, and knew I had the raw materials to achieve something for myself. I didn't want to be just another reformed junkie, waiting for every piss-poor Giro, smoking dope and hitting the Drop-In every Tuesday and Thursday morning to count my sorrows. I got four A-levels, for Christ's sake, I could do anything. But it wasn't that easy; I was shot to hell, physically and mentally. I was a *wreck!* It felt like I had spent the first eighteen years of my life putting a complex jigsaw puzzle together, and then—when it was beginning to look like the picture on the box—deciding to smash it up, trample it, scatter every last piece. I was faced with the task of putting it together again. It was terrifying. I had to find the four corners and all the edges and I didn't even know where to begin looking.

But I did find the edges; they were on page fifty-four of the *Sunday Mirror:* WRITE FOR PROFIT, the advertisement invited. GUARANTEED SUCCESS, it promised. I sent for the details, only to find that the course cost two hundred and seventy-five pounds—too much for a modest budget funded by Mr. and Mrs. Tax Payer. I consulted my counsellor. I told him about the edges. He smiled an endearing smile and assured me there was no problem—that two hundred and seventy-five pounds was a piss in the ocean, and I was enrolled on the promising WRITE FOR PROFIT course with the backing of a government scheme recognising opportunities for the unemployed.

The first thing I had to write (or rather *type*; I can hold a pen but without fingers to keep the pen steady I find writing with one too difficult. Over the years I have developed a typing style with my thumbs and can now produce forty wpm) was a personality assessment that asked searching, personal questions like: *How do you think others view you?* And my favourite: *Is there an emotional or traumatic experience in your past that you feel has influenced you in later life?* I deliberated over my answers for some time, and offered an honest, albeit abridged account of myself. Even back then, it would seem, I was sensitive to the fact that my experiences may be construed as fiction.

I was assigned a personal tutor: Lacy Chadwick, *MA (Oxon)*, a travel writer and columnist for the *Daily Mail*. According to her letter of introduction she would read my work and advise thus. My first creative assignment was to write a review on a magazine of my choice, an exercise I found both frustrating and futile. An alternative review was in order, I decided, and my choice of magazine was the October '95 edition of *MegaDrive Mania*. The 'review' I wrote articulated a bewilderment that so many people would want to play video games when there was so much fresh air to breathe. Except I substituted the words 'video games' with 'mindfucks' and the word 'people' with 'shitballs.'

Shortly after submitting this first work of creative genius, I received a letter saying that Lacy Chadwick, *MA (Oxon)* no longer deemed herself suitable in assisting my literary development and that my new personal tutor would be freelance journalist Oliver Williams, *Ph.D*. Well, Doctor Ollie didn't stay the course, either. He stepped aside after reading two of my essays, the first of which was titled: *The Pain/Exhilaration of Cutting Off Your Own Fingers*, which was followed by a gritty, introspective piece I called *Golden Wonder*. Doctor Ollie was replaced by Harry Lewis, a proofreader for a leading publishing house and the author of the bestselling political satire, *Red Seat, Blue Seat*. Harry was with me all the way, never wilting as I stretched my literary limbs, offering practical advice and fair criticism, counterbalanced with appraisals for flair and originality. It is down to him that I became a successful journalist. Harry, if you're reading this, you the man!

I sold my first article to the *Socialist Worker* three months after beginning my writing course. I am not a socialist. I do not bend to their ideals in any way, but the article expressed sincere concerns for Britain's homeless and berated John

Major's government enough to grab the editor's attention. It was Harry who advised me that, whenever considering a piece for a radical publication, not to be proud or truthful, but to write exactly what they want to read. It worked; I was paid fifty pounds for the piece. I have heard that some writers do not cash the first cheque, but have it framed. Not this writer. Fifty pounds to the unemployed man is tasty money, honey—I cashed it before the ink had dried and went to Voodoo, a popular establishment in the city's shadier district, which has exotic dancers every Wednesday and Friday afternoon.

More cheques followed: two hundred pounds from *GQ*, one hundred and fifty pounds from *Tribune*, one hundred and seventy-five pounds from *New Internationalist*. I even received payment from *Chic* for my first piece written under the name of Sarah Shaw. *What Every Woman Needs*, the article was called. I had wanted to call it, *Why all Men are Bastards*, but felt that Harry's 'write exactly what they want to read' advice would only stretch so far.

I spent a year freelancing for various publications before landing a job with my local newspaper, where I learned the mechanics of journalism. From here I moved to the *Western Post*, which paid enough to get me out of bed every morning. With a healthy income I was able to get back on track and put the past behind me. I had traversed the rocky road; that complex jigsaw puzzle was once again beginning to look like the picture on the box. With this achievement—both emotional and financial—I vowed to never look back. No more living on the streets. No more selling pieces of my soul. No more heroin. Above all else, no more heroin.

And then I met her again—*Ptesan-Wi*—floating in the rain. I met her again and everything changed.

*   *   *

Or at least she appeared to be floating. That was my first thought when I saw her ... that her feet were not touching the ground.

She wore a delicate white summer dress. In July it would flow around her, it would whisper and swell. Now, in the cry of January rain, it held to her body like a child's hand. Her perfect shape was defined. I could see the colour of her skin, and the soft black triangle of her pubic hair.

I slowed my car to a crawl as I neared her. There was a distant groan of thunder. My headlights, sweeping through the rain, washed over her and in an instant she was held, like a beautiful wild creature in the flash of a camera. When I think about her now it is this image that most often comes to mind: *Ptesan-Wi* caught in a moment of light with her dress clinging to her body, dark eyes shining as she looked at me.

Floating towards me.

I stopped the car and wiped the illusion from my eyes. This close, I could see that her feet were firmly on the ground. However, the peculiarity remained. Who was this woman wandering alone, almost naked, in the icy rain? Why was she on this quiet back road, eight miles from the suburbs and at least a mile from the nearest house? Who was she?

She crossed the road and approached my car. A blade of wet hair obscured her face, but couldn't hide the fact that she looked familiar. Another ghost. Another shadow from my past, the data erased when the Centre corrupted my mind's hard drive.

My past, you may have gathered, is not a good place. Most people recall the years that have fallen behind them with a certain fondness, even the bad times, I think. Perspective is sunshine, more often than not. When I think about my past—the parts I can remember—I see whirlwinds and blizzards. I see the colour of the cold. As her eyes fixed on mine I felt the urge to slam the car into gear and go, leaving her in the rain, in the obscure part of my past I have progressed from. Instead I buzzed down the window, smiled, and tried to hide my hands.

'Do I know you?' she asked. She had an accent: American, I thought, but this may have been how she had learned to speak English.

'I don't know.'

'Your face is familiar.'

So is yours, I thought, but said nothing. Biting rain, like exotic insects, swept through the open window. I flinched but kept my eyes fixed on hers. The inclement conditions did not seem to affect her. She stood there, oblivious, looking at me while the cold rain swirled around her.

'Do you need …?' I gestured at the empty passenger seat, thinking that the invitation sounded desperate and ridiculous, and only found consolation in the fact that anything I said would sound ridiculous. The situation was a long way from ordinary.

She smiled, moved around the front of the car, and climbed in on the passenger side with such smooth movement and grace that she seemed to be carried on the wind. I closed the window, she closed the door, and the storm was silenced. The winter wind still made the car sway and the rain hit the bodywork like bullets, but it all seemed far away. Sitting next to a beautiful woman who was not quite a stranger, the storm was just another part of a scene that was surreal and dangerous.

She looked at me, her eyes never lowering, her smile never faltering. 'You're *so* familiar,' she said.

I looked at the road, at the trees swaying in the storm like dancers in the rousing finale of a musical. A fleck of icy water trickled down the right side of my face. A tear? I sighed, and decided it couldn't possibly be. What had Graham Greene written about tears? That we only weep after we are happy … that tears are the result of something enviable.

'I have a common face,' I said. I didn't want her to remember me, and I didn't want to remember her. 'Where am I taking you?'

There was a brief but heavy pause before she replied: 'Home. You're taking me home.'

She told me to U-turn and I steadied myself to reveal my hands. I am self-conscious about them, even though the disfigurement is self-inflicted. They make people stare and children cry. They crept out of my sleeves like frightened, hunted animals out of their hiding places. I put the car into gear and turned around. I have no trouble driving. I have no trouble with most tasks—it's the little things that prove difficult: zipping a fly or reaching into my pocket for loose change. I'll never play a musical instrument or ride a bicycle again, unless it's an old-fashioned model where you have to pedal backwards to brake.

'You have no fingers,' she said, just like that.

I gave her the smile I had given a thousand times, and considered my repertoire of replies. When people ask about my fingers, I usually tell them that I was born this way. It's easier. I will sometimes respond with humour, but not this time.

'I manage,' I said, and the subject was dropped, until later.

I drove through the storm, feeling it push and pull, like an agitated crowd. There was little conversation, only the brief exchanges of strangers who feel they ought to say something. The subject of how we knew each other was not presented, or the issue of her walking in the rain wearing nothing but a gauzy summer dress. I tried to keep my eyes on the road and not on her body, which was coming through what she wore like a bruise.

After two or three miles she indicated a narrow side road cutting away to the west.

'Here. Turn down here.'

I had to brake hard. The rear tyres groaned and slipped before finding their line. My thumbs pinched the wheel, set to react. As I took the turn it occurred to me that I had never noticed this road before, despite the fact that I must have driven past it a hundred times. I didn't think it too peculiar at the time. It lacked significance, given the circumstances.

The lane snaked through two miles of countryside before plunging into a green splash of forest, broken here and there by the naked brown of elm and sycamore. The rain fell slow and fat through the canopy. I thought of Dorothy crash-landing in Oz, and how her world had changed colour. It wasn't only the savage shades of green and the way the rain was falling, it was the sound—the *feel* of the place. The wind was a fluting sigh within the trees. I could feel a new energy. It was like being in the cave behind a waterfall. I believed then—and do now—that I had driven across a ley line into … I don't know exactly … a different place, a different *time*: another notch on the weirdometer.

She never took her eyes off me. It was as if she were fascinated, like an uncivilised tribe in the heart of Africa would be fascinated by the white traveller passing through their village, dashing coins for courtesies. Her eyes were wide, wonderful wells of ebony. Her smile was like the only part of a dream you can remember upon waking.

'Pull over,' she said in a voice as rich as the colour we had driven into, 'and we'll walk from here.'

I stuttered before slowing down—my *body* stuttered, registering the invitation in her words and tone of voice, and not quite believing it. My hesitation amused her. She touched the back of my hand—light as a feather falls—and I snatched it away, a gesture as diffident as hers was wanton.

She said: 'You will walk me home, won't you?'

I stopped the car and looked around. The road curled through the woods like a scar that wants to be hidden. The trees reached to the sky with the grandeur of a child's ambition and I was aware of lightning, like wizardry, making mischief high above their green boughs.

I couldn't see a house.

She saw me looking, wondering, or maybe she read my mind. 'Come on,' she said. 'I'll show you.'

We walked in the rain and she tried to take my hand. I pulled away, but she persisted, and I acquiesced. Her touch made my hand more grotesque, like a ruined face behind a comely mask. I recalled a time when I was very young, walking through a busy town with my mother, who insisted that I hold her hand. I didn't want to but she made me and I trudged at her side, feeling awkward and helpless. I felt that same helplessness now but for a different reason: the strangeness was escalating, and I couldn't stop it.

Where did I know her? The question ran at me, over and over. Half of my mind reached for the answer while the other half blocked it—didn't *want* to know. I trailed at her hand, looking at the colour of her body through her wet summer dress. Memories flickered in my mind like images in a zoetrope. I grasped and let go, grasped and let go.

'I know you.' The trees creaked and swayed and shook their brilliant leafy heads of the rain. The wind rolled and laughed between them, stirring the wet leaves into a glitter of movement. The beautiful woman stopped and looked at me, drew me close. In the dark flash of her eyes I could see that she knew how we were connected. Her delicate lips parted. She would tell me, I was sure, and I braced myself for the fever of recollection. Instead she said: 'We're almost there,' and kissed a spot of rain from my cheek, like a tear kissed away in a moment of tenderness and understanding. She turned and walked through the woods, through the rain, with me trailing at her hand, head down and mystified.

It had been a long time since I had been intimate with a woman. I could remember the last time, like a person who has given up smoking can remember their last cigarette. Her name was Shirley and we'd fucked all night—hard animal sex—while the party hollered and howled around us, and the band played dirty rock and roll. My bandaged hands had poured blood as each orgasm shook my body. My back is tattooed with the scars she gave me (Shirley had hooks instead of hands). I've never been lucky with women; my hands scare them away, it's as simple as that. But this beautiful stranger was showing an affection I had never known before. She radiated sexuality. I could feel it, and it's all too easy to say that the only reason I could was because she was young and pretty and almost naked, but there was more: a passion in the way she held my hand; an ardour in the way her hair fell over her shoulders and shone in the rain. There was adventure in her eyes, something vibrant and powerful—and yes; I understood that there was something dangerous there, too. But I was spellbound and I followed her; I had been left wanting for too long. What man wouldn't?

By the time we arrived at her house I was cold and soaked. She may have been indifferent to the conditions but I was not, and I longed for a warm, dry room. Candlelight shimmered in the windows of her house. Maybe it was the fact that it was nestled deep in the woods, but it looked like something from a fairy tale to me.

'Is someone home?' I asked. The candlelight created strips of shadow that danced beyond the windows with a human quality.

'No,' she replied, showing me the adventure in her eyes, the danger in her smile.

'You've left candles burning. That's—'

'What?'

I wanted to tell her that it was a good way to set your house on fire, but the words were pointless. I don't know why I questioned that she'd leave candles burning in an empty house, considering I'd found her walking, barely dressed, in the winter rain. When it came to conforming to the norm, it seemed she wasn't interested.

'Come on,' she said. 'Let's get out of these wet clothes.'

Chimes outside her front door announced our arrival—blanched seashells depending from lengths of nylon, chattering contentedly in the wind. We passed beneath them and into her house, which seemed to breathe us in. When the door was closed and my eyes had adjusted to the change of light, I could see that we were in a large room: a living and dining area with a Native American influence. It wasn't overrun with crafts and ornaments. There were no headdresses standing in the corners or dreamcatchers spinning over the doors, but there was something in the colour scheme and the arrangement of furniture that gave it a native flavour. It was enhanced by the candlelight, and by the way the shadows moved.

I gestured at the walls—painted in broad strokes of russet and teal—and at a star quilt draped over one of the chairs. 'Where did ... are you ...?' I looked at the shine of her raven hair, at her brown skin and midnight eyes. 'Are you a descendant of ... you know, part of a tribe ...?'

'Lakota Sioux,' she whispered in reply. 'Pure-blooded.'

'What are you doing in England? Are you—?'

'You ask too many questions,' she said. 'You talk too much.' She moved into the centre of the room and began to unfasten her dress: a single bow at the back, which she pulled, and the garment—clinging though it was—was ready to slip from her.

'Lakota Sioux,' I repeated, and then she was wearing nothing at all; with a slight shrug the dress slipped from her shoulders, revealing her wet body, and the blush of desire. I gasped, took a step back. Naked girls were nothing new; Sebby and I frequented Voodoo, but this was different. *She* was different.

'Are you aware of what you're doing?'

'What am I doing?'

'Putting me in a compromising position.'

'So ... compromise.' She walked towards me, the rain running out of her hair and onto her bare skin, cascading where my strange hands longed to touch.

'This can't be happening.'

'Don't say anything.'

'This sort of thing just—'

'You don't have to say anything.'

I followed a single drop of rain—it looked like an emerald in the green light—as it trickled down her body, and couldn't help but to imagine a ghost-finger taking the same slow and teasing course. I staggered at the thought, blinking rain or tears from my eyes as she stepped closer. There would be too much sensation for the tip of one finger to take, trailing the emerald as it meandered down, farther down, diving into the soft nest of her pubic hair like the road had dived into the forest. How could one fingertip contain the sensation? My dazed mind likened it to pushing a finger into a plug socket; the shock would stop your heart. Even so, my hands screamed to hold her, phantom fingers flexing, wanting to trace every jewel that trickled from her hair to the tips of her toes, and wanting more: to hold her in my arms, push my body into hers, and stay there forever.

'I want you,' I said.

'I know.'

I reached out to her, thumbs sensing the way like antennae. I could feel tears gather in the corners of my eyes. She guided my palms as if I were blind, placing them on her body, and I could only stand there, trembling, staring stupidly at my distorted hands on her flawless brown skin. Tears spilled from my eyes and ran down my face in flashes, the way the rain ran down her body. She closed her hands over my own and moved them to her breasts.

'There.'

This rare pleasure, senses dancing, the heat of our bodies making me forget the peculiarity of it all. I was drowned in the moment. It didn't matter that I had found her walking, barely dressed, in the rain. It didn't matter that she lived in a house in the woods like a character in a fairy tale, and that she left candles burning while she was out. It didn't matter that she was familiar: a face from a past I had put behind me. All that mattered was the moment, and that I was lost in it and whole again—for the first time in so very long, I was *whole*.

Spellbound.

She led me to her bedroom: a beautiful room with the same Lakota influence. There was a painting of Crazy Horse on the wall and she kissed every inch of my wet skin beneath his serene gaze. I'll never forget how her lips had felt on the parts of my body that hadn't been touched by another person for so long. She made my soul tremble, and my spirit cry. I sank into the folds of her bed with her on top of me. When I close my eyes I can see her dangerous smile and feel the heat as she slipped me inside her. There was rhythm, rhythm like a chant, like a thousand drums, like two furious heartbeats. I will always feel it, and will always remember the fire in her eyes.

She didn't speak as we made love, but I looked into the fire and knew what she was thinking: *Now I've got you, now you're mine.* With the storm raging, the chimes crying, and a thousand drums beating ... I looked into the fire and knew that I was lost.

*   *   *

Dreams slide away, most of them the instant you wake, while others slide with time. Sometimes a dream can stay with you, locked in your mind through all the years, through every happiness and anguish, outliving memories of times too rich to be forgotten, but forgotten nonetheless. Dreams slide away, but every now and then ...

I am flying in the one dream I can remember. The world below me is far away, yet I determine impossible detail. I fly over rivers and mountains, and above the smoky scream of a hundred cities. I watch a train leave its station and I follow its track as it curves and shudders towards its destination. I touch the birds as they fly below me, fingers lost in the silky riffle of their feathers. I arch my back, soar higher, and find a track of my own: the vapour trail of a soaring 747, and I follow it until I am breathless with exhilaration. It is a dream, and I know it, just as I know that this rush is something I will never experience when I am awake.

And then: *Ptesan-Wi*, dark eyes wild and staring into mine, long hair dancing over my face as she moaned and gyrated. Her small breasts brushed against my chest. I could taste her sweat on my lips. We burned together, we came together, and the exhilaration of my dream was surpassed.

Her hands in my hair, both of us crying as she pressed against me and I pushed and *pushed*, absorbing her beauty. It was poetic, it was chaotic: a shimmering, tangled shape wrapped in candlelight. We ascended to orgasm and I could hear the clamour of our hearts. I thought it was the thunder, but realised—with the first paralysing sensation of orgasm—that it was the sound of a stampede: a furious herd rushing through the woods, causing the house to shake to its foundations. *Buffalo,* my exhilarated, disbelieving mind assured me. *That's the sound of the buffalo charging.* My thoughts dissipated as I came inside her, my body rigid and my mouth touching hers: one kiss, one body (intense, erotic sculpture), and the sound of our hearts a stampede.

*   *   *

'I don't even know your name. My body feels alive in a way it hasn't for so long—if ever—and I don't even know your name.'

'Is it important?'

I considered this. 'I may never see you again, and I want to put a name to the memory.'

We were lying in bed, still naked, even though an hour had passed since we had made love. She lay with her head on my chest, drawing figure eights around my navel with the tip of her forefinger. Crazy Horse regarded us with a solemn expression, as if we had partaken in a sacrilegious act. The artist had given him sad eyes, colourless, yet full of wisdom. The storm had died to a drizzle that looked like mist and the light was being chased out of the sky. I could hear the chimes singing: a sound that filled me with such peace that I didn't want to move from that moment, from her bed, and her touch. I didn't want to go back through the woods to where my car was parked on the other side of the ley line, where the world was different.

She told me that her name was Mia. 'Will I star in your fantasies?' she asked.

'Always,' I told her.

She lifted her head from my chest and looked at me. Candlelight played in her eyes. 'Will you think of me when you're alone?'

'I don't want to be alone, but if I am I'll think of you.'

'Like a movie star. What's your name?'

'For your fantasies?'

'Of course.'

My soul made music at the thought of her lying in bed, thinking of me. I told her that my name was Scott ... that I wanted to star in the movie in her mind. I wrote my name in lights with my hands, thumbs flashing. 'Scott Hennessey in—'

'What happened to your fingers, Scott?'

The words died on my lips, and the music in my soul was silenced. For the last two hours—in her warmth—I had been whole again, but now I was reduced to what I knew myself to be. Her question had not been asked unkindly, but it was blunt, and presented in a manner that demanded an answer.

My hands fell into my lap, giving up the dream. Mia took them and began to study the lines on my palms. I watched her eyes trace the meandering path of my heart-line and wondered if I should tell her the truth. How would she react if I told her that I had cut off my fingers, one at a time? We are taught that honesty prevails, but I didn't want to repel her; I wanted to see her again. There are times when honesty is better left in the dark, and I decided that this was one of those times.

I told her that I used to work in a sawmill and that my fingers had gotten inti-mate with a machine the 'old hands' called Angry Jack. This was a well-used reply, dating back to my days at the Centre, and a favourite whenever angling for sympathy.

'Poor Scott,' she said, and brought my hand so close to her face that if I had fingers they would have touched her lips. 'Poor little fingers. That must have hurt so much.'

'Not really. Only afterwards, when they were healing.' This *was* the truth; there is an inexplicable exhilaration in cutting off your fingers, a high that tran-scends the pain. I recall that I was sporting a monstrous erection for seven of the eight amputations. Bizarre, but true.

A long silence followed, during which Mia continued to pore over my tragic hands, and I tried to recapture that feeling of wholeness, even though I knew that it had died inside me. Self-consciousness took its place, that old devil with which I was all too familiar, and I tried to take back my hands so that I could hide them. But Mia held tight, and all I could do was lie there and look from her to Crazy Horse. My self-consciousness extended to my nakedness. I shifted my body and half-covered myself beneath the damp sheets.

'You have a broken life-line,' she told me, and at the sound of her voice all other sounds (I was unaware they had been silenced) fell back into place: the chimes, the wind in the trees, the hum and creak of her fairy tale house settling. It was like emerging from water.

'Broken?' I uttered. 'Is that bad?'

'It could be.' She looked at me, that familiar danger touching the corners of her eyes. 'You have secrets, don't you?'

'Everybody has secrets. Tell me what it means to have a broken life-line. Am I going to die young, or something?'

She let go of my hands and I drew them back as if they were reproved exhibits.

'The break indicates change,' Mia said. She sat up, knees drawn to her breasts, ankles crossed, as if she too were suddenly self-conscious. 'The life-line reappear-ing would suggest starting over; not simply turning a new leaf, but becoming a new person—from the soul.'

A small tear rolled from my eye, so small it became trapped by the delicate lines that have come into my face with age and hard learning.

'Change,' she whispered, turning to the face of Crazy Horse. 'The beginning of a new life, the end of old times. In Native American legend the birth of a white buffalo means the same thing: end times. The pessimist may view this as an omi-nous sign, but I—that is we, the Lakota Sioux—regard end times with only a positive spirit: the end of famine, the end of war, the end of greed. Tell me, Scott … how do you see end times, or the break in your life-line? Do you see it as a new beginning?'

'Yes,' I replied, thinking of the way I used to be, remembering how it feels to be so desperate. 'Yes I do, and I have made a new beginning. I have started again.'

'Oh?' Mia reached beneath the sheets, took my hand, and studied my palm again. The wind whipped and howled outside, sending the trees into massive chatter.

'No,' she said at length, letting my hand fall onto her thigh.

'No? What do—?'

'Your time for change hasn't come, Scott. You may think it has, but you haven't reached the break in your life-line.'

I looked at her dubiously. She stared back and there was something about her presence that I found unsettling. My contentment had dissolved. The urge to get out was overwhelming.

'You may have been through trauma, Scott,' she continued, 'but who hasn't? Look inside yourself and you'll see that you are the same person you have always been. At heart you are the same. At heart.'

'You can tell this from reading my palm?'

'No, I can tell from looking into your eyes.'

I got out of bed and dressed with my back to her, partly because of my self-consciousness, but mostly because I didn't want her to read the truth in my eyes; I didn't want her to see that she was right. I had been through the mill, I had seen and done things that could destroy a man's will to live, and had emerged on the other side, not as a new person, as I liked to believe, but as the person I had been before I went in (minus eight fingers). The idea that I had not reached the break in my life-line terrified me. Change? I didn't want *change;* my life was back on track—why rock the boat?

'I don't believe you,' I said, fighting with the fly of my damp chinos and then struggling into my sweater, which smelled of the trees and was heavy with rain-water. 'Our lives are not determined by the lines on our palms. That's bullshit. It's what we do, the decisions we make …'

'And the people we meet.'

I turned to leave but was stopped by the sight of her: this beautiful creature sitting naked on the bed, knees drawn to her breasts and her hair—as dark as a raven's wing—spilling down her back like a cloak. Who was she? Why had she seduced me? And how did she know so much about me? These questions swirled in my mind like tornadoes. I walked to the door on leaden legs. I couldn't take my eyes off her, yet in the face of my solicitude all I wanted was to fall into her warmth once again. She was a drug; she was my weakness.

Who are you? Who are you really?

I looked at the painting of Crazy Horse. His face—fantastic and beautiful, lined with the trials of war and wisdom—looked back at me, and something in the firm set of his mouth urged me to leave.

The girl on the bed smiled at me. A single feather of black hair fell down the middle of her brow and onto the bridge of her nose. She looked wild and wonderful.

A question formed in the maze of my mind and was out of my mouth before I knew I was going to ask it:

'Mia? You say you're Lakota Sioux ...' My voice was hopeless and broken, my body already surrendering. 'Shouldn't you have a name like Black Wolf or Lone Eagle?'

'I have,' she replied, and got off the bed. She stood before me, beautiful, touched by candlelight. She was barely a woman, the first I had made love to in more than eight years, and I wanted her. More than anything in the world, I wanted her again.

'I am White Buffalo,' she said, and that was enough. I tore off my wet sweater and moved towards her—*into* her again. 'I am end times.'

2

What is life? It is the flash of a firefly in the night. It is the breath of a buffalo in the wintertime. It is the little shadow that runs across the grass and loses itself in the sunset.

—Crowfoot, Blackfoot Warrior and Orator

'Do you remember the days of paranoia?' Sebby asked, rolling his chair under the table so that the footrests bumped my shins. He apologised with a blithe hand gesture. I called him a clumsy fucking cripple and he nodded in agreement.

'I miss that fucking place like a hole in the head,' he continued. 'All those nights I would lie awake, listening to the sound of pain. You should write a book about it, Hennessey: a guaranteed bestseller.'

'Too much pain,' I said. Just thinking about the Centre made my skin crawl. Write a book about it? Thanks, but no thanks. To this day I can hear his footsteps echoing down the hall: the nurse we affectionately named 'Janice.' Sometimes he would demand of me. Other times—the times for which I suppose I should have been grateful—he would have me strip naked while he stood just inside the doorway whacking off. Even touching upon it now, years later, fills me with despair. But every cloud has a silver lining: I met Sebby during the days of paranoia, when I would lie awake at night either crying or listening to others cry, knowing that the drugs they were feeding me were turning my brain to paste, but actually looking forward to the next dose because they would make the pain subside, and things wouldn't appear so bad.

Sebby was my silver lining.

The Centre. Some would call it a psychiatric institution, but the Centre is a better name. When you are at the centre of anything you are at the furthest point from the perimeter, and that's exactly how you were in that place. That's exactly how they made you feel. Maybe, one day, somebody will write about it. But not this kid, and I'll spare you the details here. I know I wrote earlier that I would not censor this account, but I will not write about my time at the Centre for two reasons: (1) It doesn't form a part of what I want to tell you, and (2) I don't want the pain.

Sebby flicked the hair from his eyes and smiled. He had a beautiful smile. It didn't make his face come alive the way a smile can for some people, because his face was *always* alive. The twenty-six years of his life were heavy with trauma, but you would never know it from looking at him. The pain was outshone by the gleam in his eyes. His smile made him more beautiful, more incredible. Imagine a butterfly—wild colour—on the petals of a summer flower. That was Sebby's smile.

'It made us stronger, Scottie. Remember that.'

'Always.'

'And we're never going back. It's behind us now.'

I raised my bottle, and Sebby raised his.

'Good times, brother.'

'I'll drink to that.'

It was Friday afternoon and Voodoo was jumping. The resident DJ was spinning classic sounds: smoky rock and Atlantic soul, making Voodoo feel like the only place to be, the only place on earth. The dancers were doing their thing, dealing in denominations of pride. Notorious had moved for us: a sensual, full-bodied wonder from the Caribbean. Epiphany was next, a favourite of ours; she would feign pity but give us her unabashed attention. Kudos for that.

We finished our beers and a waitress I had never seen before approached our table. She had a smile like lightning, but it disappeared the moment she saw my hands.

'Two more,' I said, showing her my thumbs the way Arthur Fonzarelli would. She dashed away, clearly upset.

'You scared her,' Sebby said, and laughed.

'I'm a freakshow,' I said with a smile, and then dropped a bomb: 'But at least I have a girlfriend.'

'You have a *what?*' He pushed himself away from the table and rolled back, giving the impression of being knocked back with amazement. 'I don't believe it, Hennessey. Not for one second.'

'Believe it.'

'How long does she take to inflate?'

I couldn't stop smiling; just thinking about Mia had this effect on me. 'Dream on, Sebby. She's real, and she's beautiful.'

'Are you serious?'

'As a heart attack.'

'Well come on ... I need details.' He rolled back in, bumped my fucking shins again. 'Is this why I haven't heard from you in over two weeks?'

'I've been preoccupied.'

'I bet you have, you dirty dog.'

A waitress brought our drinks (a different waitress, I noted with a wry smile). Sebby flipped open his wallet and handed her a ten pound note.

'You can keep the change if you shake your ass for me,' he said.

'I'm not a dancer,' she retorted, but she kept the change, wiggled her ass, then winked at him and walked away. Sebby howled and slapped the armrests on his wheelchair. His hair—thick black dreadlocks—covered most of his face, but I could still see his butterfly-smile.

'I think she likes you,' I said.

'I'm good for her ego.' Sebby took a drink, eyes gleaming. 'Okay, don't keep me in suspense, Scottie: I want to know about your new girlfriend. I want to know everything.'

I was still too emotional—too *taken*—to tell Sebby everything, and I certainly wasn't prepared to open my heart in the middle of a skin bar. I told him as much as I thought was appropriate, and Sebby sensed I was holding out on him.

'This reticence ... is it because you *respect* her, Scottie, or are you getting bashful in your old age?'

'Both,' I said. 'And I don't want to jinx it. She's good for me.'

'That's bullshit,' Sebby said. 'You're pussy-blind. It's been two weeks. You don't even *know* her yet.'

'You're wrong.' My voice faltered when I spoke because Sebby *wasn't* wrong. Two weeks, and I still knew nothing about her. I was afraid that knowing too much would awaken shadows, and I didn't want that. I didn't want to remember.

'Her name is Mia?'

'Yeah ...'

'Pretty name.'

'Pretty girl.'

'Have you seen her since?'

'Twice,' I replied, and recalling these moments caused my heart to move in my chest with new rhythm. They were made more memorable by the fact that she had come to me. I had looked for her, of course, but with no success. I had spent hours—*days*—blitzing Internet search engines and directories, but found no evidence that Mia existed. I tried to find her fairy tale house in the woods, but there was nothing. I couldn't even find the narrow road that led into the woods—the road with the ley line pulled across it. My body ached with frustration, my head reeled with confusion. How could she disappear? How could a house—a *road*—disappear? It was as if I had dreamt the encounter, as if Mia had never existed at all.

I looked at my hands, at my broken life-line, and remembered how she had touched them. I hadn't imagined that moment; the girl was real, and I *needed* her. She had become my heroin(e). I would think about her and tremble. I would imagine her touch and feel pain in body and mind; I was drying-out.

She found me. I thought she was an illusion: the wish of a desperate mind. She looked at me from the other side of a crowded street, and once again she appeared to be floating. Nobody noticed her, despite her beauty, despite the fact that it was the first day of February and she was only wearing the same summer dress, despite the fact that her feet were hovering twelve inches from the pavement. I raised my hand and saw her smile. My heart roared. A bus passed between us—I lost her for a split second and nearly died. I blinked, reached out, and she was there again. She smiled at me. Her feet were on the ground.

She crossed the road, put her arms around my waist, and pressed her face to my chest. I kissed the top of her head. Her hair was rich with the scent of the forest.

'Are you real?' I asked.

She kissed me, and I knew that she was.

'I've missed you,' I told her.

'I know,' she said.

We went to my place: a studio apartment with a balcony overlooking the river. We made love deep into the night, and came together every time. Charlie Parker played on the stereo, disguising the sound of our passion. But I felt Mia's heartbeat; I felt the stampede.

'Will I see you again?' I asked when we had finished, her hair lying on my body, half covering me, the night turning towards dawn like a weary traveller coming home.

'I know where you are,' Mia assured me. 'I'll find you.'

It was snowing; the city was white. Mia ghosted into my apartment and floated to me. I was standing at the window, watching the snow, and my soul trembled as I saw her reflection draw near. With the swirl of snowfall, and her dress so white, it seemed I could almost see through her.

She touched my shoulder.

'Play Bird,' she suggested in a whisper that sounded the way the snow might feel. 'Play it loud. Play it over and over ...'

She was more than an obsession. I had been obsessed before—many times—and I can tell you that my need for Mia went deeper. I framed her in my mind like an icon. She floated in my dreams in wonderful light, and I would wake up weeping, my ghost-fingers clutching the side of the bed that was nothing without her. Every time I drew breath I longed to breathe her in. Every thing I bought and every decision I made was influenced by how I thought she'd react. I imagined the sound of the buffalo charging, and would spend hours praying I'd see her again. But I would not waste my prayers on God; I would pray to Mia herself, believing I was connected to her on some astral or telepathic level. '*I know you can hear me,*' I would whisper to silent rooms and empty spaces, thumbs crossed over clasping palms. '*I want you again, I need you ...*' Praying into the night until the Amens became dreams in which she starred. Praying; she had become my religion.

With all this pain and longing, I needed something, *anything*, to ease me. I needed to stop the craving, and there was really only one thing to turn to.

'Earth to Planet Hennessey ...'

'Huh? What?'

'You've been staring into space for the last five minutes.' Sebby snapped his fingers in front of my eyes. 'Come on, get with it. You were telling me about Mia.'

'Yeah ...'

'And then you just trailed off. I thought I lost you for a moment there.'

I looked around Voodoo, at the waitresses moving between the tables. They were all wearing crop tops, jean shorts, and false smiles: a uniform to elicit gratuities. I looked at their legs: long, smooth, and shining with tan. I imagined Mia's legs, wrapped around me, urging me. All of a sudden, thinking about Mia and looking at these girls, my hands started to tremble and cold runnels of sweat trickled between my shoulder blades. Sebby looked at me, but didn't see me. He didn't see the pain.

The room wavered and I clutched the underside of my chair. The waitress who had shaken her ass for Sebby passed our table, her breasts accentuated by the design of her bra, indulging every lecherous, hungry, thirsty pair of eyes shining in the gloom. I could only see Mia, though—imagining the natural shape of her breasts, dark nipples swollen in anticipation of my touch. I could almost feel them pushed against my chest as her body rolled beneath mine, and could hear her whispering in my ear, sweet Lakota eyes flashing. I ran the back of my savaged hand across my forehead. I couldn't stop my body from shaking.

'Hey, Scottie ...' Sebby was alarmed. He reached across the table, took my hand, but I snatched it away. 'Hey, man ... you okay?'

I wanted to tell him that I was *not* okay—that I was far from fucking okay. I had become an addict, and I needed Mia so desperately that everything inside me was hurting.

'Can I get you anything?'

'No, I ...'

'You don't look good, brother.'

'Need ... toilet.' I got to my feet and swayed towards the washroom. The music changed as I rolled from left to right: The Velvet Underground giving way to Steve Earle singing 'Copperhead Row.' I remember this vividly, and I remember bumping into a table and staggering into a waitress. She called me a clumsy drunken bastard and pushed me away. I stared—trembling and sweating—at her body, at her eyes, at the tight strawberry-swell of her cunt at the top of her perfect legs, thinking of Mia and *wanting* Mia and knowing that without her next to me and loving me there was really only one thing to turn to.

To stop the pain, to soothe my desire, what could I do but chase the dragon?

*   *   *

The foremost advantage of injecting heroin is the immediate high; it goes directly into the bloodstream and—*whoosh*—flies to the brain like a rocket. There are disadvantages, of course: the telltale tracks left by the needle, and one's tolerance increasing at a quicker rate. The dangers inherent in fixing should also be considered, effected by such lapses as missing the vein, using dirty needles, or bad technique. These can include thrombosis, septicaemia, HIV, hepatitis B, abscesses, and heart disease. There are more, but this is not a dissertation. I will tell you that I knew a junkie who damaged his veins so completely that gangrene set in. Killed him in the end. Fucking *gangrene*. I thought that nasty shit only existed in places like Africa and South America.

This is not an endorsement to administer the drug in another way. You will still become addicted, your tolerance will still increase, and your addiction will kill you. The dangers are fewer, but they are still there. Equipped with this knowledge, a majority of heroin users will nonetheless opt for the more dangerous method of mainlining. I would have, given the choice. Unfortunately, this option had been taken away from me; control is an essential factor, and no fingers = no control. Consequently, I had two choices: I could snort, or chase the dragon. The former method is easier, but has never appealed to me; I knew a junkie who'd taken so much skag up his nose that he'd rotted his septum clean away—left him with a hole in his face the size of a ten pence piece.

Chase the dragon, then.

I would always struggle with the procedure, spilling precious powder as my unsightly pincer-grip negotiated a union between the foil and the flame of my Zippo. Before long the heroin would begin to cool and run to black oil, giving off its vapour. I would then inhale this vapour through a thin tube held precariously between my thumb and the tough, ugly part of my hand that is part-knuckle and part-scar tissue. My hands would tremble throughout, but inside I shimmered with the knowledge that when the hit arrived, it would be worth all the effort.

I would smoke four bags a day, sometimes more, depending on how often Mia snaked into my thoughts and crippled me, leaving me helpless and aching without her. I know what you're thinking—that I'm a gutless piece of shit, right? But know this: I never chased the dragon when I was with Mia. I didn't need to; she fulfilled that desire in me. It was only when she wasn't around and I had to fill the silent space in my life that I turned to heroin. But I never felt I was addicted to the drug, I want to make that perfectly clear. It was Mia. She was my addiction … the way she made me feel.

*   *   *

I slumped against the wall of the cubicle with one hand on the toilet seat and the other on my head, letting it come, just letting it open the door and come on in. The trembling had stopped already, my cold sweat evaporating as satisfaction filled my soul. I could hear the DJ introducing Epiphany: '… *her body is a vision, her moves are a revelation* …' and I fell across the toilet seat with a ridiculous grin on my face, knowing that the constellations were shifting—wherever the world was dark: slipping and sliding and blinking out of existence forever.

Epiphany's backing track drifted to me from some distant planet, a sexy rock/blues number I tried to sing along with. But all I could do was drool and mumble, my glazed eyes transfixed by the flame of my Zippo, which still burned and flickered like one of the candles in Mia's house.

*   *   *

'So when do I get to meet the lucky lady?' Sebby asked as I pushed him home, a long time after the girls had stopped dancing. I needed to wait until the hit had worn off before I tried walking anywhere. Sebby seemed happy to wait. He drank beer and thought about Epiphany (and Notorious, and Midnight, and Tiánah). I stared at the ceiling, not drinking beer, thinking about Mia.

'I'll arrange something,' I said, wondering when I would see Mia to be *able* to arrange something. It could be that night, or not until the following week. I even understood that it could be never. But I didn't believe that; we had just started out. We were connecting.

'Maybe we can have a party,' Sebby suggested. He craned his head around and looked at me, and I didn't care for the glimmer in his eyes. 'Just the three of us. What do you think, Scottie … a *ménage à trois?*'

'A party, yes. A *ménage à trois*, I don't think so.'

'She wouldn't go for it?'

'Not in a million years, and neither would I.'

'Well you can sit out, Scottie. I'll do the dirty work, I don't mind.'

'That's enough, Sebby.' I felt a flash of anger but Sebby didn't pick up on it. Why would he? I'd never lost my temper with him before, despite his frequent off-colour remarks. But that was his way. I expected it and loved him for it. Only this time—talking about Mia—I didn't like it. Not at all.

'I could double-dose on the rootjuice,' he said, not noticing that I was pushing a little faster. 'I'll get a hard-on that'll last until Christmas.'

'Sebby, I don't like you talking about—'

'Bang her sweet little—'

He didn't get to finish; I pushed his wheelchair as hard as I could and let go. He zoomed away from me, in a straight line to begin with, but then the little front wheels started to wobble and he veered off to the left. He would have gone into the road had his reactions not kicked in: he snatched at the rear wheels. The chair jerked, span, and then went over, spilling my crippled friend onto the pavement. He fell like a child going over in the sack race on school sports' day, the breath rushing out of his lungs and silencing his foul mouth.

I caught up to him and kicked his useless legs. Not hard, but hard enough to make me feel sick whenever I think about it. In the next instant I was down on my knees with my hands lost in his dreads. I pulled violently, noticing the tears edging from the corners of his eyes.

'Don't *ever* talk about Mia like that!'

'Sorry, Scott—*Jesus!*'

'She's not a whore. Get that into your fucking head right now.'

'I was kidding … fucksake …'

'You can pump your cock with all the chemicals you want—save your sick fucking erections for Television X. Don't even *think* about Mia.'

'Okay, okay!'

'Am I clear?'

'Yes, Christ *yes*.'

'Good.' I got to my feet, taking a step away from him, and was hit by two conflicting feelings: I wanted to leave him there—leave him lying hurt, let him struggle home by himself. At the same time I could feel my anger giving way to a resounding sense of shame that haunts me to this day. What had I done? Christ, I had never so much as raised my voice at Sebby before.

Hurt by these emotions, I looked at my best friend lying on the pavement. All at once I wanted to be anywhere but there, somewhere in the twilight with only Mia beside me, although I understood—even then—that she was the reason I felt the way I did. Every happiness, every little heartbreak: Mia.

'Oh Christ, man. Oh Jesus, Sebby, I'm sorry.' I righted his wheelchair, making this one pitiful gesture to help him. He clambered into it himself and I could only watch, feeling like the world's biggest shithead. 'I haven't been myself these past few weeks.'

'I wonder why.' Sebby glared at me, his eyes shining with shock and distrust.

'What does that mean?'

He wheeled himself away without replying, pushing hard so that I had to jog to keep up with him. When I took the handles to resume the pushing he snapped at me to leave alone—he'd push himself.

'I said I was sorry.'

'Go home, Scott,' he snapped. 'Call me when you've had the lobotomy. Maybe we can do Voodoo again.'

'Don't turn this on me. You started it by—'

'Just leave me *alone*.'

'I apologised, didn't I? What the fuck is all this about? Are you jealous?'

In one dextrous movement Sebby stopped his wheelchair and span it one-eighty so that he was facing me. 'Yeah, that's it—I'm *greeeeeeeeen* with envy. I would love to date a girl who'd transform me into a five-star fucking moron.' He was breathing hard. There were tiny flecks of spittle on his lower lip. 'She must give you everything you need. Tell me, did you enjoy the hit this afternoon?'

I was hit by the feeling that is often described as *sinking*, but is actually more like a massive shot of Novocaine; I was numb, body and soul. I couldn't move. I couldn't speak.

'I'm not blind, Scott,' Sebby continued. His voice seemed distant, slightly out of sync with the movement of his lips. 'And I'm not stupid. I can see you're back on heroin. Jesus, you've been gouching all afternoon.'

I wanted to deny it, of course. *That's bullshit, Sebby*, I wanted to say. *You're pissed off because I have a girlfriend, and all you have is a prescription for your root-juice and a few porno movies to jack-off to.* When I tried to speak I could manage only broken sounds, as if the words had shattered inside my head and fallen off my tongue in fragments.

Sebby proceeded to tell me that I looked like shit. '*Like shit!*' (He managed to italicise the predicate by speaking through gritted teeth and emphasising with his hands.) 'I suggest you take a good look at yourself,' he continued. 'Look long and hard, Scott, and ask yourself ... is she worth it?'

Some of the feeling returned: heat in the pit of my stomach, tingling in my thumbs. I was feeling emotion, specifically anger. I wanted to tip him out of that chair again. I wanted to kick him black and blue.

He wheeled around and pushed away from me. I would have gone after him, but the life was seeping into my body too slowly and all I could do was watch him go. I tried to find the words to justify my anger, remove every trace of shame, and turn the tables to make him look like the world's biggest shithead. Unfortunately, the words did not exist; Sebby was right on the money, and when faced with such an irrefutable fact the only option available—if you want to maintain at least a shred of dignity—is to keep your mouth shut.

'*You're just jealous!*' I shouted after him, duly surrendering dignity. I have learned that there is little, if any, good sense in anger.

'Your face and my ass, Scottie.' It wasn't a brilliant finishing blow. It wasn't clever, or funny, but it was enough.

My face and his ass: again, right on the money. I cursed the little bastard under my breath and walked home.

*   *   *

By the time I arrived at my apartment I had managed to dismiss the bust-up with Sebby as little more than a minor blip—the sort of inconsequential wrangle between close friends that is only to be expected when one of them branches off into a new relationship. If I was at all concerned I was doing a good job of convincing myself otherwise. I would call him later in the week and take him to Voodoo. A dose of Epiphany washed down with a couple of beers should do the trick. The thought that everything around me was starting to turn bad never crossed my mind. Okay, so I was back on heroin, I looked like shit (like *shit*, actually), I was given to uncharacteristic flashes of anger, and had fallen out with my best friend. This may sound like the beginning of a decline I should have seen coming, but I was blind, I was in *love*. You know how that can be.

Even so, Sebby's on-the-money observation that I was back on Horse had unsettled me, and in a moment of optimism (and naïvety) I resolved to go clean before it really took hold. I would use imagination to control my desire. Fantasies of Mia and I wrapped in each other's arms like Burt Lancaster and Deborah Kerr in *From Here to Eternity* were surely enough the keep the delirium tremens at bay.

I made the resolution to go clean when I let myself into my apartment—this would have been just before eight o'clock. By eight thirty-five I was looking from my balcony every thirty seconds in the hope of seeing Mia in the street below. By eight forty-five I was pacing, hands tied in my hair, eyes wild. By nine o'clock I was broken, weeping in shame and desperation as I chased the dragon. *One more time,* I told myself. *Just one more …*

When I woke the following morning Mia was there, in my bed, her body close and her fingers caressing the dark crescents beneath my eyes.

'What did you dream?' she whispered.

'I don't remember.'

'You were talking in your sleep.'

'What did I say?' I asked, wanting to know, not wanting to know.

Her lips found the full, dangerous smile I had become familiar with. 'You said that you didn't want to go back—that you were never going back.'

I kissed the edge of her smile and said nothing.

'Where, Scott? Tell me, were you running in your dream? Were you afraid?'

'I don't know,' I replied, and this was the truth; nothing of my dream had recurred with her revelation. I could have been anywhere, though I'm certain the words she heard me speak were in reference to everything—to the darkness I had worked so hard to leave behind, aspects of which I was now, inexorably, slipping back into.

'You're trembling,' Mia said. 'Was it a nightmare?'

'I'm not sure.'

'You don't remember anything?'

I shook my head. 'It was only a dream.'

'Where were you, Scott?'

I kissed her again. 'I was nowhere,' I said, and then asked her to hold me.

*   *   *

The life-line reappearing would suggest starting over; not simply turning a new leaf, but becoming a new person—from the soul.

Whenever I study my hands it is the broken line edging the mount of Venus I look at first, knowing what it signifies. The line begins to fade about one-third of the way in, disappearing altogether just short of the middle before becoming distinct again: an angry red line curving to the base of the thumb. After we had made love for the first time, Mia assured me that I was yet to come to the change represented by the break. She was right. Now, as I write this, I know that the break is behind me. I look at myself, where I am, how I think and feel, and know that I am a different person. I may look the same but inside—deep, deep down where the fire of our soul burns brightest, where our own inner-moon orbits and the river of our essence flows, I couldn't be more different. This change in me began with the coming of *Ptesan-Wi*. It is now complete; I am new.

Writing about the 'old' me feels like writing about a person I know particularly well: a brother or close friend. Still, there are times when I find it difficult to relate to the former Scott Hennessey, and more difficult to associate myself with the pain and suffering he went through. When this happens I look at my right hand, concentrate on the three sections of my life-line, and know that I was there. I felt the pain and tasted the tears. I still have the scars.

Some things never go away.

This memoir deals primarily with the break: three millimetres of skin on my palm captured in all these pages. The ball started to roll when I found Mia walking in the rain. It gained momentum when I fell into her wonderful trap, and it really picked up speed when I tasted desire—my infamous all-or-nothing attitude backing me into a corner from which the only escape was to turn to heroin. My decline was inevitable, albeit unspectacular in so much as I didn't deteriorate into the stereotypical addict/victim-of-society we have all come to recognise with the advent of heroin-chic movies and literature. There was nothing chic about my decline. I'd been through that before, during the Golden Wonder years. Maybe I had learned something from my previous addiction, though I don't believe this to be possible. My circumstances were different, I guess: I couldn't be kicked out of university again. I had savings so I didn't have to resort to crime to finance my habit. I had a job that I managed to keep, although my work did suffer (I was missing days and deadlines), but at no time did any of my colleagues take me to one side and say, *Jesus, you look like* shit. *Are you on heroin?* I maintained that emotional difficulties were the reason behind my lapse in performance, and no one could find a reason to disbelieve me. I didn't look like a man who took anywhere between one half and one full gram of heroin a day (being rumbled by Sebby had made me self-conscious); I showered morning and night, used eyedrops to take the dead man out of my gaze, and applied blusher to colour my pale skin—effective little tricks without which the real reason behind my deterioration would have been evident.

However delusive my façade, on the inside the corruption was spreading. When I wasn't with Mia the only company I wanted was my own. I would spend my days either staring out of the window or huddled in a corner with my hands over my face, listening to the fierce cries of despair inside my head. My sleep became uncertain and troubled, crammed with disturbing dreams. I lost weight and was constantly ill—a cold I couldn't shake and a headache that went right through me. I lost my temper over the slightest thing: one afternoon I took a hammer to my electric toaster after it failed to brown the bread evenly. The radio fell victim to my wrath following eight tedious minutes of boy-band songs. It occurred to me later (after the radio had been reduced to a wasteland of plastic and wires) that I could have re-tuned or hit the OFF button. I say again ... there is little, if any, good sense in anger. The incident with the neighbour's cat proved most disturbing, even to my derailed mind. It had left the remains of an unfortunate rodent on my doormat and I came along one morning and stepped into them—*barefoot!* Yeah, I got that fucking cat. I lured it into my apartment with a piece of string, and then used the string to tie its legs together. I threw it into the oven for twenty minutes on 200°C/400°F/Gas Mark 6.[1]

Throughout all of this, of course, was Mia. She came and she went, and when she came my world was fire in the darkness. I told her that she had changed my life, and she would whisper in the soothing hours of our togetherness that she was never going to let me go. It never occurred to me that she was killing me, slowly and deliberately. You could have written the fact across the sky and I would have ridiculed it. I felt that I had found the real thing, that I was complete. It was only after **PRIVATE NUMBER** was murdered and I saw the X-shots of his body that I realised Mia's deadly purpose. The memories came back with terrible clarity. I knew why she had found me. I knew the reason for her revenge.

You're mine, baby, she would tell me in moments of passion, when the lights were out and all I could discern was her perfect silhouette, and all I could hear was her voice. Relieving me, fulfilling me ...

You're all mine.

... killing me.

*   *   *

I recall, with an unusual brightness of mind, one final night of contentment with Mia. It has occurred to me since that she *made* it perfect, not only with her conviviality but with her power. The night was unseasonably warm, the stars presented fantasy, and the moon was a dream ... a diamond-white dream in a spangled sky. Every sound was intimate, every second was loaded with sweet possibility, and every breath was laughter. This perfection—unnatural, I would swear to it—was another tool of seduction, but not solely for my benefit; that night we were entertaining ...

'She's beautiful, Scott,' Sebby said to me. I could hear the deference in his voice. 'What the fuck does she see in you?'

---

1. For fan-assisted ovens please refer to the manufacturer's handbook.

'I have no idea,' I replied.

Soul music playing on the stereo, a half-empty bottle of Shiraz on the table, and the lights turned down low. Sebby's wheelchair was empty, folded, out of sight. He was sitting in an armchair, a glass of wine in one hand, and an expression on his face apparent even in the low lighting: my friend was awestruck. He absorbed Mia the way he absorbed the wine. He was canned on both.

'Beautiful.'

Mia was on the balcony, gazing at the stars. I could imagine how they were captured in her eyes, twice as alluring. She stood, holding the rail, leaning back to take in the full splendour of the night sky. Her hair swayed—moved like a dance—inches from the ground.

'She makes me believe in God,' I said. 'She makes me believe the world is good.'

Sebby looked away from Mia, but only for a second (this was all he could manage). His eyes touched upon mine. 'I'm happy for you, Scottie. I admit to being jealous, but ... I don't know, you deserve a little luck, whether God played a hand in it or not.'

I smiled; my sentiments exactly.

This get-together was Mia's idea; she wanted to meet Sebby. *I want to meet all the important people in your life,* she had told me. I replied, somewhat ruefully, that there were only two such people, and she was one of them. I had family, but had lost contact with them long ago. They hadn't come when I needed them, and weren't likely to come now. As for friends ... there were several colleagues I could place in the 'friends' category, at a push. None were especially close, and certainly not important. All I had was Sebby and Mia, and that was all I needed.

I had indicated reluctance at her suggestion, having not spoken with Sebby since our altercation. I was confident he'd be amiable, but didn't think the situation appropriate for introductions. Actually, I thought he would be an embarrassment; Sebby was vulgar at the best of times and I wasn't sure how Mia would respond. This was only half of it. I had my own issues: I was confused and angry almost all the time, and Mia was the only person I wanted to be with. I expressed my displeasure, but Mia could be very persuasive.

I called Sebby.

'Stop the press,' he sneered down the line. 'If it isn't Scott Hennessey: Hero of the Underworld.'

'How've you been, Sebby?'

'Rolling and rocking. To what do I owe the pleasure?'

'I wanted to apologise for my behaviour last week—'

'It was three weeks ago.'

'Whatever … I was bang out of line.'

Silence.

'Also, do you still want to meet Mia? She's coming over Friday. I thought, you know, a bottle of wine …'

Sebby had needed little persuading (his curiosity was greater than his anger), though he made one condition: that Mia and I didn't spend the entire evening 'canoodling.' I made a condition of my own: that he keep all profanity and innuendo to himself.

'I can't promise anything,' he said.

'Neither can I.'

The promises were kept, however, and our evening was sublime. Sebby was at his most charming. You'll excuse me for suggesting that his urbane behaviour was not entirely for my benefit. He wanted to look good in front of Mia for himself. This sounds cynical, I know, but it's the way I saw it. Who could blame him? Who is not guilty of showing off from time to time? In the few minutes we had, just the two of us, Sebby had spoken true: with his eyes all over Mia he had said she was beautiful—inciting not feelings of jealousy from me, but waves of pride. I don't think I've ever been as proud as I was that night. Mia shone, I'm telling you. The girl *shone*.

She came in from the balcony, flowing with impossible symmetry, and with the stars behind her she became, in the heartbeat it took for her to cross the room, a vision both fanciful and poetic. In that moment my body was still and silent. I heard Sebby whisper something—some breathless sigh to compliment what his eyes were seeing.

'It's amazing out there,' she said. 'Have you ever known the stars to be so vivid?'

Sebby shook his head and I said nothing. I had seen stars dance and disappear, but I said nothing.

'They are so proud. Na-gah must have tears in his eyes tonight—all that beauty below him.'

She sat next to me, kissed my open mouth, and asked me to pour her some wine. I obliged and Sebby asked:

'Is Na-gah a god?'

'He is a star,' Mia replied with a smile, touching the back of my hand as I gave her the wine, a subtle gesture that meant as much as her kiss. When she lifted the glass to her lips Sebby and I did the same; when she swallowed so did we, and together we set our glasses down and looked at the wonderful night.

'Na-gah is the only star who does not move,' she continued. 'You can always find him in the same place: on top of his mountain, looking down. We know him as *Qui-am-i Wintook Poot-see*, but you call him the North Star.'

Mia pointed. I followed the tip of her finger and could just see the North Star from where I was sitting. Sebby was closer to the balcony doors and had a clearer view, but he didn't—couldn't—look at the star for long; he was hypnotised by Mia. She told us about Na-gah and he didn't take his eyes off her. It must have hurt him to blink. I wondered if he was listening or only watching her lips move. I wondered if he even knew where he was.

'My father, Luther Big Crow, was an incredibly wise man. He had many stories, and taught me so much. I was very young when he taught me about desire, and what it can do to your soul. He woke me in the middle of the night and walked me out into the prairie. He showed me Na-gah, burning brilliantly, and then told me how he came to be there, and why he never moves. I cried so much that night, and my father held me in his arms and asked why I was crying. I told him that I thought the story was sad, and he held me tighter and said: "Every tear is a lesson. There are no sad stories, there is only *learning*." Na-gah teaches us that, sometimes, we can reach too high, and sometimes it is better to accept what we have than to push for more. But that is the nature of man, isn't it? To always want more, to *desire*. My father would say that the road of desire leads only to ruin.'

There was a fantastic silence, but only between us. The soul music still played on the stereo and the outside-world made its rolling, rumbling sound. But between us: *shhhhhh*. Sebby looked at Mia. Mia looked at Na-gah. I looked at my hands. There are times when I forget that I don't have any fingers, and then there are times—and this was one of them—when the fact moves through my mind like a poltergeist.

Shhhhhh …

'Na-gah was the much-loved son of Shinob, a god of intense power and beauty, a skywalker from the days when the earth was young. Na-gah's passion was mountain climbing. He would constantly challenge himself, always searching for the mountain that touched the sky.

"I will find it one day," he said to his father. "I will find my mountain. I will climb it, and then, father, I will walk the skies with you."

"But, my beautiful son," Shinob would tell him with a smile. "You are of Mother Earth, and you must stay there and share the beauty I gave you with those around you."

'Na-gah didn't listen to his father. He was driven by desire, and would spend all his time searching. Before long, he found what he was looking for: the perfect mountain—*his* mountain. It was dark and beautiful, its sides were sheer and smooth, and its height was lost in the clouds. "This is it," Na-gah said. "This is my mountain, and I will climb it. I will walk the skies."

'Na-gah circled the mountain, looking for a path to start out on, but there was nothing but sheer rock face. Not to be deterred, he resolved to climb it like a lizard: hand over hand, into crevice, onto shelf. He walked around the mountain again, this way and that, looking for the least footing to get him started. But there was nothing. "I *will* find a way," he promised … and that was just what he did.

'He noticed an opening in the rock face. It was small, mostly concealed by shadow. Na-gah could see that it led *into* the mountain rather than up it. He thought it might be the only way, and decided to try it. He squeezed into the hole—into the mountain. It was cold and dark inside, and Na-gah had taken only a few steps before deciding to turn back and find another way. He started to inch toward the opening, and then heard the most thunderous sound. It seemed that he had displeased the great mountain; it roared at him and sent a huge rock crashing down. It fell across the opening, blocking his way out. Na-gah was trapped, and could do nothing but venture deeper into the unpleasant darkness in the hope of discovering another way out. He walked for hours, tiring desperately, noticing that the path he walked was getting steeper, and gradually he was climbing higher and higher.

'Hours turned into days, days turned into weeks, and weeks into months. At last, crawling like an animal and an inch from death, Na-gah saw a shimmer of light ahead of him. He believed that his imprisonment was at an end, when really it was just beginning. "*I am free*," he screamed, his hands and knees bleeding as he crept toward the light.

'When he emerged from the mountain he could see that he had made it to the top. Na-gah had fulfilled his desire, and he was exultant. "Look at me, father," he cried, trembling and scared and embracing the sky. "Look what I have done."

'Shinob heard his son's voice and bounded across the sky. His heart sank when he saw Na-gah.

"*Qui-am-i*, how did you get to the top of that mountain?" Tears were cascading down Shinob's face because he knew Na-gah was trapped forever. He would never travel again; he had climbed his last mountain.

"I crawled through a hole in the mountain and found a pathway that led me here," Na-gah replied. "Now, father, take me from this mountain top. Let me walk the sky with you."

"But, *Qui-am-i*, I cannot help you, even with my power. You are there now, and there you must stay." In that moment, as Na-gah fell to his knees, Shinob knew what he had to do.

"*Qui-am-i*, I will turn you into a star, and you will shine in all your beauty, from now until the end of time. And all the creatures of Mother Earth will see you, for you are high. And all the walkers of the sky will know you, for you are *Qui-am-i*, you are my son. And in shining, you will be a guide for everyone."

'And so Shinob turned his beloved son into the star we can all see, wherever we walk on Mother Earth. He is the only star we can always find in the same place: Na-gah never moves. He is the North Star.

'Look at him now, beautiful but alone. This is what can happen when you reach too high. This is what can come with desire.'

*   *   *

I had known Sebby six and a half years, and had heard him talk about the accident that left him paraplegic only twice. The first time was at the Centre, after I had told him (truthfully) how I had lost my fingers. The second time was on that perfect night with Mia.

'I have desire,' he said, clasping the useless poles that were his legs. I noticed that he had spilled red wine on his shirt—two drops in perfect tear-shapes—and thought that he looked, with his beautiful smile, like a child … like a tragic doll. 'Is it so wrong, Mia, to desire?'

She was standing by the balcony doors once again, looking at me. 'What do you think, Scott?'

My lips were dry and I felt a terrible *need* inside. I could barely open my mouth to speak.

'I think …' Sebby's voice (sitting in the armchair, wheelchair folded, out of sight). 'I think that your father was right, Mia: that the road of desire leads to ruin. I also think that the two are closer than that. Much closer, like a yin-yang symbol, maybe: one forever flowing into the other.'

A sigh escaped me and I became the subject of expressions: solemn, questioning. I offered only the weakest shimmer of smile and lowered my eyes, not imparting that Sebby had, with his words, defined my ruined soul.

Mia moved, shifting from one foot to the other. My gaze was drawn back to her.

'Do you need to tell us something, Scott?' she asked.

I shook my head. I felt that if I started to speak I wouldn't stop, and by the time the night was over Mia would know all there was to know about me, every dark secret, every truth. I didn't want to go down that road. I wanted to drink wine, listen to the music, and absorb the warmth of the two people I loved most in the world. If there was to be a second recounting of tragedy—Na-gah's being the first—let Sebby do the talking.

I looked at his legs, at their position in the armchair—both leaning to the left, knees together. I noticed how he subconsciously drummed his fingers on his thighs, slightly out of time with the music. My gaze dropped to his feet: perfectly still. I realised that I was tapping my feet in time with the bass drum and cymbal. Up they went, down they went—*thump-cha! thump-cha! thump-cha!* Sebby drummed his fingers. His feet were perfectly still.

'What I desire,' he began weakly, as if we needed to be told. His mouth was open, his eyes far away. He held the silence for too long. 'Impossible,' he breathed at last. 'Every wish I have, every thing I want … impossible. Do either of you know how painful it is to desire something you can never have?'

I didn't; my desire was apparently obtainable. She proved this by coming to me, and sitting so close I could feel her body's vibration. She touched my face, fingers trailing from my cheekbone to the edge of my lips, and when she took her hand away I could still feel the heat of her touch, like warpaint.

Sebby was looking at us, his brilliant eyes caught in a flash behind his hair. His smile was beautiful, but sad. I had to look away.

'When I saw you standing on the balcony,' he said to Mia, 'all I wanted was to join you—to get out of this chair, walk to your side, and look at the stars together. I don't want the world …' He trailed off, voice trembling.

'Do you walk in your dreams?' Mia asked.

'I don't remember my dreams.'

'What about your daydreams?'

The sadness left his smile. It was wonderful. 'I'm superhuman in my daydreams. I have to be. My imagination doesn't need wheelchair-access, and it doesn't want a broken body. I run, I fight, and I love: a thousand women a night, all screaming my name, begging for more.'

'Is that desire, or fantasy?'

'Is there a difference? Maybe there is … but not for me. When your desire can no longer be achieved it becomes a fantasy. The idea of having sex with a thousand beautiful women is only as preposterous as the idea of standing on my own two feet. I'm not suggesting that all paraplegics feel this way. On the contrary—we've as much chance of successful living as any able-bodied person. I could be a movie star, a model, or a Paralympic legend. But I don't want these things …'

'You just want to walk again,' Mia spoke for him.

'Yeah, I just want my mountain.'

I could hear the rumble of life outside my apartment: the traffic with its irregular, insect sounds, the reassuring hum of electricity lying on the grid like a warm hand, and the river sighing through its heart, catching stars like a wishing well catches coins.

The stars: wonderful little heartbeats keeping the night alive. Hardly aware of what I was doing, I reached out as if I could scoop them, like water, into my palm. I was drawn to Na-gah (ghost-fingers fully extended), that shimmering image of light, surrounded yet utterly alone.

'This is how I lost my body,' Sebby began, and told us—just as he had told me six years before—that the accident had been his fault. It had been his idea to steal the car, and he had goaded the driver, his best friend at the time, to drive as fast as he could. 'Jamie always did what I said,' he explained. 'He was two years younger than me, and he hung on my every word like a little brother.' They'd stolen a ridiculously fast sports car. The owner, who had left the keys in the ignition, had lost a means of transportation, but Sebby had lost the use of everything from his bellybutton down, and Jamie—just a kid—had lost his life. It had taken three hours to cut Sebby from the wreckage. He had drifted in and out of consciousness, but remembered two things clearly: the first was a voice declaring that the mess in what was left of the driver's seat looked like spaghetti sauce (Jamie: fifteen years old: a baby in his father's arms one moment, spaghetti sauce the next). Sebby's other memory was of a man in a yellow coat, holding a white sack in one hand, and a small shovel in the other. 'He was scraping bits of Jamie off the road. I saw him drop something red and wet into the sack, and it was only later that I realised it was Jamie's face.'

The owner of the sports car had lost an expensive piece of turbo-charged metal that night, but if he or she had been sensible enough to take the keys with them, Sebby would still have his body and Jamie Sallis would still have his life (twenty-five years old and maybe making babies, or spaghetti sauce, of his own). I would be writing this account, but with a different complexion. It would not co-star Sebastian Cross; we would never have met, and he would be living his life, oblivious of me and my troubles. He would be running, fighting, and loving ... desire and fantasy a world apart.

I know it's wrong to hold the owner partly responsible (and I don't, not really—not deep down where the anger gives way to whatever emotion rides mostly unfelt beneath it), when even Sebby blames no one but himself. 'I saw the keys in the ignition,' he told us. 'I convinced Jamie that we should take a joyride, and I was the one screaming at him to go faster, even though I could see the needle on the speedometer touching ninety.' Equally, I think it would be wrong, not to mention unfeeling, to say that they got what they deserved. I know that some people subscribe to this Draconian logic, but they were kids, for Christ's sake, and what happened to them when that turbo-charged piece of metal span out of control ... say what you like, think what you like, but nobody deserves that.

I thought Mia would say something—a précis, perhaps, of Sebby's actions based on Sioux legend—but she remained still and silent, her hand wrapped tightly around mine, allowing my friend time to formulate his thoughts and share what he needed to.

This moment—and it lasted only seconds—was entrancing. There was a powerful triangle of energy between the three of us, and I felt the line drawn between Mia and Sebby was strongest of all. They were connecting on a level I could see but not reach. I felt no jealousy; it was not attraction, but connection. It was like watching a wave break or an avalanche slide. It was wonderful.

'Do I feel guilty?' Sebby shrugged. His dreadlocks masked his expression, but I didn't need to see his face to know where he was looking. 'Of course I do. The guilt lives in me like cancer. It wakes me in the night, and it has Jamie's voice. It's hard to sleep when you have a dead fifteen-year-old boy whispering in your ear, blaming you, hating you. But here's the thing: the guilt is nothing compared to the knowledge that I'll never walk again. This is what hurts the most—selfish fucker that I am. But deep down, in the part of my soul that can run, fight, and love, I've yet to accept that fact. Never walk again? Fuck you, man. I'll be on my feet by the summer, you wait and see. It's a little like ... I don't know, do you remember being a child, and believing you would live forever?'

His question drifted, unanswered, into silence. It was absolute silence, if only for a moment: the stereo was between songs, our triangle of energy was a soundless shimmer, and the hum of the everything outside my apartment had diminished, as if all that commotion had paused to collect itself: an instant of meditation before rumbling on.

Until, somewhere ...

I heard the cry of a car alarm. It was answered by the shudder of a distant train, and the shotgun-blast of an exhaust backfiring. The river groaned, stretched, and rolled. I could hear a TV set screaming (applause/commotion) elsewhere in the complex, and in our sublime universe Sebby inhaled, Mia sighed, and The Temptations harmonised in the key of C.

Sebby looked at me, fingers drumming on his thighs. 'Can you get my wheelchair, Scottie?'

'Why? Do you want to go home?'

'No,' he replied, and his smile was back—his beautiful smile. 'I love this fucking song. Let's dance.'

*   *   *

And so we danced, Mia with her arms around me, her lips just a kiss away, and Sebby proving to be a slick mover in his wheelchair—tilting back onto its rear wheels and spinning on the spot, even affecting a Chubby Checker twist by shuffling from left to right. I'm not sure how long we danced, but while we did we forgot about the world and knew only each other. We became equal in beauty and ability: an equilateral triangle full of soul. It was magical.

It wasn't until the next morning that the peculiarity of what I had seen occurred to me. At the time I thought nothing of it, perhaps dismissing it as a trick of the light, or the fancy of a mind that has enjoyed too much wine. Or maybe I was having too much of a good time to care.

It was our shadows: moonlight shone through the open balcony doors, as refreshing as a breeze, and our shadows made chaos against the walls, striking impossible angles and poses. Mine was tall, an unpainted marionette flailing, turning. Sebby's was a geometric wonder, spinning like a science project, and Mia's ...

I looked at her dancing, laughing in my arms. I looked at the wall, my shadow an unlikely child's shape ... and where hers should have been I could see only a rumour of movement: the ghost of a shadow. I looked twice—a cartoonish double-take—but this was my only reaction. Besides, what else could it be but a trick of the light? I may have dwelled further on the anomaly, but just then Mia took my face in her hands and kissed me hard, opening my mouth with hers, and indicating the bedroom with her eyes.

She cast no shadow. I can write this with complete honesty. I know what I saw: the moonlight passed through Mia like she wasn't even there.

She led me, still dancing, towards the bedroom. I glanced back at Sebby. The expression on my face was apologetic, yet triumphant. He knew the score and I saw no hint of jealousy on his part. Before the door between the living room and hallway closed I saw him make an A-okay circle with his thumb and forefinger, then 'kick-back' onto his rear wheels, and resume spinning. I felt a huge surge of love for him. The line connecting us burned intensely, and then Mia slammed the door. The triangle of energy was shattered, but I didn't care; I had other business.

Mia didn't have a shadow, but she had a body and she knew how to use it. She threw me to the bed and stripped me. She was violent and exciting. When she ripped off my shirt her fingernails tore across my chest, leaving severe lines that didn't fade for days. Her mouth left a trail of bite marks, and when she lowered herself onto me the night exploded. She was dry and tight—the penetration was excruciating, but blissful. My soul burned as she fucked me. The buffalo charged. She was half-dressed.

We made our music into the night with an urgency that left me hurt and breathless. The moonlight crept in on the secret, making ghosts of the white drapes, coating our bodies like a new blue skin and shining brighter as we worked harder; we were dynamos. When I came into Mia I told her, for the first and last time, that I loved her. Her response was to grip me tighter. I trembled inside her, frail and beaten.

I woke in the early hours. My face was burning and the backs of my legs were cold: the sensation that precedes the need to fix. I blinked sleep from my eyes and considered the four bags in my coat pocket. Mia stirred but did not wake. I looked at her and my craving subsided. I touched her and it disappeared.

The moonlight was a suggestion of what it had been, scarcely touching my bedroom window, but enough for me to see the beautiful young woman who shared my bed. She was sleeping in a foetal position, her hands linked as if she had discovered her dreams while praying. The dress she had worn all night—throughout our passion—had, with her movement, worked its way over her waist. I touched her thigh with my lips, not to kiss but to inhale. It was heaven. Her scent—her taste—was, I thought, the only fix I would ever need. I pressed my palms together, crossed my thumbs, and prayed:

'Never leave me, Mia.'

I want you ...

'I need you forever.'

And ever ...

'Amen.'

I lowered my hands and got out of bed. It occurred to me that I didn't have a photograph of Mia, and that this would be an opportunity to remedy that. It had, after all, been the perfect night. I needed the perfect memento.

I opened the bedroom door, just enough to allow the hallway light to spill in so that I could see what I was doing. My camera was on the bottom shelf of my sprawling bookcase. Its shelves were mostly double-stacked, from left to right, sagging in the middle—tired old things. The bottom shelf was loaded with heavy reference books and assorted paraphernalia. My camera was amongst the clutter, and I felt for it with my strange hand. It was old, and not complicated; the kind of camera I have heard referred to as idiot-proof. I took it from its case, checked the film, and switched on the flash.

Mia was captured inside the viewfinder like something first imagined, then painted. The angle I had chosen emphasised her partial nakedness, with the curve of her thigh touched by two sources of light. Her linked hands and foetal position inspired me: I would take the picture and have it enlarged to a ridiculous size. I would frame it and call it *Innocence*.

I pressed the button, stealing this moment in time—making it pocket-sized, so that I could carry it forever. The flash kissed the room, reminding me of the way the lightning had shocked the sky on the day we met. The old camera clicked and whirred. Mia's eyelids fluttered and she raised her head from the pillow. I thought she was going to wake up, and wondered what she would think when she saw me with the camera. I would tell her the truth, I decided. I would tell her about *Innocence*, and how she looked beautiful in the last of the moonlight. But Mia did not wake; she lowered her head to the pillow and was lost to her divine dream.

*　　*　　*

I wasn't going to write about what happened next, feeling it too personal, but now that I have reached it—and after more painful deliberation—I feel that I should. It does not affect me, but it does affect the truth I am trying to tell. For that reason it is important.

I wanted to check on Sebby, make sure he hadn't tipped himself out of his wheelchair spinning, drinking, dancing like he was. I wrapped a towel around my waist and edged into the hallway. The spare bedroom door was ajar. I looked in and could see that the bed hadn't been touched. Sebby could have fallen asleep in his wheelchair, but he had never done that when he'd stayed over before, and there were times when we'd both been piss-drunk, fit to collapse. I would quite often fall asleep where I fell, but Sebby always found the spare bedroom. This led me to believe that Sebby had gone home (feeling too uncomfortable with the jungle sounds coming from my bedroom), or that I would find him lying on the floor, hurt or unconscious, having spilled out of his chair.

It turned out to be neither; Sebby was still there, and still awake. He was sitting in the armchair, positioned so that he couldn't see me looking at him. There was a men's magazine lying open on one arm of the chair, not *GQ* or *Men's Health*, but the kind of publication that features coke-sold cuties and Readers' Wives in various stages of undress. On the other arm was the detritus of an addict: an empty syringe, two or three alcohol swabs, and a discarded ampoule. It was a shooting-up kit, but not for heroin. This drug was called papaverine. Sebby referred to it as his rootjuice. The car accident had fucked up the nerves essential to the arteries that carried the life force to his penis. His days of getting a natural hard-on were as dead as his chances of running the four-minute-mile. The rootjuice provided the solution: fifty milligrams injected into the shaft, inducing blood flow into the cavernous tissue of the penis. There could be some unpleasant reactions: bleeding, infection, priapism (or 'Boner of the Gods' as Sebby called it. He once had a bar-on that lasted thirty-six hours and eventually had to be brought down to earth with pharmacologic reversal). For this reason Sebby's doctor recommended the injection only be administered twice weekly—maximum. Sebby agreed but took no notice; he loved jerking-off too much. He used to joke that, if they ever made masturbation a Paralympic event, he was going for gold.

He was going for gold now, looking at his dirty magazine, occasionally flipping the pages while his right hand pumped his penis. I could see fine tendrils of blood oozing through the cracks of his fingers.

I don't know why he masturbated. Could he even feel it? Was there any sensation in the dead half of his body? I don't know, and it wasn't a subject I wanted to get into with him. Of course, any sexual act produces pleasures beyond the physical, but I can only imagine that the reason Sebby put himself through that painful injection for a ten minute shuffle was because he wanted to keep that part of himself alive, the way some people will keep a dead relative 'alive,' even years later, by changing their bed sheets twice a week and polishing their shoes. It was a matter of not wanting to let go. It was a comfort thing.

I slipped silently from the living room and walked to my bedroom. *A thousand women a night, all screaming my name, begging for more.* I felt awkward and sad, but these emotions dissolved when I climbed into bed. I pushed my body close to Mia's and kissed her sleeping eyes.

When I woke up in the morning she was gone.

*   *   *

They found George Lasky's body three days later.

His death became the buzz of the office, our biggest story of the year. Even the bloodhounds in the Smoke wanted a sniff of this one; it was just so ... *unusual.*

I distanced myself from the buzz and focused on my work: a riveting report on the growth of organic farming in the region. I kept my head down and my Walkman on (Charlie Parker—oh, memories), only venturing from isolation when necessary: toilet sorties, lunch breaks, heroin runs, the occasional indiscreet word from Tad Sandler (the *Post*'s editor, and the most condescending son of a bitch I've ever known). It was following an uncomfortable meeting with Tad, returning gratefully to isolation, that I saw a photograph of George Lasky on Ricky Wright's desk. I had a middling relationship with Ricky. He was a good journalist, but his crude humour would often unsettle me.

'I know this man,' I said, picking up the photograph. I tried to put a name to the face, or recall the association, but nothing recurred: more spaces in the mind (it must look like a squeezebox—solid at both ends, with nothing in the middle but bellows and strange sound).

'You mean *knew* him,' Ricky said. 'Past tense.'

'He's dead?'

'Where have you been, Hennessey? That's our boy. That's George.'

'*This* is George Lasky?' I looked at the photograph again, into lustreless black and white eyes ... and all of a sudden I knew (wheezy, rattling sound from the squeezebox).

What did we do, Scott? What did we do to that girl?

'Private number,' I muttered.

'Huh? You okay, Hennessey?'

'Private number,' I said again, looking at the photograph, the bellows coming together with a discordant hiss of memory. It all came back to me—every buried nightmare, every forgotten ghost—and it hit hard. I remembered what we did that night in the woods. I remembered the girl, burning and smiling.

She's back, Scott, and she's taking us out one by one.

She threw fire. She threw rage.

'Dead?' The office adopted crazy proportion: the ceiling sloped one way, the floor the other. I sagged in the middle (almost like my mind) and had to grip the edge of Ricky's desk to keep from falling over. 'Are you sure? I mean ... how?'

Ricky gave his head a little shake. 'Get with the program, Scottie. This is the story of the year, and you don't know thing-one about it ...'

'I've been preoccupied,' I said. I'd been saying this a lot since meeting Mia.

'You've been living under a fucking rock,' Ricky countered. 'This story is going to own the cover for at least three prints, and everyone's e-mail is jammed with enquiries from Fleet Street. How do you *not* know about this?'

'Just tell me how he died,' I said, trying to sound firm, but I was still too dazed and I only sounded broken, maybe even scared.

Ricky whistled through his teeth. 'Is George a former boyfriend of yours, Scottie? Did you used to blow him in college, or something? We don't know much about your past, do we?'

'I know him,' I croaked, then winced, corrected myself: '*Knew* him; past tense. Shit.'

'Private number, right? Here …' He opened his top drawer and took out a Manila envelope. **LASKY X-SHOTS** had been written in the corner where you would normally place a stamp. 'We won't be running these.'

The last thing I wanted was to open the envelope and look at the X-shots, but my deformed hands were working without instruction. Before I could stop them they had lifted the flap and taken out two colour photographs. One was a close-up of Lasky's face, the other a full-body shot. He had died on his bathroom floor wearing nothing but a pair of socks. The socks concealed the fact that he only had three toes: one on his left foot, two on his right.

'Nasty, huh?' Ricky said.

'Strangled?' I asked—another weak sound. I studied the close-up: George Lasky's face was a purple/black mask of pain, one eye wide and shot with red, the other half-closed. His throat was bruised: a thousand ruptured blood vessels spidering down to his chest. What I thought to be a shadow cast by the shelf of his jaw was actually abnormal swelling. It looked like his Adam's apple had inflamed to three times its normal size.

'Not strangled,' Ricky said, looking over my shoulder at the photos. I could feel him leering, I swear I could. 'Georgie was a chronic asthmatic—'

'This was an *asthma* attack?' I gasped, shuffling the X-shots, shaking my head.

'Don't be a bonehead, Scottie. Do you really think an asthma attack would cause this much sensation? Not a chance—'

'Murder?' I stopped breathing, waiting for Ricky's reply.

'It's been ruled out,' Ricky said. I breathed again but the colour was still draining from my face. 'At this time, police are not treating the death as suspicious. The coroner's report could prove otherwise, but I doubt it.'

'What happened then?'

'I'm *trying* to tell you. Jesus!' Ricky rolled his eyes, but he was grinning. I didn't care for his sense of propriety. 'It was a freaky-deaky accident: Mr. Lasky—survived by no one, it would seem—choked to death after swallowing his inhaler.'

'*What?* I looked at the purple/black close-up, one eye wide open, the other half-closed. I looked at the impossible swelling in his throat.

'As we go to press, the common theory is that Lasky suffered an asthma attack while going about his duties in the bathroom. He was evidently not a man to take chances; he kept an inhaler in every room of the house. He staggered to his bathroom cabinet (you can't see it in the photo, but the cabinet is open), grabbed his inhaler, and started puffing away.'

Ricky enhanced his account with a little impromptu reconstruction: bulging eyes, hands cupped to his mouth, body rocking back and forth. I could hear the whistling rush of an inhaler in the back of my mind, exactly as I had heard it when George Lasky called three months before.

I gestured, impatiently, for Ricky to go on.

'The police believe he slipped on the tiles—you know how slippery tiles can be when you're wearing socks. Great when you're a kid, but not so great when you're a fifty-two-year-old man having an asthma attack. Georgie hit the deck—*bang!* Ricky smacked his hands together to better illustrate the scene he was recreating. 'The inhaler dropped into his mouth and down his throat. He's struggling to breathe anyway, right? So now he *really* starts to panic—maybe tries to fish the inhaler out with his fingers, but only succeeds in pushing it down further. Next thing you know, George Lasky is an ex-person. Thanks for the memories, baby. The bad news is you're dead. The good news is … we got gravy.'

Ricky snatched the X-shots from me, looked at George's black-grape-face, and then, in an incredible show of disrespect, flicked the dead man right between the eyes. 'Freaky-deaky, huh?'

I was shaking my head, though inclined to agree: freaky-deaky, for sure. 'Something's not right,' I said. 'These inhalers are tested for safety. Kids use them, for Christ's sake.'

'A can of worms,' Ricky said, still grinning. 'Pass me that opener, would you?'

I cocked my thumb at the hideous black lump in Lasky's throat. 'It doesn't make sense to me. I think someone *rammed* the inhaler into—'

But Ricky was shaking his head. 'Bathroom door was locked, from the inside. The window was closed. It's the classic locked room mystery.' He adopted a hardboiled detective voice, which was actually quite good, but entirely inappropriate: 'If anybody was in the john with this sap when he kicked off … well, the only way they could've dusted out would be to disappear into thin air. I got two bits says that didn't happen. It's hooey, I'm tellin' ya—*hooey.*'

'Impossible,' I said, shuddering.

'This is what's going down, Scottie,' Ricky said, losing the gumshoe-persona. 'It's what we've all been so jazzed about for the past five hours. Welcome back to Planet Earth, and please make sure you're up to date on all current affairs from here on. In other words, get your head out of the clouds and read your fucking memos.'

He pronounced it *mee-moes*. I fucking hate that.

'I do believe the delights of organic farming await you. Now, if you don't mind, I have a corpse to grind.'

I stole one final glance at George Lasky's purple/black face. I looked into his sightless eyes and heard his voice rattle through my mind:

She's already got to the others, and now she's got to me. You're next, Scott.

Memories rushed at me like an ice cold wind, stealing the breath from my lungs. I was there again. I could feel the fallen leaves beneath my feet, taste the damp air, and smell the paraffin oil that kept the torches burning. George Lasky walked beside me, barefoot (one toe on his left foot, two on his right). Beside him was the woman with curved, glimmering hooks where her hands had once been: Shirley.

We were walking through the woods, towards the Altar of the Voice, where so much blood had been spilled. The girl walked ahead of us, naked and shimmering. Her wrists were bound behind her back, her ankles joined with a length of coarse rope (just enough play to allow her to walk). I could see two rills of sweat trickling down the curve of her spine, made orange, like lava, in the flickering torchlight.

She was whispering prayers in some exotic language.

I dropped into my seat and gazed at the ceiling, but all I could see was fire. The office buzzed around me. Fax machines whirred. Keyboards clacked. Telephones rang. Talk, talk, talk ...

'*... slipped on the tiles ... inhaler lodged ... Lasky, L-A-S ... lived on his own ... wife died in a house fire six months ... front page, we're talking maximum mileage ... beautiful story, just fucking beautiful ...*'

The sounds of my working environment were whispers next to the chaos in my mind: the roar of burning trees, the screams of dying men and women. Fear took the strength from my body and I collapsed face down on my desk.

Old wounds. Wouldn't it be heavenly to forget—to forget everything?

George Lasky had said this to me three months before. One look into his dead eyes had brought it all back. I saw it in my mind like a movie:

Flames leapt from her hands, from her body. The dead circled her, still burning. I could hear death's relentless thunder. It sounded like (*buffalo*) a stampede, and I reeled away, one of only four survivors. I dared to look back and our eyes met. I felt her heat, her danger. She pointed at me, smiling ...

The girl was beautiful, but she was death.
You're next, Scott.
The girl was Mia.

3

In the beginning of all things, wisdom and knowledge were with the animals, for Tirawa, the One Above, did not speak directly to man. He sent certain animals to tell men that he showed himself through the beast, and that from them, and from the stars and the sun and moon should man learn. All things tell of Tirawa.

All things in the world are two. In our minds we are two, good and evil. With our eyes we see two things, things that are fair and things that are ugly. We have the right hand that strikes and makes for evil, and we have the left hand full of kindness, near the heart. One foot may lead us to an evil way, the other foot may lead us to a good. So are all things two, all two.

—Eagle Chief, Pawnee

Allow me a moment to fill you in on the details. Let me tell you about the Way of the Eternal Night, and take you to where faith can be discovered in the heart of weakness. Let me show you a world of throwaway souls, and belief: blind, helpless, dancing to rock and roll music. Here there are angels. Here there is sin.

Take my hand ... let me show you salvation.

* * *

'Do you believe in angels?' the kid asked me. And he was a kid—younger than me, maybe only fifteen years old.

I opened one eye and looked at him, my teeth clattering in the cold. 'The heaven kind or the Christmas kind?'

'They're the same, I think.'

'But they're not. You only see the heaven kind when you're dead. They'll be like your relatives—the ones who have passed on, you know? They'll welcome you, get you settled in heaven.'

'Teach you how to fly?'

'Teach you how to fly.'

'And will they stay with you?'

'Throughout eternity.'

He considered this, floating away for one magical moment, to where he was held and loved. Somewhere warm. He swiped the back of his hand across his face as if he were wiping away tears, but he wasn't crying. I had never seen the kid cry. He had been dealt a losing hand, no doubt about that, but he never complained, never shed a tear. I admired him for that. I was nineteen years old at the time, the clothes I wore were warmer than the rags he lived in, and I had an education. This wouldn't get you far on the streets but it was a glimmer of light, at least. Without schooling you had nothing—the streets would be your home forever. Despite this, not a day went by when I didn't feel the sting of tears in my eyes. But the kid ... always hungry, always cold, and I never saw him cry.

'What about the Christmas kind?' he asked, silver breath floating in the cold air between us.

I gave him a reassuring smile. 'They're out there right now,' I said, pointing at the late night shoppers: a flurry of movement, this way and that, loaded with gifts, rolls of wrapping paper.

'I can't see 'em.' The kid's eyes were alive, reflecting Christmas trees and candy canes.

'Well, they're out there. Have you noticed that over the last week or so you've had a little more money dropped in your cup?'

'Yeah, I have.'

I nodded. 'Christmas angels.'

'That's bullshit,' he said after a few seconds of careful contemplation, and just the way he said it got me laughing so hard a couple of the late night shoppers actually looked down at us. He started laughing as well, his face a caricature of joy—almost unlikely in its dimensions. He held up his hand and I high-fived him. There we were, a couple of cold and hungry gutter rats, suddenly kings.

'So cold,' he said a few minutes later, huddling into the corner, hugging his body tight. He had wrapped himself in newspaper beneath his thin jacket. 'How cold do you think it is?'

I looked at my hands. The tips of my fingers were blue. 'Minus five hundred,' I replied.

Flicker of a smile. ''Tis the season.'

A pretty woman dropped a fifty pence piece into my cup. She looked at me, briefly. I wished her a merry Christmas, and I meant it. Another flicker of a smile, and she kept walking.

'Mine or yours?' the kid asked. He hadn't seen the pretty woman; his eyes were closed, he was trying to sleep.

'Mine,' I told him. The idea of splitting the money never crossed my mind; it didn't work that way.

I put my fingers into my mouth to warm them, then pushed my hands deep into my empty pockets and shuffled a little closer to the kid. I could hear a band of carol singers on the other side of the Plaza: 'God rest ye merry gentlemen, let nothing you dismay …' I closed my eyes.

'You didn't answer my question,' the kid said, just as I was drifting.

'Which one?' I murmured. The icy wind howled across our alcove and I shivered.

'About the angels.'

'What about the angels?'

'Do you believe in them?'

I thought about the pretty woman. 'I don't know,' I said. 'Go to sleep.'

*   *   *

It is never a deep sleep, and it is never easy. You turn and you shiver, you ache and you sigh. I don't know what time it was when I became aware that the small body next to mine was no longer moving. The night was still dark, but the carol singers had long since stopped and the shoppers had all gone home. The world was silent. I opened my eyes and looked at the kid. A frost had settled on the exposed parts of his body. His skin, normally brown and beautiful, was now hard and grey/white.

'Oh, shit.' My limbs cried in pain as I moved closer to him, taking his face in my hands. I peeled open his eyelid, but the dark eye behind it was not looking at me, or at anything.

'Hey, kid—'

I shook him and his body fell sideways in exactly the same position it had been in when propped in the corner. He did not stir, he did not shiver. The eyelid I had opened remained open, and the dark eye behind it saw nothing.

I stayed with him until the kind light of morning touched the sky beyond the Plaza, with his head in my lap and my fingers in his hair. When the tears on my face had dried (they were tears of self-pity, not sorrow) I took a single sheet of newspaper from under the kid's jacket and used it to cover his face. I moved his cup—half-full—next to his still heart, and put the money from my cup into my pocket. I thought about the pretty woman with the fifty pence piece.

Do you believe in angels? I looked at the kid, with his half-full cup next to his heart, and his grey/white face covered by a sheet of grey/white newspaper. I wondered if he still needed an answer to that question, and then I walked away.

It was Christmas Eve, 1989—my last day on the streets. In less than eighteen hours I would be bathed, fed, and lying in a warm bed.

And I would believe in angels, too.

*   *   *

I was close to death's door when he came. I sat in a freezing blue ball under the flyover, my hands—wrapped in the pages of an old piss-stained newspaper—over my head, as small as I could make myself. I didn't so much breathe as shudder. My heart ached. My lips were so cracked and sore they were bleeding.

The world was a continuous shriek of arctic sound: the wind whipped and whistled, and the far-off song of life in the city was like a bucket full of ice cubes. Even the cars crossing the flyover carried a raw sound. Everything seemed blue, so cold it was breaking open.

I don't know how he found me. The same way I found Mia, perhaps: fate. He was a moving part of the night: a long black coat, flowing; long black hair tied back with a strip of black ribbon. His eyes, though a different shape, held the same dangerous spark as Mia's. Looking back now, holding them both in my mind's eye, I can see that this was the only quality they shared.

'The Voice calls you,' this dark stranger said, holding out his hand. 'Your days of wanting are behind you. The Eternal Night lies ahead, and it is warm. Ah, I see distrust in your eyes. Don't ... that's it, take my hand. There ...'

He ripped the sheets of newspaper from my hands, sent them scattering to the wind.

'Are you an angel?' I asked.

He smiled. 'If an angel is defined as salvation, then yes ... I am an angel.' He lifted me to my feet, studying my hands, squeezing my fingers.

'The heaven kind or the Christmas kind?'

His reply was enigmatic, but his hands were so warm I found I didn't care. 'The Voice is the only power, and it has brought us together. Come with me, brother. You have just been saved.'

*   *   *

We arrived at his house less that an hour later, an impressive Queen Anne on sprawling grounds. In the morning I would see sweeping silver gardens, flood-lost hollows, and an army of sycamores marching to a distant war of trees. Now it was too dark to see anything other than the shape of the house, this discernible by its few lighted windows.

His car, chauffeur driven, pulled up at the steps leading to the front door. I looked at the house and saw the silhouette of a woman in an upstairs window.

'This is home now,' the stranger told me. 'You can stay here for as long as you like, or leave tomorrow, if that's what you want. While you are here you will never be hungry, and you will never be cold. There are people here, many of whom were homeless like you, or lost, or simply confused. The Voice brought them here, and they have found salvation. You should know that we do not permit drugs. Not even alcohol or cigarettes. This means that you will have to beat your addiction if you want to stay here.'

'My addiction?'

'Your eyes tell me everything. Don't be afraid, brother; the Voice will give you strength.'

I licked my cracked lips and looked at my hands, like a reprimanded child.

'You should also know that we do as the Voice tells us, *whenever* the Voice tells us.'

'The Voice …?'

'We do not question the Voice. We do not falter in its desire. Any failure to do what is expected will result in banishment from the house—back into the gutter I pulled you from. Do you understand?'

'I think so.' But I didn't understand any of it. All I knew was that I didn't want to go back to that blue breaking world. I would tell him anything if it meant I would eat a hot meal and sleep with a roof over my head. I thought he probably wanted me for sexual favours—all this talk about the Voice being part of his perverse role-playing scenario—but it didn't matter; I'd done that before, too, and for considerably less than a night in a warm bed.

This idea was reinforced when he took my hand and studied it with his dangerous eyes.

'Lovely hands. Such strong fingers, yes …'

I looked at the house again. The woman-shaped silhouette was no longer alone; a taller, male shape stood beside her. Movement at another window caught my eye: the twitching of curtains, a small hand, and a pale glimmer of face. Behind a third window a soft blue light created a stage for shadows, languorous in motion, curious in shape. I wondered what this place was—a bawdy house of gutter rats, and this consuming figure draped in black: the Pied Piper, playing his music, watching them follow.

I took my hand away, looking at him closely for the first time. He was younger than I had initially believed. There were few lines set into his face, just a whisper of silver at his temples. His eyes were clear, with a suggestion of the Orient in their shape. His lips were so thin they could have been painted on: one simple stroke.

'Who are you?' I asked.

'Yes, the questions …' He inclined his head, one finger tracing the hard line of his jaw. 'There will be time for explanations after you have rested, but I will tell you that my name is Shintaro. I am your friend, and your brother, except during Service when the Voice speaks through me. Then, in essence, I cease to be; I become an instrument, a channel, and as such I have no name.'

I was shaking my head. 'Service? This place is a church?'

'A church?' He smiled. 'Defined as …?'

'A place of worship.'

He looked away from me, gazing over his grounds, lost in the darkness. 'So defined, the answer is no. We do not restrict worship to one place. Our church is everywhere, because that is where the Voice can be heard.'

Another look at the house. More silhouettes, more curious shadows.

He took my hand again. I tried to pull back but he held tight, and he was stronger—much stronger.

'I feel your trembling, and sense your apprehension.'

Music started playing inside the house. It sounded like 'Chantilly Lace' by The Big Bopper. I raised my eyebrows at the sound, so unexpected, so peculiar. The silhouettes at the windows had disappeared but the shadows were still there.

Shintaro grinned. I saw his teeth for the first time, white and even. 'I know you will be happy here, brother. But time will tell, and if you are not …'

He led me into his house, where the rock and roll made the floorboards bounce and the doors shake in their frames. I could hear cheering and laughter. I was drawn towards these sounds but Shintaro took my arm, shaking his head. He led me upstairs and down a long landing until the clamour of the party became a background buzz. I passed only one person on the way: a girl, slightly younger than me. She smiled and raised her hand. Two of her fingers were missing.

Shintaro opened a door on a large bathroom bursting with steam. A bath had already been drawn—pink water, blue bubbles. It looked like heaven.

'I say again, your days of wanting are behind you.'

I turned to his voice. In the rolling clouds of steam he had become a man-shape, this drawing away from me, losing definition, as he moved down the landing.

*   *   *

I bathed for over an hour, drawing more hot when the water cooled, absorbing lotions, oils, and fragrances. I finally conceded its embrace, wrapped myself in towels, and stepped into the landing. Shintaro was waiting for me. He led me to another room. It was small, with a king-size bed covering most of its width. I sighed, preparing myself. This was the reason he had brought me here, the two of us alone, a huge bed. He would begin to undress now, and take the ribbon from his hair …

'Sleep,' he said, and that was all. He nodded at the bed and left me.

*   *   *

Despite the massive comfort, the warmth, I did not sleep well. The environment was foreign and my body—three hundred and eighty-one days on the streets—needed to adjust. I thought that someone would burst through the door at any moment, drag me out of bed, and throw me back on the streets. It wasn't that I thought it too good to be true, but rather a sense of alienation—that, regardless of what Shintaro said, I simply didn't belong.

Voices—whispers, really—woke me deep into the night: Shintaro and a woman. I kept my eyes closed as they stood over me.

The woman: 'Another pretty boy, Shintaro? Really …'

'He is for you. How would the unenlightened put it? Merry Christmas, darling …'

'But I already have a gift.' I heard two metallic objects being tapped together, and resisted the urge to open my eyes.

'Ah, if you don't want …'

'Thank you, Shintaro. Is he clean?'

'Only on the outside.'

'Heroin?'

'Sad. Yes, very sad.'

'A blood test, then.'

'That goes without saying.'

They said nothing for a long time, but I could feel their shadows lying like scars across my body. I could hear their breathing, and occasionally: *tap-tap, tap, tap-tap*.

The woman: 'Has the Voice spoken?'

Shintaro waited a long time before answering.

Tap-tap-tap (impatient?).

Shintaro: 'Yes.'

'And?'

'Fingers.'

I was aware of movement under the bed sheets. I felt something cold and metallic slide around my wrist, hook my arm out, and lift it.

The woman: 'Oh yes, beautiful fingers.'

Shintaro: 'The Voice has spoken.'

*   *   *

<u>Cold Turkey #1</u>

I have chosen to title this sub-chapter because I believe these two words offer you all the insight you need into my first days? weeks? months? in Shintaro's house. I could expand this account by at least twenty thousand words—describe the pain, the pleading, my fingertips bleeding from continuously scratching a locked door. But why waste time and effort when I can impart everything with two words, three syllables, ten letters?

Cold turkey.

Enough said.

*   *   *

Shintaro stood in the doorway, his skin washed in the pink evening light streaming through the window. 'It has been hard for you, Scott, but you are clean now. You are ready.'

'For what?'

'For the Way of the Eternal Night. You are ready to hear the Voice.'

He stepped into the room, one of only two rooms I had been allowed in since my arrival at the house—the other being the bathroom, to which my thrice-daily trips were always supervised. I didn't mind. It beat huddling on the street, or sleeping in the cars at Zero's Junkyard. Shintaro had kept his promise. I was always warm and never hungry, and as soon as the delirium tremens had stopped and I began to get a grip on myself, I wanted for nothing. I would spend my days reading, looking out of the window, writing poetry. Every night, on the stroke of midnight, the music would start downstairs: Little Richard, Carl Perkins, Richie Valens—classic rock and roll. The kind you would find on the jukebox at Arnold's. I heard the voices and laughter of the other members of the house, and their whispers outside my door. I had asked Shintaro about the parties. He said they were 'celebrations,' and when I asked if I could partake he told me that I would, in time.

And now the time had come.

'What is the Voice?' I asked him.

Shintaro opened his arms, fingers spread, as if the question could be embraced. 'The Voice is *everything:* creation's first vibration, and the pulse of the universe. Everything we see exists because the Voice said it would be so. Every brilliant mind to conceive a thought: Archimedes, Galileo, Shakespeare, Michelangelo, Socrates … all acted on the Voice. The Big Bang? The Voice spoke, and so was it done. Every action in every war: the command of the Voice. Famine in

Africa, earthquakes, floods, charity, religion, triumph, cancer, miracles, life—the Voice takes full responsibility. It loves and hates in equal measure. It is both good and evil. There is no mystery here. The fact that we exist as part of its great design proves that. The Voice, put simply, is the truth. Open yourself, give yourself unequivocally, and you will hear that truth. And the sound, Scott ... yes, the sound is beautiful.'

He stood, motionless, waiting for me to respond: a question, a sigh, any tell-tale body language. The rebel in me wanted to ... well, *rebel*—tell him that, if bullshit could power rockets, he'd reach the moon. I considered his rambling reply little more than an embarrassing cliché. But still, inexplicably, some part of me—surely cousin to the all-or-nothing attitude that had already caused so much trouble—was drawn to what he was saying. His words, however trite, had a certain attraction.

I went with it, playing into his open hands. 'You mean the Voice ...' I frowned, deliberately baiting. '... is like God.'

Shintaro winced. '*God?*' he coughed the word: a bitter taste in the mouth. 'God is a character of the Voice's design, an aid for those too afraid to hear the truth. He is an imaginary friend, and no more.'

'So this is a sect?'

'Defined as?'

'A faction: followers of some ... idea.'

'Ah, essentially the answer is yes. But the Voice is not an idea, Scott. It is the *only* power: an all-knowing, ever-encompassing force that demands reverence and worship.'

'Sacrifice?'

'Defined as?'

I laughed. 'You tell me, Shintaro. I mean, we're here in this house, always warm, plenty of food, rock and roll parties seven nights a week. What's the catch?'

The evening light had faded from the room as the sun fell away. Shintaro's skin appeared ashen, and his eyes more dangerous than usual.

'There is no catch, Scott, but any belief carries an element of sacrifice, be it time or money, or physical sacrifice such as fasting, flagellation, or asceticism. I am not only referring to religious beliefs. A man will work his fingers to the bone to fill his home with the things that will make him comfortable. An artist will work through the night, depriving himself of sleep, so that he may finish his masterpiece. Even love is a vessel for sacrifice; if we do not give ourselves entirely, then it is not love at all. And so sacrifice, defined as giving in order to receive—yes, the Voice may demand ... some small part of you.'

He sat on the edge of the bed, his fingers dancing close to mine. 'You are not a prisoner here, Scott. You do not have to become a follower. If you want to leave, the door is open. Yes, I will even have my driver take—'

'I want to stay.' The firmness of my voice surprised me, compelled by memories of addiction, desperation, and fear. I remembered how the winter winds would seep into my bones and make them creak and cry. I recalled the derisory sound a coin will make when it hits the bottom of an empty cup. I considered the contempt of the fortunate, and the guilt of those who turn the other way. But more than anything I remembered the kid (*Do you believe in angels?*), the way he had never shed a tear, and his dark eye staring, seeing nothing.

'Are you sure?'

I looked at Shintaro and once more had an image of the Pied Piper leading the rats out of the city.

'I want to stay,' I said again, and his hand found mine, squeezed my fingers.

*   *   *

I was drifting into sleep when someone knocked on the door. No, not someone, some *thing*; I recognised the unnatural quality in the sound. I thought, *tap-tap, tap-tap*. I sat up, looking at the line of light under the door, broken into dashes. Someone was there. At that moment the music started downstairs, heralding midnight. I could feel every enthusiastic slap on the double bass vibrating through the bed posts, and then the door was creaking open ...

'Hello, Scott.' I recognised her silhouette at once: loose hair spilling over her shoulders, a slender waist; I had seen her standing at a window on the night I arrived at the house. I recognised her voice, too—placed it a second later: the woman with Shintaro on that same night (*tap-tap, tap, tap-tap*). I remembered the cold metallic thing coiled around my wrist, lifting my arm from beneath the bed sheets.

I was about to ask who she was and what she wanted, but was stopped by the sight of her arm unfolding from her silhouette, reaching out to me. I then saw the reason behind the unnatural-sounding knock on the door. I saw the reason behind the *tap-tap-tap*—the metallic thing that had slipped around my wrist ...

'The celebration has started, Scott,' she said, and although I couldn't see her face I could tell she was grinning. 'Take my hook. Let's go.'

*   *   *

It cannot be defined as SRA: Satanic Ritual Abuse. Reason #1: In the three years that I lived with Shintaro and the gang, the big red guy with horns never made an appearance. He was just another character of the Voice's design, the bad guy in the God epic. Reason #2: In the true definition of Satanic Ritual Abuse (also know as *Sadistic* Ritual Abuse), it states that a victim is involved: an *unwilling participant* (usually an infant) in acts of sexual and/or physical abuse. This wasn't our way. For a start there were no children (no one under the age of eighteen. This was one of Shintaro's rules of recruitment). As for victims … only one that I recall: an exquisite beauty with soft tan skin and raven hair, who was held in the house against her will, who was tied up and systematically abused by each of us in turn, who prayed in Lakota as we shaved her head and burnt the black feathers of her hair.

You could argue that we had been manipulated to the will of a madman, and in that sense we were victims, but we were not unwilling participants. I could have left the house at any time, and I cut off my fingers with understanding, and acceptance, of the residuum. It was far from complex, after all: 8-1=7, 7-1=6, 6-1=5. When Shintaro said that the Voice would demand some small part of me, he meant it.

This brings us to the category of self-mutilation, also known as self-harm, or self-injury. It is strongly associated with suicidal teenagers, and involves cutting, burning, wound interference, scarring, and picking as a release from anxiety, fear, and emotional pain. This is more closely related to what we were doing than SRA (most of us were troubled teenagers, after all), but it's still a long way from home. Amputation is not associated with the disorder, and this was our rush. We were snipping off fingers and toes, band-sawing hands, lopping off arms and legs, and awarded merit according to the degree of our disfigurement. The awful truth of this has never been uncovered, or at least not revealed. As far as I am aware, mental health professionals have not been afforded the opportunity to pick at the bones and give it a label. So we can call it whatever we want. How about RSA: Ritual Self-Amputation? Hey, it's got a beat and you can dance to it.

The earliest suggestion of this was the girl who had waved at me when I arrived at the house, and revealed that two of her fingers were missing. Shirley's hint was less subtle: hooks instead of hands. As she led me to the celebration I began to suspect that there was more to this place than rock and roll, but what I was about to discover would terrify, revolt, exalt, and enchant me: emotional tsunami.

I was swept away.

We came to a large room—almost a hall—illuminated by wild colour and strobe lighting. The effect, moving further into the room, was like being trapped in a physics experiment. The floor thumped with the music, as if it had its own heartbeat. The walls swam with psychedelia: Chinese hieroglyphs, swirling light shows, and paisley smiles floating all around like rare bacterium seen under a microscope. I felt hands touching me, inspecting me, and strange faces swimming in and out of focus. It was nightmarish, and divine.

Suddenly I was alone; Shirley had unhooked herself and was weaving across the dance floor, looking at me over her shoulder.

'Enjoy yourself.' I couldn't hear her voice, but was able to determine what she said by reading her lips. She moved and gyrated in the strobe lighting like a computer generated image. Her hooks kicked off blinding stars of ultraviolet.

'*I'm getting the fuck out of here!*' I yelled. It was too weird, just too …

And then I took a proper look around, as if an invisible force had control of my body and was turning me in circles, training my eyes.

To begin with, it wasn't a stereo providing the sounds, but a band: a bona fide rock and roll six-piece. And they were good, sounded like the real deal. Shintaro was on guitar and … and …

'That can't be right,' I said. 'Oh fuck, that *cannot* be …'

The pianist was a double below-knee amputee; she worked the pedals with wooden pegs. The saxophonist (currently blowing the solo on 'Yakety Yak') only had one foot, and was standing in front of his monitor amp like a flamingo. The drummer didn't miss a beat, despite the fact that he was missing numerous body parts (one ear, one hand, both feet). There was a horse-faced woman playing double bass, but her equine expression was overshadowed by the fact that her right arm ended just south of the elbow. She slapped the strings with an odd prosthesis strapped to her shoulder. It looked like a small paddle. The vocalist had the moves and grooves of Elvis. He rolled his pelvis and sneered in all the right places. Even his hair was perfect. Ignore the fact that he had no hands and hey, Love Me Tender, baby.

But the oddities did not stop there. The invisible force continued to turn me in circles and I saw Shintaro's legion in frenetic bursts of light. I would estimate only one-tenth of the assembly was, for want of a better word, *complete*. The remainder—perhaps as many as eighty people—was malformed in some crude and deliberate way, and made no effort to conceal its deformity. On the contrary, most paraded half-naked, skin painted in glowing swirls that drew attention to absent body parts. They were walking, dancing, shrieking, breathing art exhibits. Imagine Damien Hirst on acid.

The music stopped with exquisite timing, and I enjoyed a moment of silence before Shintaro's followers exploded with applause. They howled their appreciation. Those with hands clapped, those without stomped their feet. I could see Shirley in the middle of the dance floor tapping her hooks together. The sound made my fillings ache.

Shintaro came to the mike. The furore died to a murmur, and then an anticipatory quiet …

'Whispers Coletti on sax,' he said, his voice booming, set-off with an effective little kick of feedback. The crowd exploded again (*tap-tap-tap*). Whispers hopped forward, acknowledging the accolade by rippling off a dizzying arpeggio, and then blowing the 'smoke' from the bell of his sax.

Shintaro held up one hand and within moments that excited silence had fallen again.

'Brothers, sisters, and lovers … tonight we welcome another into our perfect warmth. He is a deaf refugee from the streets. With our love and support, and if the Voice wills it, he will soon hear the most beautiful sound of all.'

I became aware that I was the only person looking at Shintaro; everybody else was looking at me. I was surprised to find that I liked the attention.

'Let us welcome our new brother,' Shintaro boomed into the mike. 'Let us be loud, let us be proud. Come to me, Scott … look out on true beauty, and be loved.'

Blistering applause shook the room and I was pushed and prodded towards the stage, followers urging me with their hands and prostheses. Shirley snagged a hook through the belt-loop of my jeans and tugged me along. I would have gone willingly; after living on the streets and facing the supercilious expression of the world, this affection was exhilarating.

I was hoisted to the stage, and I turned to face them. The psychedelic lighting made it impossible to see them all, but I could feel their energy, and it was like a cure. I smiled and gripped the microphone stand with both hands.

'I'm Scott Hennessey,' I said, and the applause went through the roof again. I was a superstar. I felt that whatever I said would be met with two hundred decibels of all-out admiration. What a fucking *buzz!* My smile became a beautifully stupid grin. I held up one hand the way Shintaro had, and that same excited silence fell.

I tilted the mike towards my lips (very cool) and was about to say … what? I suddenly realised that I didn't know what to say. The questions that had been flying through my mind (regarding deviants and freak shows) seemed inappropriate now.

The muscles in my face made a slight adjustment, turning my grin into a grimace. I felt a line of sweat trickle from my hairline to the corner of my eye—could almost *hear* it, crashing through the pores like the run-up of a wave. The silence stretched and I caught multicoloured glimpses of questioning expressions. I could sense the adoration shifting.

I was saved by a memory: my father spinning his old 45s and me, only six or seven years old, singing along, using our upright vacuum cleaner as a microphone. I remembered my father's rare love as he laughed and called out to my mother: *Hey, Laura ... we've got The Killer here. Jesus please us, come and look at the boy.*

They regarded me, expectant and silent. Filtered light played on their disfigurement. It was like looking at a pile of broken dolls.

We've got The Killer here.

I looked at Shintaro. 'Do you know 'Great Balls of Fire?'' I asked, and the room erupted. The ceiling appeared to tremble on the four walls like the lid of a boiling kettle. The followers howled like animals, already dancing: a flicker of strange movement in the disco lights.

Shintaro grinned. He turned to the rest of the band and counted us in.

*   *   *

Man, I *rocked!* I sang three numbers—Elvis on backing vocals—and came off stage a hero. I was lifted onto the shoulders of the followers and paraded around the room.

'Hey, Scott ... welcome, brother.'

'That was unbelievable—so cool, baby!'

'You're gonna love it here.'

'My name's Hannah. Good to meet you, Scott.'

'Fucking sensational, man!'

And that's how it happened—how I came to belong in Shintaro's house, where I found friends and lovers, and became a Follower of the Voice. The love around me was boundless and brilliant. I was kissed and held and the cold city streets were a million miles away.

From that moment on ... Great Balls of Fire, I was rocking, baby!

*   *   *

Acrotomophilia: a condition pertaining to a sexual obsession with amputees. The acrotomophile (or *devotee,* as they prefer to be called) has no desire to become an amputee (this would be a different, though related, paraphilic condition known as apotemnophilia), but will derive stimulation from the disfigurement of others. The psychology of the devotee's 'control' and 'mastery' over the amputee need not be argued, but there are other theories behind what makes him or her tick, from the obvious (insecurity) to the abstruse (a fascination, in the case of a double full-leg amputee, with the prominence of the genitalia).

I'm not sure if Shintaro's psychological profile fits that of the acrotomophile—there are both similarities and inconsistencies—but I think it's close enough to work with. He was certainly demented, and incredibly wealthy—always a dangerous combination. In the Followers of the Voice he had established an empire and a religion, and had installed in us aspects of his madness. He never aimed for the stars. He was a coward in that respect, preying only on the weak, mainly street kids. He had us exactly where he wanted us: following some clichéd concept of a determining power, which gave us warmth, security, and rock and roll parties every night, while simultaneously satiating his disturbing fetish: watching us devoted fools eagerly cut off parts of our bodies.

I was in that house for three and a half years. Eight fingers.

What the fuck was I thinking?

My memories from this period—most of them, anyway—had been wiped clean. Two years at the Centre was all it took: a few beatings and a constant supply of neuroleptics and … well, you didn't know who you were, let alone what you'd done. Looking back, I can see that the Centre hadn't erased anything. The memories had simply been stored in a kind of mental recycle bin. Seeing George Lasky's purple/black face in the X-shots had been like clicking 'restore.' *Do you wish to restore three and a half years of memory to your Active Desktop?*

And there it was, back again.

But despite the drugs and the beatings, some memories remained: I never forgot the way Shintaro held his warm hand out to me as I sat shivering under the flyover; I never forgot the mechanised feel of Shirley's hooks, or how they peeled the skin from my back when we were having sex; I never forgot the honed edge of the sushi knife—the *deba bocho*—I used to chop off my fingers, one at a time.

Again, deliberation. I'm not sure how much detail is needed here. The important thing to know is that we believed in what we were doing. First and foremost it was ritualistic, an offering to the Voice. Cutting off a healthy part of your body served as an initiation for the novitiate, and a method of elevation for everybody else. Not that we had established a ranking system in terms of giving and following orders, but we did have respect for those who had offered more to the Voice.

We may have been brainwashed, crazy kids, but I'm telling you ... we really did believe in what we were doing.

Deliberation: the gruesome details. What more do you need to know? There was an altar, and there was blood—*buckets* of blood. We donned black robes for our ceremonies, we burned torches and chanted. Nobody bled to death; we had effective methods of stemming the blood flow. The body parts were offered—that is, they were burned in the 'Ceremonial Fire.' Shintaro did not speak in tongues. There were no pentagrams, no incantations, nobody drank the blood and, as I've already mentioned, the big red guy with horns wasn't invited. And what were we promised for our dedication and worship? The Eternal Night, of course. Not heaven, not hell, but a transition of the soul to the greatest rock and roll party of all time.

Three and a half years. Eight fingers.

No wonder I ended up in a mental institution.

Followers came (wasted, hungry) and followers went (some silently, others screaming). I can't remember them all, but wonder how I ever forgot some: Dixie Moon, who taught me to trust the weight of the *deba bocho,* and how to cut through the bone with one quick movement; Whispers Coletti, who stood like a flamingo and played the saxophone like a dream; Hannah Lawson, a beautiful friend and a delicate lover; and George Lasky, who arrived closer to the end. I didn't think George would cut it (the term we used for those who stayed with us. The pun was intended), I thought he'd be a Screamer. He'd been unlucky—a riches to rags story on account of a cataclysmic investment. He was tossed to the streets, picking through dustbins and puffing his inhaler—and there was Shintaro, playing his pipe: come with me, brother, you have just been saved. Yeah, I thought George would be a Screamer, but I underestimated him. He took to our religion with breathtaking enthusiasm. Maybe there was a streak of the bizarre buried deep in his conservative heart. It's not exactly unheard of, is it? But more than anything, I think George—and so many others—took to us because we were having a blast. I know that must sound insane given that we were surrendering body parts, but you have to embrace the positives: we didn't have to work, we were into free love and free expression, and there were kick-ass parties every night. The Church would disapprove, but for the sadomasochist it was Utopia.

Shintaro brought Mia to the house in the summer of 1993. *She is my gift from the Voice,* I remember him saying. *I found her fragile. I found her floating.* He soon developed a powerful obsession, and we didn't need to hear her terrible cries or the sounds of abuse to know that she was being held against her will.

His empire languished. Many of the followers—the wise ones—left the house, taking the open door option not extended to the girl in Shintaro's room. Twenty-eight remained. Four would survive the fateful night. Three have since died.

Shintaro's state of mind (already questionable) bowed to ruin. He would walk naked through the house, barking orders, sneering, drooling. His appearance deteriorated along with his mental health: unshaven, unclean, his long hair loose, split, and dirty. After several weeks his possessive behaviour changed and he moved to 'share' his gift with the remaining followers. *She needs to hear the Voice,* he would say, his eyes lustreless, hazy with madness. *Make her hear it. Do whatever you have to.*

I remember her lying on Shintaro's bed, tethered by rope to the posts. She was helpless, and broken. I trailed my stumps along the perfect arc of her back and she shuddered at my touch, recoiling as far as the rope would allow.

'The Voice calls to you,' I said.

She turned to me with tear-struck eyes. She was beautiful, like the world is beautiful, but she was hurt … again, like the world. I remember her words (*now* I do) very clearly: 'I have spoken with Great Spirit, and you will burn brightest of all.'

It was late summer and the sky was full of crimson when the end finally came. Shintaro announced that we were taking Mia into the woods: an offering to the Voice. Not her fingers, not her toes, but *her*—all of her.

'The Voice has spoken.'

'But, Shintaro—'

'*THE VOICE HAS SPOKEN!*'

We shaved her head and she chanted in Lakota: the language of the Western Sioux. We burned her exquisite hair, and with her hands *imploring* the flames she cried and prayed. We bound her wrists and ankles and walked her to the Altar of the Voice, a journey made long by her restricted movement. When we arrived I noticed that the ropes had broken her skin. Blood coursed over her feet and into her palms, and I thought the symbol apposite to sacrifice. This was the last of her suffering, however, and the beginning of ours. We could never have foreseen the horror that was about to unfold.

Shintaro's precious Voice was silent and powerless. *Ptesan-Wi's* rage was deafening. She was all-power, and Shintaro was the first to burn.

*   *   *

I remember running … and running …

Three followers ran with me: Hannah Lawson, George Lasky, and Bobbi Sugar. I used to believe we were the lucky ones, but now I'm not so sure. We may have survived that night, but our suffering was far from over. George Lasky suffered a terrible death. Hannah Lawson and Bobbi Sugar, too. I'm the last man standing. My suffering continues, but I'm not running anymore. Luther Big Crow has told me that there will be a ceremony, and that *Ptesan-Wi* will come.

Mia will come.

And so I wait, my body a tower of fear and my mind a furnace of memories: I can see Mia floating in the rain, and feel her body as we loved. I close my eyes and she is in my arms, dancing without a shadow, whispering in my ear: I am White Buffalo. I am end times.

'What's going to happen to me, Big Crow?'

'Only *Ptesan-Wi* can decide your fate.'

'What if I run … keep running?'

'She will find you.'

'Is there anything I can do?'

'You have done all you can. Now … just wait.'

Waiting …

… and you will burn brightest of all.

I'm not running anymore.

*   *   *

I could write more about this extraordinary page in my history. Indeed, I believe it deserves its own book, but time is not on my side. I had started to detail Mia's furious spirit—how she had silenced the Voice forever—but the writing was frustrated by emotional roadblock. I deleted the two paragraphs I had managed and resolved to return to it later, given time and heart to do so.

And so … back to the three millimetres of skin separating the curve of my lifeline. Back to the break.

*   *   *

'Is there a problem, Scott?'

I lifted my face from my hands and saw Tad Sandler frowning at me, the one person I didn't want to see. I think that if I could have formed a fist I would have punched him. The thought made my phantom fingers tingle.

'Problem, Scott?' A little louder this time. I glanced around the office to see if we had an audience (there are few things more entertaining in the workplace than watching a colleague being hauled over the coals), but everybody was absorbed by the George Lasky exclusive. I watched Ricky Wright flip the X-shots to our distribution manager, then throw his hands to his throat and pretend to choke. I could have punched him, too.

Tad's frown was w-shaped. It was turning from lower to uppercase as I watched.

'No problem,' I lied, then twitched the left side of my mouth in what I hoped was a convincing smile—quite the achievement considering the massive fear that had turned my bones cold.

Tad thumped the top of my desk. The mouse jumped on its mat and the screensaver gave way to the sum total of my day's efforts: *Report on Organic Farming by Sarah Shaw (link with pic. Caption): THE WAY FORWARD? Farmers prepare for the coming season with an eye on the fast growing popularity of organic produce.*

'Then perhaps you can tell me why you have only managed …' He clicked on word count. '… thirty-one words since you decided to roll in at ten-thirty this morning … late … *again.*'

I was tempted to tell him the truth. Poor, sheltered Tad, who had probably done nothing more daring than a shot of tequila. The truth would blow him out of his Hush Puppies.

I got in at ten-thirty, just like you said. I plugged into my Walkman so that I wouldn't have to listen to you fuckwits hop and jive, I wrote these thirty-one words, and then I went to the washroom on the third floor to chase the dragon. Do you know what I mean by 'chase the dragon,' Tad? Of course you don't. Allow me to educate you: it's the method of inhaling fumes from heated heroin, usually through a tube. I still have a bindle in my pocket that I intend to toot as soon as I can, which isn't soon enough. Don't try to understand it, Tad; it's just the way I'm operating at the moment. Anyway, I got back to my desk at around midday—I can't be sure, could've been eleven-thirty—but I was too wired to work. So I listened to my Walkman again, stared at the screensaver, and dreamt for about an hour. Then I went to lunch. I met Sebby at Dino's Bar and Grill (I didn't eat; I can't eat), we talked about my girlfriend, and I came back here at about two-thirty. That's when you called me into your office and gave me another of your overweening lectures—you fucking prick—and when I was walking back to my desk I saw a photograph of George Lasky. This triggered a memory that, simply put, rocked my fucking world: my girlfriend, sweet little Mia … turns out she's the girl we tried to sacrifice in the woods seven years ago. But this is no ordinary girl, Tad. She has a power you wouldn't believe—some kind of Lakota witch, makes the sky rain fire. She killed twenty-four members of our sect that night, and since then has killed three more. George Lasky was her latest victim, and I'm next on the list. And this, you loathsome fucking sleazeball, is the reason why I've only managed thirty-one words since rolling in at ten-thirty this morning, and as far as I'm concerned you can take those words—in fact, take this whole detestable job—and cram them up your corn hole.

'Preparation,' I said. 'It's all been—'

'Horseshit!' Tad cut in, uppercase W, pointing at me with one manicured finger. 'This report shouldn't take more than a couple of hours. You're losing your way, Scott. You ... thin ice ... *comprende?*'

'*Sí, señor,*' I said.

He snaked away and I gave him the old Billy Shakespeare gesture ('*Do you bite your thumb at us, Sir?*'—'*I do bite my thumb, Sir.*'), then boarded the next rocket to Sony Walkmania. The bloodthirsty sounds of my professional environment were eclipsed: Charlie Parker cradled me in 4/4 time, and I drifted farther away with every note. I closed my eyes: instant midnight, with Mia—both of us—close and naked. I held her in my arms and we caught starlight like a jewel.

Remember me now, Scott? Up and down, her dangerous smile pressed to my eyes, blinding me.

'Yes, I remember you now.'

And are you ... afraid of me?

'I am afraid, but I—'

Good, Scott. That's good ...

I opened my eyes and looked at the cursor blinking on the screen: faithful, ready to proceed with the report even if I was not. I stabbed the delete key until my work had been undone, thirty-one words unravelling as if formed by a loose thread. I was left with a clean white screen and my thumbs hammered into action: fear, thoughts, confusion ...

> **White Buffalo ... my mind is ripped my soul is broken. did you kill george Lasky? Are you really goinf to Kill me? Will I burn brightest?? are you ... White Buffalo.... .are yoj Mia. Mia. MiaMia. Mia. Mi a.mia.Mia Mia ... Mia. Mia. M Ia XXXxxxxXX**

Other emotions came, with teeth and with chains—flashing and bruising: grief, anger, heartache. These I vented not through words but through tears. I lowered my head so that my colleagues would not see me, trying to keep my shoulders from hitching, trying to catch the tears in my ruined hands.

*   *   *

I was in the washroom on the third floor within twenty minutes, locked in a place somewhere between chaos and bliss. All emotions were still present and angry but I had distanced myself from them. They now carried a discomforting quality, like the sound of your neighbours quarrelling. I knew I would have to face them once the hit wore off, but for now ...

I would have stayed there all night, I think, if it hadn't been for the cleaner knocking on the cubicle door, dispelling my absorption.

'You okay, fella?' he asked.

'Mia,' I said, and there was the heartache. It hit me like a harpoon, with successive shots of grief, disbelief, and confusion. Fear returned, a pressure pushing at my chest from the inside. I had to link my thumbs in a tight X to keep my hands from shaking.

I looked down and saw the cleaner's shoes in the gap under the door, his shadow flickering in the doubtful hum of the fluorescent lighting.

I asked him: 'What time is it?'

And he said: 'Eight-twenty.'

This meant that I had been in the washroom for—my mind span, reluctantly doing the math—at least four hours, probably closer to five. What was I doing to myself?

'Just wanted to check that you were okay,' the cleaner added.

I picked up my refuse—an empty, blackened square of foil, my tube, my Zippo—and staggered out of the cubicle. The cleaner reached to steady me but saw my hands, saw *me*, and thought again. I sneered at him and swayed towards the door, then out into the third floor corridor. I caught sight of my reflection in the tinted glass of an office window and stopped. My soul shuddered. My heart screamed. I dropped to one knee.

What had I become? This image of me ... drawn and hanging. My eyes were inscrutable punch-holes, my face like Halloween: a skull mask with a bleeding nose. I appeared to float in my clothes like a scarecrow in rags. My tie was undone, my shirt unbuttoned. I made some movement and this ... this *ghost* of me made the same. I closed my eyes. My reflection disappeared and I knew that I was dying.

... *she's taking us out one by one.*

'No,' I whispered. 'Not me.'

I opened my eyes.

Mia was floating behind me, her gaze meeting mine in the glass. I watched her lips form my name and I screamed, turning—still down on one knee—pathetic hands clamped to my chest.

The corridor was deserted. There was no sign of Mia, but I was sure I could smell the forest, the green and earthy fragrance I associated with our closeness. I stood, legs unsteady, and flinched again when the heating switched on: a click-clack, followed by a hum that moved through the floor, through the walls, too loud in the stillness. I looked left and right and into the dark glass again. It was just me and my scarecrow reflection.

'Mia?' Just to be sure. I still expected her to come floating out from somewhere.

Alone.

I walked to the stairwell as fast as I could, shooting panicky glances over my shoulder. As I took the first flight I could smell the forest again. My skin crawled. I called her name and heard her whisper in reply:

'*You can't run from me, Scott.*'

I turned in a clumsy circle, sure that I would see her. I had heard her, I could smell her; she was *somewhere*. My shadow was my only company: a crippled star-shape on the wall, arms cast for balance.

'Where are you?' I yelled—*tried* to yell, but the words were broken sounds. Tears ran from my eyes, cold against my skin. I stumbled down the stairs, falling at the bottom … picking myself up quickly, hurting. And then I froze.

Mia was there, a ghost in the second floor corridor. She pointed at me, and came at me, shadowless, white and black fire, silent.

I closed my eyes and waited for her kiss, and then my mind was seared by the thought of **LASKY X-SHOTS**: close-up, one eye open and bloodshot, that ugly protuberance in his throat. This image kicked the fight into me and gave me the strength to turn and run. I took the stairs down to the first and then the ground floor two, three at a time. I didn't stop. I didn't look back, but I knew that Mia pursued me all the way. I could almost feel her touching me, and hear her whispering, always close:

'*You can't run, Scott.*'

My heart clamouring, tearing me inside.

'*I'll find you.*'

Throwing open the door, staggering into the street.

'*I'll always be there.*'

Still running, still crying, pushing people out of my way.

'*I'll always be with you.*'

Darkness … running into darkness until my legs gave beneath me …

*   *   *

(And there I was—with heart-rending familiarity—face down on the city streets, dressed in rags with tears in my eyes.)

*   *   *

It was after midnight by the time I crawled back to my apartment. I fell across the threshold and locked the door. Everything was broken. My mind was a vortex of hurt and disturbing imagery and I lay in the hallway, too afraid to open my eyes, and more afraid to close them.

I need a hit, I thought, understanding (somewhere deep, where the seldom heard voice of my conscience fought to gain an audience) that this was exactly what Mia wanted. This discernment was overwhelmed by dependence: a black, voracious cloud—*feed me. FEED ME!* I flipped onto my stomach, gained my knees, and crawled again: a starved stray, head hanging. There was a polythene envelope in an odd grey sock in my underwear drawer and I was sure I had enough Horse to get me through the next few hours. I reached my bedroom, threw myself at the chest of drawers, found the odd sock, the envelope … and it was empty, fucking *empty*. I didn't have the energy to cry. I just crumbled, my face buried in the underwear I had pulled out to get to my stash. I felt myself wilting, like a dying plant.

I called my contact at five-fifteen A.M.—couldn't wait any longer; my body was a bruise and I had spent an hour puking blood and bile.

'Do you *know* what fucking time it is?'

'Sorry, I just … you know …'

'Fucking *woke* me up.'

'Yeah, sorry. I just …'

'What the fuck gives *you* the right—?' After he had stopped raving we got down to business: two G's, twenty hits. '*No problemo, amigo.* It's grade alpha, and nasty as a bastard.'

'Can you bring it to me?'

'Fuck you, buddy. That's *not* the way it works.'

'I can't get to you. You know how it is.'

'What the fuck? You think I'm running some kind of fucking *delivery* service? Is that what you think? Fucking *FedEx?*

'I'll pay extra.'

He was at my apartment by six-thirty. Money talks and bullshit walks. In junkie/dealer associations this is not so much a truism as a credo. I gave him one hundred and seventy pounds. He gave me a polythene envelope containing twenty 'bags' of a dirty brown opiate/glucose composite. Each bag was a hit: a tenth wrapped in a cigarette paper, sealed with plastic wrap. No thank you. No goodbye. Exchange made, door—*slam!*—closed. Business done.

It was mid-morning before I came around. The trembling had stopped, the pain had stopped, and I was able to think again. I took a shower and called work. I told them there had been a death in the family and that I wouldn't be in, not knowing then that I had finished at the *Post*, that I was finished as a journalist. My life was about to go in a very different direction.

I turned on my computer and went online. I wanted to know what I was up against.

The following information comes courtesy of fourteen hours (and three bags) of hard surfing, searching through hundreds of entries on people with the same names as my old friends, and hitting the archive-links of local, national, and international newspapers. I found additional information by running through spools of microfilm at the city library. I kicked up the dust, gave myself a headache doing it, but I found what I wanted in the end.

Bobbi Sugar was the first to die: May 17th 1997. Nothing freaky-deaky about her death, not on the surface, at least. She blew her brains out with a .44. No suicide note, and no reason to suspect foul play; Bobbi shot herself in the bathroom. The door was locked and the window was closed.

She had returned to her home in the USA at around the time I admitted myself into the Centre, and for two years lived what appeared to be a successful and happy life. She became involved in gay rights and met her lover at a rally in Washington, DC, the acclaimed singer/songwriter Sookie Ghosh. They were 'married' three months later. Bobbi learned guitar and collaborated with Sookie on the album 'Sugarville,' which went gold within a month of its release. The couple was working on their second album when Sookie died. Sookieghosh.com details the mystery of her death: this brilliant woman taken from us in her prime, who'd written songs for Tom Jones, KD Lang, Sheryl Crow, Sting … a figurehead in the American gay movement of the nineties. Dead at thirty-two. There had been a fire in her motel room and all efforts to determine the cause of the blaze had drawn blanks. It wasn't an electrical fault or a gas explosion, and although Sookie had been known to partake in a little of the old weed from time to time, it was unlikely that a carelessly discarded joint had been the cause. The evidence created by the blaze suggested that the point of origin was nowhere near obvious sources of ignition. '*She went up like the goddam Challenger space shuttle.*' This was an off-the-record remark by Lead Fire Investigator Chad Peruzzi of the NFPA. '*Almost like she doused herself in kerosene and struck a goddam match.*' Gay rights activists claimed it was the terrorist activity of anti-gay zealots, but their accusations had no substance and could gain no audience; investigators found no suggestion of arson. The possibility of spontaneous human combustion was entertained, but given little in the way of column inches. After all, people didn't just explode into flames, did they?

Bobbi was dead ten months later. She used an unlicensed Colt .44 to blow a hole through the back of her skull. At approximately nine-fifteen on the night of May 17th 1997 neighbours heard a single shot from the house that Bobbi had shared with Sookie. Nobody was seen leaving the premises. The police arrived and found Ms. Sugar's body in a locked bathroom. The .44 was lying beside her. There was no suicide note, and the feeling among friends and fans was that a note would only have told them what they already knew: Bobbi had lost her way since Sookie's death. She had cancelled a national tour and abandoned a follow-up album. I discovered several interesting threads on various forums, each suggesting that Bobbi had shut herself away from the world after becoming obsessed with the ghost of her lover. This theory has been substantiated with the discovery of a DAT containing recordings of two unpublished Bobbi Sugar songs. On one of them she screams the same lyrics over and over: '*Beautiful woman, my beautiful ghost. Hold me in your arms, don't leave me, don't leave me.*' The second song is an unsteady instrumental plucked out in the key of D-minor. Bobbi introduces it as a 'love-fusion' called 'Lakota Summer, Lakota Girl.'

I followed a link to www.nastyman.net and found a police photograph of Bobbi's corpse—an X-shot, if you will. Bobbi's face is turned away from the camera. The back of her head has disappeared. There is only a black, ragged space and a few stained straggles of hair. Perhaps the most disturbing thing about the photograph is the caption beneath. It reads (in a bubbly cartoon font): *The bullet from Bobbi Sugar's .44 blew the moody songster clean out of her artificial legs. One of them was found—still standing—at the scene.*

Beautiful woman, my beautiful ghost.

I had to dig deeper to find out what happened to Hannah Lawson. It made for bleak reading. In the five years between her departure from the Voice and her death in the summer of '98, Hannah lived a tragedy. Here's the abridged version:

She went from Shintaro's domain to the streets of London, where she turned to prostitution. Her pimp and sometime lover was East End mobster Ernie 'No Neck' Castle. Besides pimping, No Neck was also involved with drug-running, dog-fighting, car-cloning, bare-knuckle boxing promotion, forgery, and pornography (child and fake-snuff). He made good money selling explicit photographs of Hannah to various underground publications. Like me, Hannah had amputated her fingers (I used to call her L'il Sis). Her deformity was always the subject of the pictures, never her nakedness.

Before long—and God only knows why—Hannah Lawson became Hannah 'No Neck' Castle, in a no-frills civil service in Bethnal Green. No Neck, clearly of a romantic persuasion, arranged for his new bride to shoot a series of pornographic movies. Hannah soon discovered that heroin suppressed the degradation, and succumbed to addiction. She fell pregnant after finishing *Our Men in Havana* (starring Havana). No Neck—assuming the mantle of responsibility—told Hannah that she couldn't do skag while expecting his child, so he hit her in the stomach with a cricket bat. Hannah filed for divorce after losing the baby. This rather expensive development proved too much for No Neck and he arranged to have Hannah taken out of the picture for good. Unknown to him, the hitman he approached turned out to be the central link in a chain called Operation Angel. At one end of the chain was Ernie 'No Neck' Castle and his criminal legion, at the other was a team of brilliant minds from New Scotland Yard. No Neck was hauled in on too many charges to mention here. He currently resides, At Her Majesty's Pleasure, at Wormwood Scrubs in London. Sources indicate that it will please Her Majesty to keep him there for a great many years to come.

Hannah emerged from this episode financially stable, but emotionally wrecked. She submitted to rehab following a near-fatal overdose, and this is where husband #2 enters the tragedy: Jack Hollow was Mr. Wonderful—a tender, patient counsellor who helped Hannah beat her addiction. They fell in love, there was a June wedding, and baby Indigo was born a year later. From the information I gathered it seemed that, for a short time, everything was peaches. The family moved to a new home in Roehampton, Jack's income took an upward leap after he landed a job counselling drug-torn celebrities at a nearby clinic, and Hannah started to write poetry—winning several cash prizes with her efforts.

Due in part to her association with one of Britain's most notorious criminals, but mostly because of her ignoble 'acting' career, Hannah had attained some small celebrity. I discovered the following headline in the archives of the nationally circulated *Sunday Sport*: TROUBLED PORN STAR BATTLES FOR CHILD. It transpired that Jack wasn't Mr. Wonderful, after all; he'd been having an affair with a mysterious young woman (I spent an hour searching for this woman's name, with no luck), and had decided to leave Hannah and take Indigo with him. Hannah fought for her baby—she pooled her resources and took it to the wire, but the court had no choice but to award custody to Jack. He was an upstanding member of the community, a proven Golden Heart, who volunteered

for The Samaritans, had raised close to thirty thousand pounds in organised charity events, whose lawyer produced seventy-two letters from people attesting to his
solicitude and understanding in their fight and subsequent victory against the evil
of drugs. Hannah ... well, her history was somewhat lacking in encomia. The
Judge offered his deepest sympathy, and remarked that it was 'tragic to a point
that beggars belief' that Mr. Hollow's regard for humanity did not extend to his
wife.

Her decline was both swift and terrible. She sought solace the only way she
knew how (there are no ex-addicts, after all; there are only addicts). Her final
months were spent scrawling mad poetry and sending hate mail to Jack. Fearing
for himself and Indigo, he went back to his lawyers, who hastened to court, and
succeeded in having an injunction placed on Hannah. They needn't have both-
ered; Hannah was dead before the ink had dried on the paperwork.

She had three poems published posthumously. Here is a verse from one of
them:

> Shatter: a touch to *coooool* me.
> I had forgotten your fire.
> Shatter: I always knew you would
> *wooooo* me. White Buffalo ...
> I remember you now;
> your charge runs through me.

There was no dignity in Hannah's demise. No bullet in the head, no X-shot of
a body sprawled on a bathroom floor. Hannah Lawson, my best friend during the
three and a half years I spent with the Followers of the Voice—L'il Sis—died of a
heroin overdose. She crawled into a rubbish skip to die.

And so to George Lasky, who realised, albeit too late, exactly who Mia was,
and whose warning provided me with the link to this knowledge, even if he
lacked the courage to be explicit. Without his bizarre telephone call I would have
seen his death as others saw it: a freaky-deaky accident. But I knew—I could
never prove it but I *knew*—that Mia was with George when he died, that she had
overpowered him and forced the inhaler down his throat. I knew that a beautiful
Lakota spirit had floated into Sookie Ghosh's motel room and burned the
renowned songwriter from the soul out, and ten months later had slipped the
barrel of a Colt .44 into Bobbi Sugar's mouth, making it look like suicide when
in reality it was more sinister. I knew that Mia had floated into Jack Hollow's life,
upending Hannah's perfect world, driving her back onto the streets, back into
heroin, and headlong into death. Mia was behind it all, her furious spirit exacting

revenge without suspicion. She is an unspeakable force, ancient and beguiling, forcible enough to summon fire from the sky, delicate enough to float through locked doors. How long had it taken George Lasky to realise the danger he was in? Did comprehension dawn before or after his wife burned to death in a 'mysterious' house fire?

And now it's my turn.

Her passion had blinded me. My desire had ruined me. How long before I lost my job, lost my home, and found myself back on the streets? How long before my addiction killed me? Would I die alone, or crawl into a rubbish skip to die with the rats?

Was it too late to save myself?

All this ... running through me like stripped wire. It was too much to think about. I disconnected in two ways: from the Internet and from reality; I smoked the dragon's tail while my universe trembled, drifting ...

Drifting away ...

*   *   *

After Midnight.

I lay in the half-dark of my computer room with loose sheets of information scattered around me, partially submerging my body: a man drowning in printed pages circled here and there in red, highlighted names and dangers. I would have stayed there until morning but the sound of movement in the living room pulled me from my collapse. I sat up with a gasp, everything crystal, throwing one hand to my chest and in doing so gathering a sheet of A4: underscored typeface and looping, angry arrows—no longer simply words but a symbol of thoughts and fears. I looked down at it and in the light bleeding from the monitor was able to read:

> Beautiful Woman, my <u>Beautiful Ghost</u>.
> Hold me in your arms, don't leave me,
> <u>Don't leave me</u>.

I listened carefully, my head angled, my body curled like a question mark. For a long moment there was only silence and I started to believe I had imagined the sound, and then I heard it again: a sigh, like a thirsty breath, a little louder—a little nearer—than before.

Was she here? Had she come for me?

An icy finger ran down my spine. It wasn't a shiver, running top to bottom wave-like; it was a line of coldness, thin as a blade and constant. I got to my feet, my body still curled. I must have looked monstrous, a soundless thing bent double, my expression that horror film O-stare of terror. I took a single tiptoe step. The floorboards made a sound like a tree falling, a splintering cry that held me to the spot in a moment. I dared not breathe. I was the ghost of a dandelion, trembling in the breeze.

I heard the sound again, and it *was* closer. It was followed by another: the sigh of two silken fabrics moving together, hair against skin or dress against thigh. I could see her in my mind's eye, feather-light, moving through the living room on a current of air. I listened for other, more definite sounds, but the silence was broken only by a rumour of presence: a breathing sound that could have been air in the pipes, a murmur of silky movement that could have been my imagination. I *wanted* it to be imagination, but knew better. It was Mia (the bullet in the gun, the fire in the soul, the heroin in the vein). She had come for me.

I spoke her name, standing straight, so that my shape in the half-dark became something else, from monstrous to man-shaped, something prepared. I moved towards the door, kicking up pages of information, articles, photos. They lifted before me like startled birds, see-sawing in my wake before settling—face up or face down—like tired lovers.

I stepped into the hallway and looked towards the living room. The door was standing ajar and I could see only a slice of the room beyond: the arm of the sofa, the edge of the TV screen, a triangle-shaped section of rug. I studied the gloom to see if it would deepen or flicker. I waited for a shadow to fall, muted in the streetlight shining through the balcony doors, and then remembered how—on that last perfect night—Mia had cast no shadow. This recollection brought pain in so many ways. I wiped sweat from under my eyes, took a step towards the living room, and then I heard that sound again: a hush of secret movement, the sound of an open mouth.

'Mia?' I was surprised at the cool blue sound of my voice, imagining myself drawn red with alarm, my words hissing like steam.

No reply. I watched the darkness, took another step.

Movement ahead of me, so swift it barely registered. I replayed it in my mind in slow motion: a shape, long and thin, drifting—*floating*—across the living room. I played it again, deciphering the detail of its shape as it edged out the arm of the sofa and blacked out what I could see of the TV screen. It was a Mia-shape, with flowing hair and arms wide open. It was her.

This information computed in the time it took my left foot to roll from heel to toe in its stepping action. In the next second I was cowering with my hands over my head, terrified. I waited—a dandelion again—for her to make a move.

The sound of her breathing … and I could imagine her hovering in the gloom, lifted like the poisonous head of a cobra.

'I know who you are,' I said. There was nothing cool about my voice now. My words were as frail as autumn leaves.

'*Scott …*'

I shuddered at the sound of my name, and her voice—the same as it had been when she whispered in my ear during the hours of our heaven, yet distorted in its bleak intonation: from passion to pain, like tragedy.

'*Are you ready to face your pain?*'

I felt my legs weaken and had to fight to stay standing. I reached out for the hallway wall, needing its support.

'*Scott …*'

'What do you want from me?'

'*I want you to be brave.*'

'Listen …' I tried to steady my breathing, my legs, my heart, but everything was betraying me. 'Listen, Mia, what we did to you … what we did, I'm sorry. I'm so—'

'*I want you to burn.*'

I caught another glimpse of her, raised from the floor, the streetlight shimmering in her eyes. As before, I replayed it in my mind, slowing it down, and saw her to be—as I knew she would be—beautifully wicked.

I couldn't run and there was no fight in me. I couldn't crawl into a ball and wait for it to be over. I was without a prayer, standing there. I was at her mercy.

'I'm so sorry,' I said again.

She came at me then, swooping in the dark like an owl, and had her hand around my throat before I knew that she had moved. I was thrown against the wall, lifted from the floor. My wretched excuses for hands made their fight: clutching, snapping, pushing, ineffectual. Mia squeezed harder, her grip encircling my windpipe, narrowing the vital passage until my breathing sounded like a wind instrument with a split reed.

She said my name. I looked into her eyes and saw fire. Shintaro was there, burning and screaming. I felt the heat and looked away.

'*Take me home,*' she whispered. I didn't understand what she meant. I hissed and struggled, pleading with my eyes, weeping and sorry.

She squeezed harder. How powerful was this woman, physical enough for love and pain, spiritual enough to glide like a ghost? Could she be real? Could she be anything but?

I made a final effort to push her away but everything was fading—*I* was fading. I knew she wouldn't kill me. Eventually, yes, but not now. She could burn me in a heartbeat (I would go up like the goddam Challenger space shuttle) but she wanted me to suffer, just as Hannah, Bobbi, and George had. A mercy killing was not in the game plan.

I stopped breathing. My pulse slowed, booming in my temples like distant bombs. Mia relinquished her hold and I fell into a heap on the hallway floor. I tried to breathe again but there was nothing. My vision swam in and out of focus. There was Mia ... and then gone again ... there was Mia, floating above me with the fluid motion—and almost the shape—of a manta ray.

And then gone again.

Fading ... slowing.

Her voice: '*Wherever you are, I'll be there.*'

I managed a dry, gasping breath. My thumbs scratched at the carpet. My back arched.

'*Wherever you go ...*'

I closed my eyes, breathed again.

'*... I'll be waiting.*'

*   *   *

In the pink blush of morning light this episode seemed improbable. The marks on my throat proved otherwise: five perfect semi-circles—four on one side of my windpipe, one on the other—all dark with bleeding. Five lines raced down to the hollow of my throat where they converged in a single rusty teardrop. I touched this teardrop and it flaked away. I traced the race-lines with the side of my thumb, felt the ridges of torn skin. The marks were real, the pain was real.

I was held for a moment by the mirror, looking at what I had become (I gazed beyond the yellow exterior to the grey, shrunken thing cowering inside me), and I knew that, if Mia didn't get me, the heroin would. This was her design: to fill me with desire, and lead me to ruin. I was Na-gah; she was the mountain.

This was twenty-four hours after my dealer had brought me twenty bags of (cut-to-fuck) Horse. I had sixteen bags remaining: a four-day supply. I stood in my bathroom with all sixteen bags in the palm of my hand. I told myself that it wasn't heroin I was holding, but fate: a gram and a half of dirty brown destiny.

What was I going to do? Chase the dragon and stay on top of my mountain? Or flush the contents and see if I could find a way down?

I'd like to be able to tell you that my decision was spirit lifting, full of determination, that I flushed the heroin with a war cry and faced the battle with resolve. But it wasn't that way at all. I cried for a long time. I twisted into the tiles on my bathroom floor, full of hurt and sickness. I confronted my reflection, each visit to the mirror revealing a sight more helpless than the last. The spotlights above the mirror were like knives in my eyes, but still not as bright as the conflict inside.

I prayed, recalling in the hot flats of my mind how I had once prayed to Mia, when she was my religion. Now I crossed my thumbs and prayed to God, to the Voice ... to whatever power makes things happen: that vibration, that first shudder in the great big nothing, resounding to create life. I prayed to this faceless, shapeless hum for the strength and courage to fight. I prayed to live, to be delivered into each new minute.

I pounded on the walls.

I hissed animal-like at the creature in the mirror.

I paced and screamed and lost the shape of the day as I moved from room to room, hating the enclosure of my apartment as much as I hated myself. The information I had gathered remained scattered on the floor of the computer room. I picked up the pages and taped them—at crude angles, some upside down—to the walls throughout my apartment. Highlighted words leapt at me as I paced: *herself with a .44 ... I always knew you would wooooo me ... in mystery blaze ... her charred remains ... faced the horror of ... Shatter ... bizarre accident ...*

White Buffalo

Everywhere I looked, wall to wall ...

Beautiful Woman, my Beautiful Ghost.

I thumped the mirror with the flat of my hand. The mirror broke. I saw myself in a thousand pieces (*Shatter*). I paced ...

I decided, eventually, to compromise: one last bag, and then I flushed the remainder before I could change my mind. As I watched the blue water swirl it occurred to me that, if I wanted it—and I *would* want it—a fresh supply was only a phone call away. I had the cash; it could be here within the hour. What I lacked was the will to resist.

I picked up one of the mirror fragments and looked into it. One eye and part of my face was reflected in a knife blade shape. On the verge of slipping into the warm waters of my fix, I said:

'I have to get out of here.'

I saw nothing of this ambition in the piece of my face reflected in the mirror shard, and nothing in the way of a response. It was as if that broken part of me didn't understand.

I fell backwards, through the open bathroom door and out into the hallway. *Run ... just get away,* I thought. The pages of information taped haphazardly to the walls challenged me, but the idea was forged and it buzzed like poetry—a romance between being and doing that followed me down as the day turned to grey, as it took me to its heart and mothered me.

*   *   *

I packed some clothes, my passport, my camera, and drove to the airport. I planned to enquire at every desk until I found an available seat. I didn't care where I was going, only that I *was* going. I moved through the terminal with fierce energy, rolling my shoulders like a boxer before a title bout. The rush of adrenaline was intense. Mia had said that I couldn't run but I was running anyway. Tomorrow I would wake up under a new sky. I wasn't just running, I was *flying.*

I was on the west coat of Ireland three hours later, standing on the Cliffs of Mohair. I watched the sun bleed into the Atlantic, turning everything red. I inhaled deeply of the clean air and imagined myself with a hard lacquer of bronze, like a statue. The ocean was a hologram, perfectly still until I inclined my head left or dipped right, and then the depth and colour was accentuated by the subtle change of perspective. This panorama presented a freedom and possibility I never knew existed. It rendered me minuscule, yet vital. The sun melted into the horizon, glorious to the last. It painted the impressive cliff faces below and to the left of me with flashes of gold and violet, making them appear, with all their ageless standing, vulnerable and bruised: the flesh of the earth against the universe. I was there, alone and at the edge of the world. My tiny size was given emphasis by my elevation, or by the fact that I was but a single step from a mighty fall.

Even then I felt the pull: an attraction to the west, something magnetic and divine that called to me from the red horizon. It was all I could do to keep my feet planted, resisting the urge to plunge into the thermals and surrender, bird-like, to that distant pull. I thought I could hear drums.

I found a comfortable hostel in a nearby coastal village. It was clean and trustworthy. I took a single room and paid for one week. It was more expensive than the dorms, but better to air my frustration to four walls and a bed than to half a dozen backpackers and a band of travelling musicians who smiled too much.

I had no difficulty sleeping that first night. The efforts of the day had exhausted me and I lay down my head and succumbed to a deepness only a shade removed from comatose. I imagine myself supine in the narrow bed, my only movement the regular swell of my chest as I breathe (unusual considering my preponderate stillness, like a watch ticking on a dead man's wrist). I imagine the room finding light as morning breaks, and my skin warming from grey to orange. Life happens outside my window: the gulls loop and cry, people amble back and forth, a bumptious dog barks at every passing car. I am oblivious, purged of all senses, a foreigner who has found himself as much a part of the scenery as the old-man-shape of the trees and the black cliff faces raised against the ocean.

I am cradled, dreamless, drowned.

The sun is drawn to its zenith. The world continues.

An unnatural sound drew me back into living, telling me where I was before I opened my eyes: the cartoonish heartbeat of a bodhrán—one of the musicians practicing in the dorm down the hall, sweeping the beater across the face of the drum and whistling to give it more character. I looked around the room, blinking sleep from my eyes and wondering what time it was. I was sure it was early but something about the quality of light told me it was late morning. I climbed out of bed and experienced the first crippling pangs (the *needies*, as Sebby sometimes called them). I dropped to my knees and let out a long breath, drew in another, knowing all I could do was ride it out. There was no dragon to chase, no dealer to call … and no Mia to touch and love. I had to ride it out—that was why I had flown.

*   *   *

Cold Turkey #2

The first stages of withdrawal usually begin six to ten hours after your last hit. I had gone close to twenty-four (due mainly to the extraordinary depth of my sleep), but the effects made up for lost ground in that they were, or certainly seemed, twice as harsh. I didn't have shakes, I had quakes. I didn't have aches, I had a body ruined and beaten. I lay in bed as the chills set in, fully dressed with the blankets pulled over my head, listening to my teeth bang. I stripped naked when I had the sweats, threw the window wide, and soaked my body with cold water. Consider, also, the cramps, the bizarre bouts of sneezing, the muscle twitches, the involuntary jerking, the sickness, the dizziness, the crying, and the diarrhoea—oh my *God* the diarrhoea—and you have an indication of what I went through. It doesn't happen at once; there were times, even during that first day, when I believed I could face the world. There were moments when I felt almost ordinary, but then the suffering would begin again—maybe with a searing, knife-blade pain behind my eyes, maybe with an itching sensation somewhere inside, somewhere I could never quite reach. Within minutes I would be pacing, or curled in a ball, or broken on the floor. It was punishment, but it was more, as if *I* was the pain—the bruise on the skin or the fracture in the bone: a living, aggravating hurt looking for something to attach itself to. I had become bodiless, soulless. I was the suffering.

Time didn't make it easier; the slow revolution of days didn't stop the pain. It was Mia. It was *Innocence.*

*   *   *

In the light of recent events I had forgotten about *Innocence*: that moment stolen from time, when Mia lay sleeping in my bed, caught between the light from the landing and the glow of the moon. It was only when I was digging around in my bag (I was looking for heroin) and I happened upon my camera that I remembered.

'Mia.' Her name was on my lips, like her body had been during those moments when hope seemed infinite. The eggshell part of me—fragile with desire—reached for her again. I closed my eyes and tried to remember her evil (the marks on my throat had since faded). I breathed steadily for the first time in so long, and tried to remember her love.

She was here: in my hands, *inside* the camera. The thought was altogether wonderful, absolutely terrifying. My passion to fix was immediately quenched. I started to cry, remembering how happy I had been when I had taken that photograph. But happiness does not last; it is just another emotion, and we ride these like we ride trains between destinations. We get off, we get on. We ride ...

I spent the remaining exposures, then unsnapped the camera and clasped the film in my palms, caught like an insect. I imagined it to have a heartbeat, and why not? It had captured life, after all. It even *felt* alive. I didn't want to let go.

Innocence. I recalled the image: her foetal position, her hands linked as if she were praying, and the light playing faithfully on her skin. Seeing it in my mind was not enough; I needed the photograph—to look at and touch whenever I felt the urge. I had no idea if this would help, but I was too weak to resist.

Suddenly I had focus, something apart from the pain. A little of my spirit returned and I stood up straight. It was as if the real Scott Hennessey had regained consciousness to find an impostor at the wheel and was fighting, albeit weakly, to regain control. I dropped the film into my pocket and left the room, surprised by how easy it was, given how confined I had felt. I walked to the bathroom down the hall, where the man in the mirror looked no worse than I was expecting, and no better. I remembered my reflection on the day of revelation: that scarecrow shimmering in the tinted glass of the office window, something pitiful and wretched dressed in the clothes I had worn to work that morning. I had become the *shadow* of that scarecrow—twenty pounds lighter, a suggestion of a man-shape. My eyes seemed too large, their natural light extinguished. My skin was the colour of bone and it creaked like new leather when I tensed the muscles in my face. Two spots of light glowed on my cheekbones like a second pair of eyes. I touched my beard and felt the shelf of my jaw beneath: an angry right angle. Green veins jumped at my temples, almost reptilian. I poked out my tongue to see if it was forked.

I walked into the village, and the sadness of my appearance was underlined in every face I passed. I heard their conjecture; I was ruined but not deaf. Two teenagers weighed down by their backpacks staggered to the other side of the road when they saw me approach. I heard one of them say something about cancer. They stared at me. I poked out my tongue and I think it must have appeared forked because they scurried away as quickly as their packs would allow. A burst of French trailed me when I passed a group of pretty youths, and I was glad I couldn't understand it; the emphasis implied that it was far from complimentary. A whisky-coloured Irishman swinging his walking stick like Charlie Chaplin informed me that I looked like the dead, then blessed me and stumbled on his way. After this I couldn't look at their faces and I tried not to hear what they had to say. I walked with my head down, my shadow behind me as if ashamed. Whenever I felt like turning back—crawling beneath my rock to die—I hooked a thumb into my pocket and touched the camera film. I thought of Mia. I remembered *Innocence* and kept walking.

There was one shop in the village that developed photographs, but they didn't provide a one hour service. The best they could do was next day. I asked the girl working the counter if I could have my photographs developed quicker. She suggested I drive to the nearby city of Galway, where they have many one hour photo booths.

'I don't have a car,' I said. 'Is there a bus?'

'Bus runs Friday,' she replied. A glance at a newspaper on the counter told me it was only Tuesday. I handed her the roll of film, and she gasped when she saw my hands. She had moved to take the film from me, but snatched her hand back and indicated the counter top with her eyes. She looked at me—anywhere but at my hands—and really saw me for the first time. Up until then I had been a voice in clothes, another uninteresting customer. She looked into my eyes and saw an extension of my deformity: a ghastly invention of skin and bone. I would think about her later, her rouged, chubby face fighting for composure. She would tell her friends about me, and would prefix her story with the words: *Oh-My-God.* I tried to smile. It felt like trying to whistle through dry lips.

'Be careful with that film. It's important,' I said to her. 'I'll be back tomorrow.'

When I left the shop the roll of film was still on the counter. I imagined she had waited for me to leave and then handled it wearing rubber gloves, as if it were a biohazard.

I discovered the appetite to gleam later that day—a sign that my spirit was on the road to recovery. I stayed in the shower until the water turned cold, gathered in suds that carried the scent of everything homely. I violently brushed my teeth, spitting more blood than toothpaste into the sink. I shaved my ratty growth of beard. I deodorised, splashed myself with cologne, and dressed in clean clothes.

Despite this cosmetic lift I remained a broken man, but one who has seen the war and emerged as opposed to one who lies defeated at its heart. I was not cured (my need to see Mia, if only in a photograph, was proof of that), but for the first time since discovering who Mia was, I thought I could face the future.

I slept reasonably well, and managed a light breakfast in the morning. My strength was returning, but slowly. It felt like the progress bar of a heavy download. I walked to the beach, noting that the people I passed didn't stare at me the way they had the day before. Now I was just a thin man, an ill man. Yesterday I had looked, as the whisky-soaked drunk had so barefacedly informed me, like the dead.

I stayed on the beach for the duration of the morning. It was awfully cold. The westerly off the grey/brown face of the ocean chilled me to the soul, but it was invigorating. I sat on the rocks and watched lovers as they struggled hand in hand across the awkward brash, laughing and kissing. I skimmed stones into the calmer water between waves. I bought a loaf of bread and fed the gulls. They surrounded me, a snap of grey and white impatience. When the packet was empty I balled it up and put it in my pocket. The gulls followed me back to the hostel, and some were still circling when I left an hour later to collect my photographs. They followed me again, swooping and crying. I reflected on this inarguable sameness in all of God's creatures: how, once we have the taste for something, we want more.

*   *   *

I wasn't going to wait until I got back to the hostel to look at the photograph of Mia. I could hardly wait until I got out of the shop, tearing at the envelope in my clumsy way, scattering the photos as I shuffled through them with my inexpert hands. Dread and excitement swept through me. My heart was cannon-blasting.

Snapshots of a world I knew, important enough to be recorded but meaningless now: the view from my balcony at dawn, red touching the smoke stacks, the rectangles of the city; a vandalised telephone box; Sebby drinking cheap white wine straight from the bottle; Sebby slumped in his chair, eyes glazed and smiling. I computed these images in a fraction of a second (as long as it took to flip to the next one): a car fire, the onlookers orange ghosts and smoke-like; a pyramid of beer bottles; a house with broken windows (destruction, it would appear, has always been a preoccupation of mine); and *Innocence*. I recognised my bed at once, the arrangement of the sheets, the two kinds of light converging in a line the colour of a soft flame. I saw these things in a blink, but it was the subject of the photo that held my attention, what I had captured in the middle third of the frame.

I wiped my eyes, sure that they were fogged by tears. But they were dry and I was not seeing things.

Mia was not in the photograph. There was only a smoky smudge in the centre of the shot, as if the camera had been out of focus in that point only. The rest of the picture—my bed, the corner of my bedside table, one of the drapes hanging down the left side like a margin—was perfectly clear. I could even define the creases in the sheets. But my subject was lost. It was as if someone had smeared their thumb over the middle third of the print while the developing solution was drying.

I don't know how long I stared at that empty photograph, but I could feel the air getting colder and the light seeping from the sky. My battered coherence sought explanation, when even my senselessness knew there was none.

What are you? My memory superimposed her image onto the print: her foetal position, the curve of her thigh. *Are you real?* I recalled how we had danced in the moonlight, and how my shadow had danced alone. *Am I losing my mind?* I could almost hear the gentle singing of the wind chimes outside her fairy tale house, and taste its native flavour. *Did I imagine you, Mia?*

I had touched her body. I had heard her voice. I had known her sex. Her hand around my throat ... I had felt it; Mia was real. George Lasky. Hannah Lawson. Bobbi Sugar: three graves told me she was real. Twenty-four man-shaped piles of ash. Fire from the sky. Shintaro screaming.

She was real.

Cold drops of rain spattered the photograph in my hand, breaking its gravitational pull. I turned my right palm to the sky and was haunted by another memory: Mia reading the lines on my palms as candlelight danced in her eyes and Crazy Horse regarded me with a portentous expression. This was just after I had given her my body and (let her in) shown her my soul. I recalled what she had told me: how the pessimist may view end times as an ominous sign, but the Lakota Sioux regard it with only a positive spirit.

Tell me, Scott … how do you see end times, or the break in your life-line? Do you see it as a new beginning?

I looked at my life-line—that broken thing—and reasoned that, if the line grew strong again after the break, so could I. This realisation offered the beginning of hope, and I reached for it. I looked from my hand to the photograph, seeing what I was running from, and knowing there was a way out.

Thunder rippled through the sky. I turned to the north and saw, between wind-torn clouds, Na-gah standing on his mountain.

'*I'll find a way down*,' I shouted. The clouds ripped a little more—a ragged window in which the star shone in his solitude. I held out my hand, the one holding *Innocence*.

'I'll find a way down.'

Another thundercrack. It seemed to reinforce my promise. The window stretched, then was gone. Na-gah was gone.

I tore *Innocence* in half and walked back to the hostel.

*   *   *

My optimism was shattered when I called Sebby later that night:

'Hey, man. How've you been?'

A pause. I could hear a siren wailing in the background. I pictured Sebby's house with its wide doorways and ramps. He would be sitting in his living room next to the phone. I could imagine the windows washed with blue as the police car (it was always a police car in Sebby's neighbourhood) raced by. The television would be on, the volume down low. Sebby was one of those people who always had the TV on, no matter what he was doing. He could be out in the garden or in the bath, but the old TV would be quacking away to itself—another of those comfort things.

'Scottie? That you?'

'Of course it's me. Nobody else calls you.'

'I suppose. You sound different.'

'How do you mean?'

'Different. I don't know. Where have you been? I've tried calling you.'

'I took off without saying goodbye. Sorry, Sebby—I would've let you know but I had to leave quickly, before I could change my mind.'

'Where'd you go?' I heard tension in Sebby's voice for the first time, and I paused before answering, waiting for his silence to reveal more.

'Scottie?'

'Yeah?'

'Where'd you go, man?'

'You feeling all right, Sebby? You sound a little—'

'I'm rolling and rocking, Hennessey, as always. Are you going to tell me where you've been these last three weeks—?'

Three weeks! Had I really been gone that long? I lowered the receiver from my ear and swayed on my feet, thinking about the days I had spent in that simple room, trying to count them. I thought about the darkness, its depth and silence. I had a vague memory of a change of sheets, and of giving the couple who ran the hostel another payment, but how much and for how long I couldn't say. I recalled my reflection, bearded, dead in the eyes, and so thin my bones seemed artificial: a xylophone ribcage, drumstick arms. Three weeks didn't seem right, but that reflection spoke to me in its ghost town drawl and I knew that it was.

The telephone beeped like an alarm clock, telling me that it wanted more money. I fumbled coins into its waiting mouth and lodged the handset back into the nest between shoulder and ear.

'… still there? Hey, Scottie …?'

'I'm still here. Sorry, I—'

'So where've you been? Are you home now?'

'Ireland,' I said, and thought, *three weeks*. It was as if I had woken up from a long sleep. 'I'm still out here. I—'

'When are you coming home?' The question jumped down the line, tearing through my words like an icebreaker. The tension was obvious; Sebby sounded like a guilty man.

Silence was drawn between us. I imagined our connection: a vibrant coil stretching across the Irish Sea, close to breaking point. I wanted to ask about his guilt but I let it go. If Sebby had something to tell me, he would, and in his own time.

'I'll be back,' I said, deliberately vague.

'You don't know when?'

'Maybe tomorrow. Maybe next week.'

'Not very specific.'

'Does it matter?'

'Not really. What have you been doing?'

'Suffering,' I said, and closed my eyes. The word was out of my mouth as soon as the thought entered my head. There was another silence as Sebby waited for me to elaborate. 'I've been trying to get clean. It's hard.'

'I'm glad,' Sebby said, and that was all. To this day I don't know whether he meant that he was glad I was trying to beat my addiction, or glad that it was hard for me.

'Also ...' I breathed deeply, tasting the dirty plastic of the handset on my tongue. 'Also, I—'

The telephone beeped again. I flinched and dropped the handset. It fell like a condemned man, bouncing on its coiled wire, swinging and spinning. I fed all my change into the box and retrieved the handset. Sebby was waiting for me in silence. I imagined his environment again, the grey walls and the murky windows, the TV set: action without words. I saw Sebby in his chair, rigid with tension, holding the handset like a man with a weapon.

Silence.

'Mia,' I said.

'What about Mia?'

'We've ... kind of split up.'

'*Kind of?* What the fuck do you mean *kind of?*

I had never known my friend so bitter. I decided not to wait for an explanation.

'Do you have something you need to tell me, Sebby?'

I heard him sigh, and that was when I knew. It came from that fount of intuition: an unpleasant, rising surprise. It felt like a shark attack, savage and powerful, taking me in its jaws and dragging me under.

'My God,' I said. I was propped against the wall with the handset—my best friend's telling silence—caught between my shoulder and my ear, but the life went from my legs and I slumped to a sitting position. Resolve drained from me: blood from a wound, leaving me weak and pale.

'Sebby,' I whispered, now knowing the reason behind his tension, his bitterness. Fear edged in, and an inexplicable green strip of jealousy. The walls of the hostel hallway suddenly seemed too high. I was small again. I was nothing.

'What do you want to hear, Scottie?'

'No, Sebby.' My breaking voice, eyes misted with tears.

'She came to *me*. I couldn't turn her away.'

Tears rolled down my face as I remembered, as I so often have, our special night: starlight glimmering, Motown on the stereo, our equilateral triangle. How bright was the line connecting Sebby to Mia? A breaking wave; an avalanche. I thought about Bobbi Sugar's lover burning like the goddam Challenger space shuttle. I thought about George Lasky's wife screaming as the house ripped into flames around her, black smoke filling her lungs—sooty, desperate handprints on the walls, the doors ...

She killed my fucking wife. I know *it was her.*

'We're just friends,' I heard Sebby say. 'We're taking it slow, that's all.'

'No, Sebby.'

'I'm sorry, Scott. I don't want to fall out over this—'

'Listen to me,' I gasped, closing my eyes against the rising walls. 'She's dangerous, Sebby. Stay away from her.'

'Dangerous? What the fuck are you talking about, Hennessey?'

'I mean *dangerous.* Why do you think I ran away? She was killing me, Sebby—*killing* me.'

'Do you even *remember* her, Scottie? I don't think you do. You've spent the last three months either jonesing or fixing. Not cool, man. So you'll excuse me if I don't take your warning too seriously. Jesus H!'

'Sebby, please ...'

'I don't have time for this. Mia will be here soon and—'

'You're seeing her tonight? Oh Christ, Sebby ...'

'What's your problem, Scott?'

'My problem is that she's dangerous. Stay away from her, I'm not kidding. Stay the fuck—'

'I don't *fucking* believe you!' His bitterness had turned to venom. I could see him in his chair, twisted with rage and disappointment, his wheels moving as his upper body trembled. 'For the first time in my life I've found someone with enough courage and kindness to see beyond my disability—to see me as I am: a man with feelings, a man with love to give, who *wants* to love. And *you* have to play the jilted-ex. Please, Scottie ... *please* don't ruin this for me.'

'You're missing the point, Sebby. I'm concerned about you—'

'I can look after myself.'

'This is different. *She's* different.'

'Just because it didn't work for you, doesn't mean it won't work for me.'

'Jesus Christ, Sebby, will you just listen—'

'No, Scott. I know this is hurting you, but I have needs, too.'

'She's going to fucking kill you, man.'

'That's where you're wrong; she's bringing me back to life.'

'Sebby—'

'Who's jealous now, Hennessey?'

I had no response. The beeps sounded again, emphasising our frail connection. I heard him make a sound in his throat, somewhere between a sigh and a groan, and I knew that he was crying. I wanted to tell him to be careful, that I loved him, but the credit ran dry. Our connection was broken and all I could hear was its breaking: a dead line, more final than the silence.

*   *   *

I couldn't sit there feeling sorry for myself, feeling helpless. All I wanted was to hide, but Sebby needed me. He didn't know it, but he did. I was forced to act. Within minutes of our connection being lost I was on my feet, my bag was packed, and I was heading back to England.

I was a ghost in the dark, in the rain, riding my thumb. I caught a ride after twenty minutes, but only as far as Ballyvaughan. A second hitch took me to Glennascaul, just outside Galway. I ran from there to the airport and made the late flight to Dublin, where the heavy rain (even now I wonder about the source of that storm) delayed my connecting flight by almost seven hours. It was mid-morning before I touched down in England.

The journey, every mile of it, was torment. I craved for my drug, and was plagued by thoughts of Sebby with Mia—lewd imaginings punishing me with fear and jealousy. I saw Sebby lying like something broken, hastily repaired, on the damp comfort of his single bed. I saw the empty syringe on his bedside table, the dry ampoule with the word **PAPAVERINE** printed on the label in neat capitals. I saw Sebby with a cleansing swab carefully wiping the blood from the tiny hole made by the needle. My mind throbbed—a white, painless headache—when I imagined Mia in her thin summer dress, pulling the bow at the back, letting it slip slowly from her shoulders …

(*You okay, sonny?* the driver who had picked me up just outside Ballyvaughan had asked, looking at me as I trembled in the passenger seat. I replied, truthfully, that my soul was bleeding, and we drove to Glennascaul without sharing another word.)

My anxiety was blinding. I could taste it in my mouth like blood. I prayed for Sebby every time I thought about Mia's burning vendetta, and the drone of every passing car became a scream. The jealousy ran deeper, I am ashamed to admit. I preferred, in my blackness, the cries of the innocent to the thoughts of Sebby with Mia. My tears ran more freely when I imagined her putting life into his body, her nakedness held over him like a rose over a honey bee. It was easy to conceive, from my own experience, the way her long hair fell across his face, rich with the aroma of the wild. I saw him tasting her hair as she rolled and bucked on top of him, exquisite movement, his full hands running patterns up and down her back while his ludicrous legs trembled according to the motions of her body. Whenever I became drowned by thoughts of their intimacy, I tried to concentrate on the rattle of the rain against the windscreen, of how much it was like the sound of fire.

*   *   *

I picked up my car at the Park and Fly, determined to be home by lunchtime. I ran into gridlock on the motorway: a jackknifed truck had closed two lanes, creating an eight-mile tailback. I came off at the next junction, took the A-roads at breakneck speeds, and reached Sebby's place just before two o'clock.

I knew, even before my car had fully stopped, that I was too late. Looking back now I think I knew this from the moment our brief and angry telephone conversation had ended, but it really only hit me then. And it hit me hard. I got out of the car, looked at Sebby's house, and something in the façade told me the house was empty. It is strange how, even during the day when no lights are on, we can often tell when no one is home; the house appears lifeless, somehow. That feeling was stronger now—sinister, almost. It was like driving a section of road where a fatal accident has recently occurred, and that moment of reverence you have. I trudged up the path to his front door and rang the bell. There was a frosted window set into the door and I pressed my face against it, hoping for some movement in the hallway, knowing there would be none. I rang the bell again, hoping he was in the bath, or still in bed. I called his name, my heart sinking fast, and thumped the door so hard the letterbox snapped like a wild trap. Nothing.

I can't remember what thoughts spiralled through my mind while I waited; there were too many alarm bells going off, emergency lights flashing and spinning. There must have been some thought process, like those rare moments of calm—perhaps when the wind shifts indecisively—during a storm. I possessed the presence of mind to walk across the lawn and peer through a gap in the living room curtains. My eyes adjusted gradually; the room was so dim. What went through my mind when I saw the TV in the corner, turned off? Did I know that something terrible had happened when I saw Sebby's only wheelchair sitting empty by the living room door? I think there remained a thread of composure. There was no sign of a fire, after all (I was sure, as I raced the A-roads, that I would find a smouldering ruin where Sebby's house used to be). Just because Sebby wasn't in his chair, just because the TV wasn't quacking away to itself, did it really mean that I was too late?

I rapped against the window with the back of my hand. I stumbled back to the front door, using my sleeve to wipe the tears from my eyes, and rang the bell. I held my thumb on the button and let it ring ...

'Sebastian. *Sebby!*'

'You're wasting your time, young man.'

'Come on, Sebby, open the fucking door!'

'Hey. *Hey!*'

I was aware of the voice, but I wasn't really hearing it. It was only when I felt a hand on my shoulder, another on my wrist, easing my thumb from the doorbell, that I gave up and turned around. It was Mr. Wye, Sebby's elderly neighbour, who would tend Sebby's little garden, and whose wife had baked for him when she was alive. He regarded me with kindly eyes the colour of a June sky. His easy touch kept me standing.

He wiped the tears from my eyes with unabashed compassion. My ailing heart moved for him.

'What happened?' I asked. The emergency lights were no longer flashing. Now there were only the white, bare wastes of an aftermath.

The old man shrugged. 'I don't know. His home-help found him this morning. An ambulance came, then the police. I asked them what happened but they wouldn't say. They told me I'd read about it in the *Post*.'

I flinched, knowing the vulgar manner in which the *Post* would handle the story. I saw Ricky Wright pretending to choke. I saw him flick the X-shot of George Lasky between the eyes. A feeling of sickness joined my grief ... my sense of hopelessness.

I asked, though I knew the answer: 'He's dead?'

No word from the old man, just those June sky eyes, their sad light doing all the talking.

'You *know* he's dead?'

He nodded. 'I saw them wheel out the body. I'm sorry, son.'

'He was my friend.'

'Yes, I know.'

'My best friend.'

'I know that, son. I'm sorry.'

I fell against the front door and slumped to a sitting position, just as I had the night before, when the reason for Sebby's tension became apparent—when he had still been alive. I wept huge, rolling tears of contrition. The pain was immense.

'Sorry, Sebby,' I cried. I couldn't catch all the tears; they fell like rain, splashing on my jeans, on the front door ramp, splashing on the old man's slippers. 'I'm sorry, man. I'm so sorry ...'

Mr. Wye squeezed my shoulder and I looked at him. He seemed so tall, so strong. It was age, not years, that had made him a man. I thought about God, and how we always envision Him as old.

'Come on, son,' he said, lifting me to my feet. I felt so small. 'You need a drink. Come with me, come on.'

I went with him, my head on his shoulder and his arm around my waist. I looked back once as we shuffled down the path like lovers, seeing the front door through my tears, still expecting it to swing open—to see Sebby sitting in his chair with his dreadlocks hanging over his face ... his beautiful smile.

Sorry about last night, Scottie, he would say, and I would run to him and embrace him. I would lift him out of his chair and hold him like I never wanted to let go. *You have nothing to be sorry for, brother,* I would tell him. *Everything is good. Now, how about we hit Voodoo for beers and Epiphany? That a plan, Stan?* And Sebby would say that it was indeed a plan, Stan, and everything would be back to how it used to be. Everything would be rolling and rocking.

I reached out, but I don't know to what—this feeling, perhaps, this dream. The old man took my hand and held it tight.

'Sorry, Sebby,' I said, and the old man held me tighter, soothed me.

'I know, son,' he said. 'I know.'

*   *   *

I received a call two days later from Tad Sandler at the *Post*. He wasted no valuable breath on niceties; he was only after one thing. I could almost smell his shameless bloodhound breath over the line.

'Will you be coming back, Scott? You haven't called or provided a doctor's note. Do you mind telling me what's going on?'

'I don't think I'll be back, Tad. Don't keep my job open.'

'Listen ...' I could hear the background sounds of the office as Tad composed what he wanted to say—that nasty buzz of commotion: voices as sharp as glass, keyboards chattering, printers shuddering, the monkeys rattling the cage, the lions licking their lips. Sebby's name would be on every monitor, his death the subject of every fax. There would be photographs doing the rounds. One would be the print-shot: Sebby grinning, wearing sunglasses, his dreads tied back in a ponytail. The others would be kept in a brown envelope (**CROSS X-SHOTS** would be written in the corner where you would normally place a stamp) in Ricky Wright's top drawer, and Ricky would show these to the Features Editor, to the Sports Writer, to the fucking tea-boy. *Take a look at this horror show,* he would say, rolling his eyes. *Freaky-deaky, huh?*

'Listen ... I can hold your job, not a problem. But I was wondering ...'

Don't even think *it, you insensitive cunt.*

'... Sebastian Cross ... a friend of yours ... yeah?'

I was silent, except for the sound of my teeth grinding.

'Were you close?'

'What are you getting at, Tad?' As if I needed to ask.

'I'm thinking: you ... major article ... national coverage. We'll get you away from that Local Life flapdoodle you've been cranking out for too long. And we're talking *major*, Scott. It's a front page guarantee: *Sebastian Cross—through the eyes of a friend.* A story like that will generate serious coin. It's a seller, buddy, I'm tell-ing—'

That was enough. I hung up, and then grinned in spite of everything. Fewer things have given me more satisfaction—ever—than hanging up on Tad Sandler. I think if I ever see that little motherfucker on the street I may not be able to stop myself from slapping him. I am not inclined towards acts of violence, but—as you know—nor am I one to resist temptation.

*   *   *

The freaky-deaky circumstances of Sebby's death made the pages of every major newspaper in the country. It was the *Post's* second bizarre death in a month. They fed on it like vampires, making me feel ashamed to have ever been associated with them.

My best friend bled to death in his bed. According to the coroner's report, he injected his penis with an 'outrageous dosage' of papaverine, inducing over-exces-sive blood flow into the corpora cavernosa, leading to tissue rupture and massive haemorrhage. In layman's terms, he pumped his cock so full of rootjuice that the fucking thing exploded. When I read this in the *Times* I couldn't shake the image of Bugs Bunny inserting his finger into the barrel of Elmer Fudd's shotgun and inviting him to pull to trigger. I think Sebby's expression must have been like poor old Elmer's after the smoke had cleared ... and what they were left holding similarly damaged.

His funeral service was a quiet affair, despite the press attention. A rabble had gathered outside the crematorium chapel, loaded with notepads and cameras, but inside the peace was absolute. The mourners were few: a stepbrother he hadn't seen for three years, an ex-girlfriend, Mr. Wye (who dabbed his damp face with the same ball of tissue he used to blow his nose). Sebby's coffin lay on the conveyor. I couldn't take my eyes off it as the minister conducting the service made his rumbling sounds, inflection in all the right places. It looked so small, like a child's coffin. I found it difficult to believe that my friend was actually lying inside it, grey in the face, restored in death to a full-body shape. As the minister rumbled I held my own silent service: I remembered Sebby at Voodoo, banging his bottle on the table whenever the dancers came near. I remembered the way his dreadlocks would fall across his face, and his eyes would shine through them like flecks of glitter. I remembered the way he looked at Mia, and how he had danced—*I love this fucking record*—spinning on his wheels in the moonlight.

I delivered the eulogy, one of the hardest things I've ever had to do. I stood next to Sebby's too-small coffin in a suit that no longer fit, looking ridiculous, like a charity shop mannequin. I had chased the dragon earlier that morning (how quickly we lapse) and was deeply grateful for its glow, facing the small gathering of mourners with their set expression, wearing their dusty best. It was like facing a painting—some two-tone abstract, the kind you walk away from asking questions about yourself.

The heroin had steadied my body but it couldn't keep the emotion from my voice. My delivery was a labour of fragile praises and silences that seemed more like apologies. I finished with Prospero's line from *The Tempest:* 'We are such stuff as dreams are made on, and our little life is rounded with a sleep.' I prayed my friend's dreams would forever be sweet.

A discreetly hidden stereo system played Sebby's favourite song. The conveyor started to move as its lilting intro filled the crematorium, carrying his coffin forward. I pictured him lying inside once again, his dreadlocks like vines against the lining, his body shuddering with the movement of the belt. Mr. Wye dabbed his face. The ex-girlfriend looked at her shoes. The stepbrother stared at the back of one hand. I wondered what he was thinking, and if he was truly sad. When I looked back at the coffin it had reached the parted curtains, edging gradually from view. Mia was standing beside it, floating in angel-symbol. Her arms were held out to her sides, as if in levitating she had lost some confidence in balance. As always, her hair lay in violent contrast to her skin, falling between her shoulder blades like folded wings. It was the first time I had seen her since the night she had left her mark on my throat, and had whispered the truth I was perhaps only just realising: that wherever I went, she would be there. Still, I never faltered. I regarded her with the eyes of a man who wants an end to his suffering, whatever that end might mean. I was ready.

Sebby's coffin was carried away. The curtains marked its passage with slow, respectful drawing. His favourite song faded too early. The quiet that replaced it was like snow in May.

And my heart: an irregular rhythm, beating with a kind of voice. I listened to it as I looked at Mia—cruciform Mia, *Ptesan-Wi*. I felt the *pull* moving through me: a chant, a song. It told me where to go. It told me what to do. And I looked at Mia, and I listened.

4

From Wakan Tanka, the Great Mystery, comes all power. It is from Wakan Tanka that the holy man has wisdom and the power to heal and make holy charms. Man knows that all healing plants are given by Wakan Tanka, therefore they are holy. So too is the buffalo holy, because it is the gift of Wakan Tanka

—Flat-Iron, Oglala Sioux

The Pine Ridge Reservation—an elbow of some two million acres of prairies, dirt roads, and Badlands in southwestern South Dakota—is, by any standards, a place of desperation. This is not only written on the faces of the Oglala Sioux who call it home, it is everywhere you care to turn your eye: in the skeletons of the car wrecks, twisted and abandoned where they flipped off the rutted roads; it is in the sun-bleached boards and shattered windows of shacks and ranch houses—most of which are without electricity and running water—dotted at the end of lanes or in the shadow of forlorn willows, like headstones in a mostly-empty graveyard; it is in the Grassroots Oglala slogans sprayed on road signs, on walls and discarded banners; in the broken Budweiser bottles and dented bumpers and useless car parts and refrigerator doors and window frames scattered here and there, glim-mering like scars on the land; it is in the voices of feuding lovers; in the fists of fighting neighbours; in the crying of a child; it is in the rheumy eyes of the drunk sitting on the hood of his car; it is in the colours of the torn, dust-eaten Oglala flag marking the reservation border, signalling the occasional breeze like a tired hand waving; it is in the air.

This is the America you don't see in the movies—the superpower nation of blinding skylines, stretch limousines, big money, big attitudes—where you can be whatever you want to be. The Pine Ridge Reservation is one of America's dirty secrets, the *real* Land of the Free, the *real* Home of the Brave. It is the country's poorest area, with close to ninety percent of the population unemployed and a per capita income less than one-fifth the national average. There is no industry and no natural resources for industry. Hundreds are homeless, those who are not live for the most part in overcrowded shacks and trailers. It has the highest infant mortality rate in the USA. Heart disease and cancer are like shadows outside every door. Diabetes is virtually an epidemic. Alcoholism is unbridled: a modern curse that lives in every family like a mean old relative.

But if there is desperation in the faces of the Oglala Sioux, there is hope in their hearts. This is their land, after all—all they have left of it after numerous wars and forced treaties—and they are proud. They are the descendants of great Americans, men like Crazy Horse, Red Cloud, and Nicholas Black Elk, who praised the gift of the land and knew hope in its simplicity. This hope remains, generations later. It is in the coming of each season, the birth of each new day. It is in the smiles of the people you pass, in the kisses of lovers, in the handshakes after the fighting, and the happiness of children. Hope is in the pursuit of heroes: the original American Dream.

This is the Pine Ridge Reservation, hope and desperation entwined. It is where I have been living for the last six weeks, and it is where—very soon now—I will meet my destiny.

*   *   *

I had no map, no directions scrawled on a scrap of paper; I followed my heart here—I followed the *pull*, the voice of the land. It's as simple and illogical as that.

I touched down at JFK in New York City the day after Sebby's funeral, armed with my savings, a credit card, and a change of clothes. My calling was further west—I could feel the unnatural pull of it, almost whispering my name—but I was too weak to answer the call immediately. I checked into a hotel in Hell's Kitchen and asked the bellhop if he knew where I could score some Horse. A new twenty bridged the distance between us. There was a knock on my door forty-five minutes later. Three white teenagers dressed like Snoop Dogg entered my hotel room. One of them let me know that he was armed. It suddenly felt like I was in a movie; I had wandered out of my own life and onto the set of the new Tarantino blockbuster. It should have been terrifying but I knew the role I was playing, I knew the script. I could handle it.

'We heard you needed a l'il sum'tin', home.'

'You could put it that way,' I said.

'Hey, he fokkin' talk all funny,' the guy carrying the .45 down the front of his Tommy Hilfiger jeans said. 'Like Australian or Irish, some mo'fokkin' shit like that.'

'English,' I said. I was smiling, falsely.

'Yeah, I fokkin' knew it was some shit like that. Hey … say sum'tin'. Say sum'tin', man.'

I obliged. I told them what I wanted.

'I need to see some green, home.'

'How much?' I asked. The kid with the gun was grinning. He had a diamond set into one of his front teeth. I didn't have to see that grin to know that these kids were wannabes. It struck me that, whether I knew the script or not, dealing with them was not such a good move.

'That thing loaded?' I asked, hooking a thumb at the butt poking out of the kid's jeans. It was a stupid question—another mistake, but in America a kid with a gun is more dangerous than an adult with a gun, no doubt about it. I didn't want to appear vulnerable. I needed to take control.

'This,' he started, his grin becoming wider as he laid a hand on the shape of the .45, 'is my Siamese bro, home. We go ever'where together.'

'Is it loaded?'

'Bet your white ass.'

'Put it on the fucking bed.' I looked at the kid who I took to be the leader. He had a crude tattoo on his arm that read RAGE-NYC. 'I'm not dealing with you while he's got a loaded .45 in his jeans. It's your decision.'

He looked uncertain. They all did. I pressed my advantage.

'What do you think I'm going to do? Grab it and pull the trigger?' I showed them my hands and they recoiled, as if I were the one with the .45. 'Look, I'm too tired to play games. Put the gun on the bed and we can do business. That's what this is about—business. There's no trouble here.'

Rage-NYC gave his 'homeboy' a signal. He reached for the .45.

'Slowly,' I said.

And, slowly, he pulled it out of his jeans and tossed it on the bed. It didn't look so threatening lying next to the room service menu. It was like looking at a king cobra in a glass box. Not that the danger had completely passed—it was only a few feet away from the kid, but I felt that I was in control now, and that was important.

The kids looked at me—wannabes, for sure; a pro wouldn't have surrendered his gun, but then a pro wouldn't have shown that he was packing in the first place. I nodded, not letting them see how scared I was. I had thrown away the script and was operating on impulse, quite unable to believe my own arrogance.

'Good,' I said. 'Now we can talk.'

They were gone less than a minute later, two hundred dollars richer, and I had a deck of heroin in a glass vial. I had my Zippo on me, a broken hotel pen served as a suitable tube for inhaling, and the green foil wrapped around one of the complimentary chocolate mints made for an adequate cooking surface.

I had to wait before I could chase it; my hands were shaking wildly—not because I needed a hit (though I *did* need a hit; I was back to four bags a day since Sebby had died), but because of my movie-set environment: noise and light and gun-toting supporting roles. The reality shook me: a heavy, dark thing full of strange sound, like a piano falling from a great height. I sat on the edge of the bed with my face in my hands, feeling that irresistible pull to the west, knowing that Mia would be there, and the end of suffering.

I picked up the vial and looked at the brown powder inside, like an hourglass waiting to be turned: time's steady death. I thought about Rage-NYC and the kid with the diamond in his tooth, and I knew that I didn't want to deal with any more crazy punk wiggers with loaded .45s pushed into the waistbands of their designer jeans.

'I have to make you last,' I said to the heroin, having a sudden and too-brilliant image of my own X-shot, and of Ricky Wright laughing and flicking me bang between the eyes.

*   *   *

I headed west the next morning. I got on a Greyhound full of clichéd Americans: old people in plaid shirts, chinos, and white pumps; kids with baseball caps turned backwards; college jocks wearing letterman jackets; a fat guy wearing shorts, taking up two seats and gnawing on a wing that looked like it could have come from a bird the size of Foghorn Leghorn. I had the misfortune of having to sit next to a Vietnam Vet, a pale specimen, his hair hanging to his shoulders in greasy strings. He wore a fatigue jacket decorated with patches and buttons. One of them was a peace sign, another a hand giving the Winston Churchill V, painted in stars and stripes. Another button read GOD-DAMN-VIET-NAM.

He offered me one of his cigarettes. I declined and pointed out that it was a non-smoking bus.

'They can kiss my ass,' he said.

I looked out the window, watching New York give way to the state of New Jersey. I caught a glimpse of the Statue of Liberty standing in the water between the two states, like a girl at a party who can't decide which boy she wants to go home with. We entered New Jersey: chain-link fences, boxlike houses with rotted porches and torn screens, old Buicks and Chevrolets up on blocks. The Vietnam Vet smoked and spoke throughout the journey. He told me that he was going to Mount Laurel to meet an old buddy, then they were heading to Atlantic City ('*Gonna play those tables and get me a whore.*'). He offered me a cigarette. I declined. He asked if I was Australian. I told him I was English. He told me he had a friend somewhere in Australia who still owed him two hundred bucks. Then he asked what had happened to my hands, wiggling his fingers as he did. I told him I was born this way. 'Lookit this,' he said. He hoisted his left leg onto the seat and rapped his knuckles on it just below the knee. It sounded like someone knocking on a wooden door. 'Que Son Valley, '67,' he informed me with perhaps justifiable bitterness. 'Motherfucker, huh?'

When I looked out the window again, the squalid neighbourhoods had given way to Interstate 95. We arrived in Mount Laurel a short while later. The Vet got off, still smoking. I said goodbye to him and he flashed me the peace sign before blowing a smoke ring into the driver's face. I was grateful to have the seat to myself for at least part of the journey. We got onto Interstate 80 and crossed into Pennsylvania. In Pittsburgh the seat next to me was taken by a fat kid who listened to rap music on his portable CD player, his eyes closed. We never exchanged a word. I got off in Youngstown, Ohio. I had been on the Greyhound eleven hours at that point. I was sick of its smell, its feel. I was tired of the Interstate and I needed a fix.

*   *   *

I checked into a Super 8 for the night. There was a bar on the next block called Yellow Creek Tavern: another slice of American pie, with Coors Light and Bud advertised in the windows in fizzing neon, and a line of pickup trucks parked outside. A sign over the door read: IF U AIN'T TWENTY-ONE U BETTER BE GONE. ID-ZONE.

America welcomed me on the inside: two blue pool tables lined with beers and quarters, the players wearing baseball caps and Levi's. TV screens mounted over the bar and in the corners were all showing the same baseball game, all except one which was tuned to CNN. Springsteen thundered from the jukebox. A half-dozen blue-collar old boys, all dressed in denim, sat at the bar, mumbling every now and then in the direction of the game, supping on Buds. Posters lined the walls, advertising Jack Daniel's and Virginia Slims and, of course, Budweiser. There was a framed photograph of Bill Clinton amongst them. He was smiling but he looked somewhat out of place, the way he would if he were to be there in person.

I ordered a Bud (when in Rome ...), pushing two quarters into the tip-trough running the length of the bar. I found a table and sat down to watch the game, thinking that, if I watched it for long enough, I might be able to figure out what was going on. I was on my second beer when a voice at my shoulder said:

'Mind if I join you?'

I turned around and saw a tall man with a smooth, almost feminine face. His long black hair was tied back with a leather band decorated with coloured beads and white feathers. His skin was darker than Mia's but the shape of his eyes was the same.

He took the empty seat and gestured at the line of TVs with the neck of his bottle. 'Goddam Yankees. No one's gonna touch them this season, believe me. They're killing the Indians tonight, but ain't that always been the way?'

I blinked, as if he had spoken in a foreign language, which, in a way he had. 'I don't follow baseball. I'm here for the beer.'

He smiled beautifully, reminding me of Sebby. 'Are you English?'

I nodded, taking a long pull from the bottle. He noticed my hands and I saw the thin veil of shock pass over his expression. His smile remained as his eyes flicked from my hands to the TV, then back to me.

'What brings you to Youngstown? Work?'

'No, I'm ...' I listened to my heart over the sound of the jukebox, the purposeful crack and roll of pool balls. 'I'm only here one night. Back on the road tomorrow, headed west.'

'How far west?'

'I'm not sure.'

'You're not sure?'

'I'm travelling by instinct. When I get there, I'll know. At least I hope so.'

He nodded. 'It sounds like you have a little real American blood in you, buddy. That's what my people used to do in the days before Columbus: travel, listen to the land, and stop when they felt it was right. The land had that power, and still does. It spoke to us, and gave us good grazing for our horses, clear running water, fishing, buffalo ... we wouldn't have survived long without the buffalo.'

'Are you a Sioux?' I asked. It was the question I had been burning to ask since he sat down.

'A little snake? Shit, no.' He shook his head. 'I'm a Chippewa—we used to fight the Sioux. Not me personally, you understand.' He drained his bottle and signalled to the waitress. She came over—no, *danced* over. I could imagine her twenty years ago: high-school-pretty, and captain of the cheerleader team. Now she had a beer belly, a butterfly tattoo, and too much make-up.

'You want a refill there, friend?'

'Yeah ... thanks.' I gave my empty to the waitress, who took it without touching my hand, then danced back to the bar to get our orders.

A Yankee batter hit a home run, rousing the old boys at the bar into groans of disapproval. 'Those *damn* Yankees!' one of them exclaimed, throwing his cap to the ground and stamping on it. John Mellencamp succeeded Springsteen as King of the Jukebox. The waitress brought our beers. We touched bottles and introduced ourselves. His name was Graham LaVerse, but everyone called him

Chip—short for Chippewa. 'It's kind of insulting,' he told me. 'But it beats the hell out of Graham.'

Six beers later, and we were talking like old friends who hadn't seen each other in years. Chip told me he came from the Red Lake Reservation in Minnesota but had been working in Youngstown for two months. 'I needed a change of direction,' he said. 'I used to work in the casino on the rez, making sure the old folks didn't shake the machines too hard. I'll go back for the summer. That's powwow season: party time. That's when the tourists come, and where there are tourists, there's money; everybody wants their picture taken with a red man.' He went on to tell me that, if I was heading west, I could do worse than to check out Red Lake.

'This feeling I have, this *pull* ... it's leading me to an Indian Reservation. I'm not sure which one ...' I remembered the painting on Mia's bedroom wall, those dark and wise eyes. 'Crazy Horse was a Sioux, wasn't he?'

Chip nodded and finished his beer. I ordered two more. 'Oglala Sioux,' he said. 'You'll have to go to the Pine Ridge Reservation in South Dakota if you want the Oglala, but I don't recommend it.'

'Why not?'

'It's hell on earth, that's why not. All those crazy Oglala do is crash their damn cars, get drunk, and cry over their precious Black Hills. I may be biased because I'm a Chippewa, but I'd stay away from the little snakes altogether. Go to Red Lake, or if you want a real Indian success story, turn around and visit the Mashantucket Pequot in Connecticut. They have the biggest goddam casino in the world up there—all of them millionaires, driving Ferraris and Porsches. They'll show you how to have some fun.'

'I'm not after fun.'

'What are you after?'

'I don't know ... I think it's more a case of something being after me.'

Our drinks came and we gave them time, lost in our thoughts. I looked at the TV. The Yankees were up seven to nothing, bottom of the eighth—not good for the Indians. The old boys had abandoned hope and gone home. The one who had thrown a tantrum had forsaken his cap (the waitress was wearing it now). Bruce Springsteen was back on the juke. The pool tables rattled and banged. The bartender sat flipping beer mats, idly watching the game.

Chip said: 'If you truly feel you must go to a Sioux reservation, there are others besides Pine Ridge. They have the Lower Sioux in Morton, Minnesota, and some of the communities on the Great Plains are okay. There's the Wiciyela of Crow Creek, then you have Cheyenne River, Rosebud, Lower Brule ...'

I held up my hand and he trailed off. 'I don't know where I'll end up. I have to go with this feeling.'

'I understand,' he said. 'But avoid Pine Ridge.'

We watched the game's unexciting conclusion. Chip got to his feet and dropped thirty bucks on the table to cover his half of the bill. He looked at me as if he were about to say goodbye, then stooped and leaned in close, one hand on the table and one on the arm of my chair.

'Do you want me to tell you why I sat next to you, Scott?'

I didn't answer; I *couldn't*. My eyes were wide, staring into his. I was impressed, once again, by his almost feminine beauty.

'The green lights,' he said.

'Green ... lights?'

'My grandfather was a great Chippewa medicine man. I'm not saying I have his ability—not anything like it, but every now and then I get a *burst*. It's like seeing with a different pair of eyes. I walked in here tonight and *pow!* He struck the table with the flat of his hand. 'You stood out, Scott. You were buzzing like that goddam Budweiser sign in the window: green lights. Someone's trying to put a hurt on you. The spirits are angry.'

'I know,' I said.

'Yeah ... you haven't told me most of what you know and that's fine. That's your business. But take my advice: listen to your heart, listen to the call of the land, but if you hit Pine Ridge—no matter what you feel—keep driving. Just keep driving. There's nothing good in that place.'

He stood, offered me a strong smile, and held out his hand.

'*Jawenda goosiwin.*'

I took his hand. 'What does that mean?'

'Good luck,' he said.

I watched him leave, then ordered another beer and drank it in silence. The Yankees/Indians had given way to yet more baseball: a game in the Pacific Time zone. The jukebox played early Bob Seger, but I wasn't really watching or listening. I sat on my own, looking at my arms and legs, looking for green lights. When I had finished my beer I collected Chip's money and paid the bill. The bartender looked at me, seeing the consternation in my expression but misreading it.

'Damn Yankees,' he said.

*   *   *

I was at the Greyhound bus terminal at seven A.M., carrying a heavy head, my eyes half-closed. I hadn't slept well, despite the beer. My mind had been restless with disquieting imagery: Mia floating in the corner of my hotel room, watching me, or my body emitting a fierce green glow like the radioactive fallout seen in old science fiction movies. I was glad to check out of the Super 8, and glad to check out of Youngstown.

'Good morning, sir. What is your destination?' There was a map of the United States on the wall behind the lady at the desk. I looked at it, trying to see if any one place jumped out at me. I listened to my heart, and felt the pull.

'West,' I croaked.

'West?' she said, frowning. 'Anywhere in particular?'

I remembered what Chip had told me: there was the Lower Sioux in Morton, Minnesota, or I could turn around and have some fun with the Mashantucket Pequot in Connecticut. I looked at the map, listened to my heart, and said:

'Pine Ridge, South Dakota.'

Her frown deepened. 'I don't think ... let me check ...' She tapped her keyboard, waited, shook her head. 'I'm sorry, sir, Greyhound buses don't operate out of Pine Ridge. Let me see ... there's Sioux Falls, or Pierre. I guess Rapid City would be the nearest major city.'

I nodded and gave her my credit card.

As my ticket was being processed I heard Chip's voice again, telling me to avoid Pine Ridge, that there was nothing good in that place. He was silenced by the sound of my heart. The feeling was so strong that I almost fell over.

'Your ticket, sir,' the lady said. I took it from her and tried to smile. She told me to have a nice day, and that I have a beautiful accent.

*　　　*　　　*

Thirteen hundred miles to Rapid City. Thirty-five hours on a bus. West out of Youngstown onto Interstate 90, through Indiana and into the Central time zone, then up through the north-central states. Thirty-five fucking hours sitting next to fat kids, young mothers with screaming babies, flatulent old people who called me 'sonny,' Beavis and Butt-Head clones with faces full of acne, a college kid doing his homework, his books resting on my lap ('*Sorry, man ... hey, sorry.*'), a five-year-old flicking around with an annoying GameBoy, who'd say 'Sum-*bitch!* every time he lost a life, a teenage girl with a mouth brace like a medieval torture implement drivelling into a mobile phone ('*Yeah, like I mean suuuure ...* '), a woman reading a Bill Bryson book who made a nasal clucking sound when she laughed, a gangsta-rappa who rapped along to his Walkman, and another Vietnam Vet who insisted on showing me the scars he'd gotten at Khe Sanh. One thousand, three hundred long miles. Two transfers. Not one minute of sleep. When I'd boarded in Youngstown I still had close to two G's left. When the bus finally rolled into the depot at Rapid City, South Dakota, the glass vial I had picked up in New York City was empty.

*   *   *

I checked into a Days Inn and slept like I had in Ireland that first night: body shutdown. I woke like I did in Ireland: needing a fix. I didn't deny myself; I had given up giving up. I went into the city—following my nose, not my heart—and found a dealer in a downtown sports' bar. I heard Mia again: *Wherever you are, I'll be there,* and thought about Hannah Lawson, broken by the drug, crawling into a rubbish skip to die. We made the deal—a surreptitious exchange in the restroom, not nearly as threatening as my experience with the punk kids in Hell's Kitchen. I did what I had to there and then: just enough. I floated back into the bar and sat in front of a huge TV made up of a lot of smaller TVs. Another baseball game. I remember asking someone if the damn Yankees were playing. The next thing I remember was closing time.

*   *   *

I stayed in Rapid City for three days (in the Chill Zone, as I called it), before listening to my heart and answering the call. The pull was like a song; I didn't need a map to follow it. I rented a car and headed out, taking lefts and rights by instinct. An hour after leaving Rapid City, I came to a sign that read:

PINE RIDGE RESERVATION
Home of the Oglala Sioux
DRIVE SAFELY—WHY DIE?

The Oglala flag—eight white tipis arranged in a star shape on a red background—drooped from a wooden pole. I stopped the car, stepped out onto the rutted shoulder, and looked across the craggy rises of the Badlands. I took a moment, breathing the heat and the dusty air, trying to gain a sense of the history that gave this part of the world its daunting quality, its magnificence. But all I could feel was the pull, to the southeast now, urging me on.

'I'm coming, Mia,' I said. A warm wind came from nowhere, whispering over the Badlands. A tumbleweed bounced across my path and the Oglala flag rippled, dust rising from it like a smoke signal.

I drove on, wiping sweat from my eyes. The road through the Badlands was hard going. The rental lurched and shuddered, kicking up dust. I tried to steer around the worst of the potholes but it wasn't always possible. I started to notice markers on both sides of the road, growing more frequent as I drove deeper into the rez—white X's, flashing their warning in the sun, placed by the state to mark the spot of fatal car accidents. More signs that read WHY DIE? and DRIVE SAFELY and DON'T DRINK AND DRIVE flashed at me between the X's. You couldn't drive past one without seeing another in the distance.

The Badlands tapered to dry stretches of prairie, the road became easier and I felt, for the first time, that I was nearing the source of the pull. My heart pounded harder the closer I got, as if it were somehow aligned with the land. I stopped in the small community of Loneman. I was tired of driving, my head felt like one of those white X's flashing in the sun, and my thumbs were throbbing. I looked for a bar, thinking that a cold beer was just what I needed, and this was when I learned my first lesson about life on the rez: there are no bars or liquor stores in Loneman. In fact, there are no bars or liquor stores anywhere on the rez. The sale of alcohol is strictly prohibited. Despite this, alcoholism remains an inescapable problem. It can be bought over the border, in towns like White Clay, two miles south of Pine Ridge Village. This tiny development has a population of just twenty-two and, regardless of numerous protests, its four liquor stores sell close to four million cans of beer to reservation residents every year. Alcohol related deaths in Pine Ridge are nine times the national average.

I bought a fruit juice at a small convenience store and sat on the edge of the sidewalk to drink it. I couldn't relax, though; the pull was getting to me, willing me on. I was close.

I passed two car wrecks as I continued south towards Oglala Village. One of them was recent: a Chevy pickup that had flipped onto the prairie. It lay on its crushed roof in a scar of dirt and juniper. All four wheels had gone, taken for spares. An evil-looking bird was perched on its chassis, feathers bristling, watching me as I passed. I came upon a second wreck a little farther on: an insane scatter of debris marked with three glimmering X's. It was it impossible to tell how many cars had been involved. A large sign had been posted in the centre: PLEASE DRIVE WITH CARE. I thought it superfluous, almost parodic, given the scale of ruin. Chip's words came to me again, so clearly I could almost smell the beer on his breath: *All those crazy Oglala do is crash their damn cars.* And in a whisper that gave me a chill despite the heat: *There's nothing good in that place.*

My head was ringing and my poor hands were tight with pain. I pulled onto Highway 18, southbound, and tried to shut out the image of my car spinning off the road and flipping impossible routines: another shimmering X on the prairie. This was no time to falter. I was nearly there, I could *feel* it. The land was singing and my heart was keeping time, every rhythmic beat bringing me closer. The sound hit a crescendo five miles south of Oglala. I jumped on the brake, slewing halfway across the northbound lane.

Where are you? I thought, getting out of the car. I looked north to south along the highway, then east to west across the prairie. She was nowhere. There was nothing. I took a burning breath and licked my dry lips.

'I'm here,' I whispered to Mia, and to the land, knowing that both could hear me. I turned in a slow circle. 'What now? What do you—?'

The pull again, very faint, from the east. I looked in that direction, then a horn blared and I snapped around. There was a pickup truck tearing up the northbound lane. It swerved to miss the rental, a screen of brown dust coughed up by its right wheels. There were three Indians bouncing around in the box of the truck and one of them threw something as they screamed past. It missed me by inches and struck the car with an angry thud. I heard another passenger yell: '*Wasicun* motherfucker!' and then they were fishtailing back onto the highway, the pickup's horn sounding a wild salute as they sped away. This happened so fast that for a moment I could not move; I stood stone-like as the dust cleared around me, a kind of shell-shocked hum buzzing through my bones. When the pickup was little more than a puff of dust on the northern horizon, I wiped the grit from my eyes and looked to see what had been thrown at me. There was a dent in the driver's side door, as if someone had struck it with their fist. A half-full can of Budweiser was rolling across the northbound land, leaving a shaky trail of beer on the asphalt.

I walked over and picked it up. The last dregs of beer spattered between my shoes. I looked at the truck-speck on the horizon, and felt the pull once again: a powerful hit that turned me to the east, lifted my chin, and directed my eyes. The last clouds of dust were whipped away and there, almost lost in a shimmer of prairie heat, stood a matchbox town of shacks and trailers. I could see a thin thread of smoke rising into the beaten blue sky, and a larger building that looked like a ranch house or small barn. I tracked the stretch of prairie between the town and the highway and saw the supports of a small bridge. A dirty ribbon of road snaked away from this, joining the highway less than one hundred yards from where I was standing.

The pull was coming from this tiny community: huge waves of energy drawing me in, like a strong tide. The realisation took the pain from my head, from my hands. I tossed the empty can to the side of the road, half-expecting it to be caught by the pull and dragged towards the matchbox town, just like my empty soul.

I'm coming, Mia, I thought—the mantra that had been running through my mind since Sebby's funeral (and maybe, if the break in my life-line means anything, since the day I was born). I got in the car and drove to where the ribbon of road met the highway. It was little more than a rutted track winding through the prairie grass. I took it slowly, and eased up even more when I came to the bridge: a brittle structure spanning a glistening strip of river. I considered leaving the car and walking the mile or so into the village, but my heart and the land were making a music I couldn't resist. I willed the car across, whooping like one of the *Dukes of Hazzard* when I got to the other side. Three minutes later I passed a sign lying in the dust at the edge of the road. It was sun-bleached, riddled with bullet holes. I had to get out of the car to read it:

SHINING RIVER VILLAGE
HOKAHE!

I looked at the spread of ramshackle dwellings, the dirt roads littered with debris, a plume of smoke rising from a pile of burning trash. A skinny mongrel nosed at a fence post, cocked its back leg, and then disappeared behind a crumbling shack. A little farther down a rust-eaten pickup truck sat in an overgrown yard, its rear end on blocks. A beautiful brown child played at the wheel, exaggerating left and right turns. There was a teenage girl standing in the doorway of a nearby trailer, the baby in her arms playing with her hair. An argument flared in the trailer next to hers. I heard something break, then the door flew open and a man wearing torn blue jeans stomped out. He had a beer in his hand and was shouting over his shoulder. He saw me and grunted: '*Hau,*' then sat at the edge of the road and drank.

I swallowed hard, breathed deep. I could taste the poverty in the air. The smoke from the fire was stinging my eyes. I wiped my face on the sleeve of my shirt, and it was only then that I realised that the pull had gone, that the land had fallen silent.

*   *   *

Shining River has a population of anywhere between one hundred and forty and one hundred and ninety people, depending on the time of year (powwow season is always busy) and the birth/death rate. These people are crammed into twenty homes, most of which have only two or three rooms, no electricity, and no running water. That's an average of nine-point-five to a house in peak season. Make no bones about it; the poverty here is on a Third World scale.

There are two other buildings in the village. One of these is an open-front shack that sells handmade crafts and indigenous foods like frybread and wasna. The other—the larger, barn-like structure I could see from the highway—is the Shining River Wildlife Reserve and Buffalo Breeding Ranch. This is home to a scattering of white tail deer and elk. There's an impoverished-looking timber wolf, a sleepy bobcat, and a few Rocky Mountain goats. The star of the show is a bald eagle that was rescued after it was hit by an RV on Route 407.

The wildlife reserve is hardly a success story (it makes only enough to buy the animals their feed), but it is positively thriving compared to the Buffalo Breeding Ranch. This hopeful enterprise was established in 1992, looking to ride the great American train and cash in on a growing and extremely lucrative industry. In Shining River, this hasn't happened. They started with a small herd of fourteen buffalo: four bulls and ten cows. This number has depleted over the years; the healthier buffalo have been sold to keep the ranch running. A single bull and three cows remain. In the last four years these dejected creatures have produced only three calves. Two of them died at birth. The other was sold to a ranch in North Dakota.

There are no banks in Shining River, no post offices or schools, shopping malls or hospitals. They have these facilities in Pine Ridge Village, six miles south. There are only twenty-two rundown dwellings in Shining River. At night, standing in the middle of the village with the shacks and trailers all around, you can hear the prayers being whispered: one hundred prayers—for strength, for courage, and thanks for the things they have been blessed with. The soil in Shining River may be wet with tears, but it is *their* soil, and it is rich with hope.

I maundered through the village, wondering why I had been brought here. I was sure I would find Mia (the thought delighted and terrified me) but there was nothing but heat and curious expressions. Feeling somewhat dispirited, I returned to the car and found a middle-aged Indian man sitting behind the wheel. He had the window open, a Bud in his hand (there was a six-pack sitting on the passenger seat), and the radio tuned to a Lakota station. He didn't appear to notice me as I approached. He looked at the road ahead, happily singing along with the radio:

'*Nake kola cemayaye, nake kola ...* '
'Excuse me ...'
'*Lakota ki toki ilale ...?*'
'Hey!' I banged on the roof.

He stopped singing and, without looking at me, reached into the passenger seat and peeled off a Bud. 'Hello, Scott No Fingers,' he said, then cracked open the beer and handed it to me. 'My name is Joseph Dreaming Bear, and I dreamt you were coming.'

His eyes flicked up to mine, just once, and just long enough for me to see the depth of wisdom in them. Then they went back to the road, to the overcrowded shacks and trailers of Shining River.

'*Nake kola cemayaye ...*'

*   *   *

'I have to take you somewhere,' Joseph Dreaming Bear said. He dropped the beers into the footwell on the passenger side and gestured for me to get in. 'Come on, I'm driving.'

'How much have you had to drink?' I asked, remembering the ominous signs posted throughout the rez, all those white X's.

He laughed. 'Don't worry about that, *kola*. But if you want to drive ... hey, that's okay, I guess. The roads are bad around here, though—even worse where we're going. You'll need to hold the wheel tight. I hope you have a good strong grip.'

'I can manage,' I said, and—right on cue—dropped the can I was holding. Warm Budweiser spattered between my shoes for the second time in less than an hour.

Dreaming Bear roared with laughter, slapping the steering wheel with one of his big hands. 'Scott No Fingers,' he said. '*Hoka hey!*'

'What does that mean?' I asked.

'It means: today is a good day to die!'

'You can drive,' I said, and went around to the passenger side. I thought we'd head back to the highway, but we continued east. Even when we ran out of road we continued east, taking the car onto the prairie, cutting through the high grass and bouncing over the terrain.

'Aren't you glad I'm driving?' Dreaming Bear asked. 'Hey, is this a rental? It sure is a nice automobile. I haven't driven a car since I crashed my sister's Topaz six weeks ago.'

We lurched to the right as the prairie dropped away. I braced myself, sure we were going to roll, but Dreaming Bear seemed to know what he was doing; he jerked the wheel with a '*Whoa there!*' and edged us onto smoother ground.

'You should've rented a truck,' he told me with a smiling, sideways glance. 'A big old gas-guzzler with an off-road suspension and four wheel drive. Shit ... this would be a whole lot easier with four wheel drive.'

I killed the radio, wanting as much of his attention as he could safely give me.

'I have a question for you,' I said.

'Fire away, *kola*.'

'Where the hell are we going? And how do you know my name?'

'That's two questions. Which one would you like me to answer first?'

Another lurch, this time to the left. Beer splashed the crotch of my jeans.

'My name,' I said. 'How do you know my name?'

'I told you, I—*whoa there!*—I dreamt you were coming.'

I opened my mouth to tell him that I didn't believe him, but found that my scepticism had been reduced to nothing. How could I doubt anything after what I'd been through and the things I'd seen? The mystery here—in this land and in its people—is real, running parallel with its beauty. And like beauty, it is not for me to understand, or even try to understand.

'What happened in the dream?' I asked.

'You'll see, Scott No Fingers. I wouldn't want to spoil the surprise.'

'Do you know why I was brought here?'

'Of course; the dream told me this, too.'

'Was Mia in the dream?'

I studied his face. His eyes were unflinching, telling me nothing. He smiled thinly and I waited ... flushed and trembling, clutching the beer can with both hands while my body seemed to clutch my heart. It occurred to me that I hadn't chased the dragon since leaving Rapid City that morning. That need—that destructive desire—was crawling up on me again: a living thing with claws and a heartbeat, but it was nothing next to my need for knowledge.

I asked again: 'Was Mia in the dream?'

Dreaming Bear looked at me. His eyes were the light in his expression, casting shadows beneath his cheekbones, making the lines in his face appear as deep as the ruts in the land. They shone with pain and strength, with truth.

'Mia Floats Softly has been dead for thirty-two years,' he told me, then turned back to the prairie, clutching the wheel, doing what he had to do to keep us from rolling.

*   *   *

We arrived at the shack soon after, a small building of loose boards and shutters with a crumbling porch and a woodpile at one end that appeared to keep the structure upright. A few thin chickens complained behind a screen of mesh fencing, a trickle of water could be heard coming from a well in the yard, and an old dog that had been sleeping in the shade of a yellow pine pricked up its ears as we approached and started to howl.

'Don't worry about *Ota Kte,*' Dreaming Bear said, nodding at the dog. 'He hasn't bitten anyone for two years. I think he's forgotten how.'

We got out of the car. The dog padded over to Dreaming Bear, tail flapping. It offered me a derisive glance as it passed, then inclined its head so that Dreaming Bear could scratch behind one ear.

'Hey, boy … yeah, you like that, huh?' Dreaming Bear looked at me, one hand shielding the sun from his eyes. 'His name's *Ota Kte*. It means Plenty Kill. When he was a pup he got into a tangle with a fully grown coyote—got the better of it, too; the coyote took off with its tail between its legs. Can you believe that, Scott No Fingers?'

I nodded. 'I can believe anything.' I was still reeling from what he had told me about Mia. My world was only just returning. One side of my brain felt detached and clumsy, the way your arm can feel when you've been sleeping on it.

'Yeah, *Ota Kte* has never forgotten that day. That's why he howls. He wants us to think he's still bad.'

I stepped forward, looking at the shack. Two of its windows were broken, boarded up. Another had a crack sealed with duct tape.

'Who lives here?' I asked. 'Is this where you wanted to bring me?'

'This is where my dream told me to bring you.' He started towards the door. I hesitated before following. *Ota Kte* sniffed at my heels. I shooed it away and it howled again.

'Respect now,' Dreaming Bear told me as we reached the door. The humour had gone from his voice. 'This man is old. His eyes have long been blind but his heart sees everything. He is carved from the land. He knows its secrets and its movements, just as you would know the ways of a lover you have been with all your life. He knows who you are and why you've come. He'll tell you more than I can. Respect now, Scott No Fingers; this is the home of Luther Big Crow: Mia's father.'

He opened the door and entered. I stood on the threshold, wanting to run, wanting to die. The darkness of the shack seemed like a cave to me. I heard a rustle of speech: something in Lakota, a voice like the sigh of an old tree swaying in the wind. It hit me hard and I staggered. I could hear Mia in it, could almost smell her in that darkness—a scent I knew so well. And then Dreaming Bear was there to keep me from falling, and then—whispering—translating what the old man had said:

'Luther Big Crow says that your fear sings like a bird in the morning, but that you should not be afraid. He wants you to come in. He has been expecting you.'

Every part of the shack seemed to creak—the walls, the window frames, the floor, like an old man trying to get comfortable. The light was poor. It came through in stripes, showing dust and age. There were a few meagre pieces of furniture: a crate for a chair, a woodstove with nothing in its belly but ashes. I saw more detail as my eyes adjusted: the open doorway to the other room, a prayer wheel hanging on the wall, the bucket from the well standing in a puddle in the corner. Dreaming Bear took my arm and eased me forward. A blue ghost of smoke swirled in the shadows before me, and at its heart was the glowing, trembling tip of a cigarette. It seemed to float in the air on its own, like a magic trick, until I was able to see the shape of the old man holding it, drawing on it, and then blowing more of that ghost into the air. He stood as I approached and we came together in a warm bar of light.

'*Yah tah hey*,' he creaked, holding out his hand. I took it as if it were made of glass, looking to Dreaming Bear for a translation.

'Luther Big Crow welcomes you to his home.'

He was small, bent at the waist like the old tree his voice resembled. His hair was long and white, some of it tied back but most hanging loose. Huge eyes, washed blue by their blindness, were turned up to mine. His skin was pale, his mouth just another deep line set into his face, discernible only when he opened it to pull on his stub of a cigarette or to speak.

He released my hand and gestured for me to sit. I found the crate, pulled it up, and gingerly trusted my weight to it.

The shack creaked.

Ota Kte howled.

Luther Big Crow spoke only in Lakota—Dreaming Bear providing the interpretation on both sides. For the sake of simplicity, I submit only the translation of our conversation here.

'Mia was born in this very room on a beautiful August night in 1950. I thanked Great Spirit for her coming. I wrapped her in a star quilt and held her in my arms. I've never cried such tears of pride. I took her outside to show her to the night. I said to the stars: 'There is a beauty here on earth to challenge yours now.' And the stars agreed. They danced for the child in my arms, burning across the sky in wonderful trails. I lifted Mia higher, weeping proudly. I knew then that she was a holy child.'

A transparent fan of hair had fallen across his face. He swept it behind his ear with a trembling hand and I saw a tear fall, glimmer in the bar of light, then hit the floor between his bare feet in a tiny puff of dust.

'Her name, of course, was Mia Big Crow, but from an early age we called her Mia Floats Softly because she looked just like a butterfly. Sometimes, when she walked, it was like her feet barely touched the ground. She certainly lived up to her name. When she was five years old I told her the story of White Buffalo Calf Woman, how she came to the Lakota Sioux in the Black Hills two thousand years ago, carrying the Sacred Pipe, offering spirituality and prayer, and teaching us the seven sacred ceremonies. Before leaving, White Buffalo Calf Woman told our people that she would return. Mia listened to this story. She was hypnotised by the tale of this holy woman, and when I had finished she asked me to tell it again. When I had finished the second time she looked at me closely—she seemed to look inside me, at my heart, and she asked if I thought White Buffalo Calf Woman would return. I said that I was sure she would, and that she would bring goodness to our people—to all people—and prosperity to our beautiful land.

'Mia had a dream that night—a powerful dream in which she had been running fast across the plains. When she looked at her legs to see why they were moving so fast she saw that she had four legs, and that her fur was as white as the snow. When she looked at her shadow she saw the shadow of a buffalo. She had tears in her eyes when she told me about the dream, and when I asked why she was crying she said that, looking through her White Buffalo eyes, the land was like a rotten apple and the people she saw had a great darkness inside them. She told me that she believed she had been born because Great Spirit wanted her to bring colour back to Mother Earth, to touch the people, and to take the darkness from their hearts. That was what she said, and only five years old!'

The smile on Luther Big Crow's face pushed all his other lines into smiles. His tears raced between them, moving across the texture of his face, the way the stars had moved across the sky on the night that Mia was born. His time-faded eyes found me in the gloom, without sight but not without expression; they were turned up at the edges, and then hidden as that fan of hair fell across his face again.

'Are you familiar,' he continued, 'with the prophecy of the Second Coming?'

'That Jesus Christ will return to earth,' I replied. 'That he will assume a physical form, renewing hope and glory.'

Luther Big Crow nodded, taking a last puff on the cigarette and stamping it out against the wall. 'Yes, Jesus Christ. He lives on the rez, too. We have churches in Pine Ridge: Catholic, Body of Christ, Seventh-day Adventist. But our Lakota beliefs run deeper, like a vein. Ask any of the Lakota here in Pine Ridge, Rosebud, or up on the Cheyenne River Reservation—ask them about the Second Coming and they will not say it is the return of Jesus Christ, but the return of White Buffalo Calf Woman.'

(Dreaming Bear: 'Luther Big Crow has just asked me what the Second Coming means to me, and I told him what I believe—that it will be the return of *Pte-san-Wi*: White Buffalo Calf Woman.')

'Mia Floats Softly believed from the age of five that *she* was the Second Coming. She told me that she would dream every night of running fast across the land, her white fur blowing, and her buffalo shadow rippling at her side. She said that she wanted to gather all the evil and turn it into a pile of bones. She said that one day she would chase the darkness as the wolf chases the rabbit. I remember how her young face would turn old with anger when she told me these things. She had so much *anger* inside her, Scott No Fingers, it used to frighten me. She even started to call herself Mia White Buffalo, and would bleach buffalo fur and tie it into her hair. As she grew older she began to study the holy ways. She offered prayers to Mother Earth, to the sun and stars. Children would come here and Mia would delight them with stories. She told them how the fawn was given his spotted shirt, how people learned to fish, and she would teach them the important lessons within these stories. By the age of twelve she was a gifted medicine girl. She knew more about the healing properties of the land than any Sioux for miles around. The sick and dying would travel here from all over the Dakotas, offering their pain to her holy ways. Some she couldn't heal, and she would tell them that they should not be afraid—that it was their time to walk with Great Spirit, and to walk proudly. She would say a prayer for them. She once told me that if she could take their pain into her own young body, she would.'

Big Crow hooked the fallen hair behind his ear again. His eyes moved around the room, and I could imagine the darkness of his vision beating like a bird's wing as they moved from the shadows to the light, then back to the shadows. He said something in Lakota that Dreaming Bear didn't translate. I sat between them on the creaky crate, everything I knew—my soul—falling around me like the old man's tears. I kept seeing him with a baby in his arms, the stars racing in spectacular celebration. And then I would see Mia with her head down, her wrists and ankles bound, flanked by darkness.

'I'm sorry,' I whispered, my tears joining Big Crow's on the dusty floor. 'I'm so sorry.'

'Your pain is the colour of a sunset,' Big Crow said to me. He reached over, took my hand. His grip was weak but warm. 'Your suffering shines. It is like the sharp edge of a knife.'

'I hurt your daughter,' I said to him. 'I am the darkness she told you about in her dreams. It was a long time ago. I was confused, scared. I was …'

Dreaming Bear translated as I spoke. Big Crow listened, the lines on his face shining with tears. He nodded and squeezed my hand …

'Stop, Scott No Fingers. Stop there. I don't need to hear your grief when I can feel its colour. Would you have someone describe the ocean while you stand there looking at it? I didn't call you here to listen to your confession. You are here for a different reason, an important reason, and I will tell you that soon. For now, you must know that you didn't hurt Mia Floats Softly, or even touch her. It was her *spirit* you encountered and tried to hurt—the part of her that is caught in the wind, chasing the darkness as the wolf chases the rabbit. Mia Floats Softly, my daughter, the holy child, left Mother Earth to walk with Great Spirit when she was eighteen years old. I will tell you about it now, though it won't be easy; my pride is a mountain, but my memories are a lake of tears.'

He gave my hand a final squeeze and sat back in his seat, losing himself in the shadows. I could just see the moon-glow of his shining eyes and, as he wept, the zigzag descent of his tears.

Dreaming Bear whispered to him. Luther Big Crow closed his eyes and disappeared. I watched the shadows and waited. For a moment there was silence, and then Big Crow drew his hands into the shadows and I heard his voice: words whispered with rhythm and balance. I looked at Dreaming Bear and saw that his hands were together and his head down. I realised that they were praying. I crossed my thumbs and looked down at the dust between my feet, where my tears had made a shape like a smile.

The silence was broken when the old man popped a match with his thumbnail. A flower of orange light threw the shadows against the walls. He got the tip of his cigarette burning and blew smoke at the match to extinguish it. In the second before it sputtered out, it resembled a streetlight flickering in thick fog.

'Do you know what lies at the heart of darkness?' The words spoken in Lakota had the rhythm of another prayer. Dreaming Bear translated and it took me some time to find the answer, even though I *knew* the answer. From bitter experience, I knew.

'Desire,' I said.

Big Crow nodded. The glow from his cigarette smoothed some of the years from his face. I could see Mia in him for the first time.

'Desire, yes. Greed, avarice, lust … it has many names. I used to tell Mia that the road of desire leads only to ruin. It's the reason you're sitting here now with a pain in your body as bright as the setting sun. Understand this, Scott No Fingers: Mia's restless spirit, as it floats on the wind, uses desire in the same way a hunter will use a trap. She catches darkness, and she turns it into bones …'

I looked at my tears and remembered how the wet summer dress had slipped from Mia's shoulders, catching my darkness. I imagined her enraged spirit hovering over the world, like a hawk, preying on its pestilent desire. I remembered how loud Shintaro had screamed.

'I was sitting in the yard when I learned that Mia had gone to walk with Great Spirit,' Big Crow said. 'It was a cool night. I had just built a fire, and was thinking about the sun dances I used to perform at powwows when I was a young man. Suddenly, a great pain hit my heart. I rolled onto my side and started to tremble. I managed to call out to my wife, Mary Walking, but she was sleeping and didn't hear. I thought that my time had come, so I spoke my prayers and held the land. The pain spread into my stomach, then into my limbs. I lay on my side and wept, sure that I would soon feel Great Spirit's hand … but all at once the pain subsided. A great stillness fell over my body, like the calm after a storm. It lasted only a moment before the ground beneath me started to vibrate. I recognised the rhythm—knew it was the thunder of a charging animal. I wiped the tears from my eyes and got to my feet, and the light from the fire was cast upon the most sacred of all creatures: a white buffalo calf. It was running fast across the prairie, into the night, chasing the darkness. And then, like a dream, it disappeared. This was when I knew that Great Spirit had called Mia Floats Softly to His side.

'I got in my truck and listened to the land—just as you did, Scott No Fingers, to find us here. I drove a mile south of Pine Ridge Village, then was forced to pull over and run where my truck would not go: through sagebrush and pines, over rocks as high as this shack, across the old-man-skin of the prairie. My heart hammered harder with every hard step, and the land was like a song. At last I found her … my beautiful daughter. She had been raped and beaten—bound by her wrists to the branches of a willow tree. Her hair was hanging in dirty flows. Her sacred body was pale and soulless.'

Big Crow exhaled a glowing cloud of smoke. When it cleared I could see the tears cascading down his face. Dreaming Bear placed a hand on his shoulder, and I noticed a glistening seam circling his wrist, like a bracelet. I realised it was the ghostly trail of a tear; Dreaming Bear was crying, too.

'I'm sorry,' I said again. Big Crow gave no indication that he had understood, and Dreaming Bear offered no translation.

'I cut the binds and brought her body back here. She seemed as light in my arms as the night she was born. We prepared a traditional Lakota ceremony. Her body was kept in this shack for four days while we built a burial scaffold outside. Mourners came in their hundreds, from all over the rez, laying flowers and gifts at the door. When the four days had passed, Mary Walking, my sisters, and three half sisters, wrapped Mia's body in a bundle and carried it to the scaffold. It was lifted high and surrounded by her passions: her books and paintings, and the star quilt she had been wrapped in as a baby. In this way, Mia's holy body was offered to the sun, the sky, and the wind. This ceremony is known as the *Wacekiyapi*. Her body would remain on the scaffold until it had turned to dust and blown away.

'I was woken that first night by the sound of a stampede. It sounded like many horses running wild, and I was sure, when I went outside, that I would see them charging across the plains, flank to flank, as if startled. But the flower moon cast her light on only one animal, running so fast, and with such fury, that it sounded like many ...'

'A white buffalo,' I said, knowing the sound Big Crow was talking about.

'She *glowed*, Scott No Fingers ... beautiful and dangerous.'

I nodded as Dreaming Bear translated; I knew this, too.

'My heart was filled with hope and elation. Tears poured from my eyes and I held out my arms as the white buffalo charged across the plains. I watched until her perfect, glowing coat disappeared on the western horizon, and then I turned to the burial scaffold, knowing what I would see.'

Big Crow cast his blind eyes in my direction, as if he could see my trembling shape in the gloom.

'Mia's star quilt was still there,' he said. 'Her books and paintings were still there, but her holy body was gone. I looked again at the point on the horizon where the white buffalo had disappeared, and then fell to my knees and prayed.'

Big Crow sat silently for a moment, finishing his cigarette and stubbing it out on the wall. Most of the light had gone from the shack, though outside the sky still held the sun in its palm. It filtered through the boards and shuttered windows in fingers that couldn't quite reach.

'I believe that Mia Floats Softly was the Second Coming,' Big Crow continued, his Lakota coming across in strained and tired whispers. 'Her life ended before her divine work was completed, but her sacred spirit lives. It charges across the rotten apple of the land, and it is furious.'

I imagined Sebby bleeding to death, and heard Shintaro screaming.

Big Crow was nodding. 'So angry,' he said.

The only sound was my rapid breathing. I could feel the old man's blind eyes tracking me in the dusty light, and wondered what colour my pain was now.

I have spoken with Great Spirit, and you will burn brightest of all.

I wondered if my fear was brighter.

Big Crow continued: 'A white man came to see me before the strawberry moon was in the sky. He was one of three men who had played a part in Mia's death. His guilt made the air sour and his fear was almost too bright to look at. I asked him what he wanted and he fell to his knees and started to beg. "Tell her I'm sorry," he implored. He was crying like a scolded child but he stank of sweat and piss. "Tell her I don't want to die." If I hadn't been so disgusted I would have laughed in his face. He told me that his friends—the men who had been with him on that terrible night—were dead. One had been killed by a drunk driver over the Nebraska state line. The other had been trampled by a spooked horse. "I'm next," he told me. "I *know* I am: your daughter came to me last night, floating in the air like a butterfly. She pointed at me and smiled. I know she killed my friends, and now she's coming after me." He continued to weep and beg and tell me how sorry he was … how he didn't want to die.'

'What did you do?' I asked.

Big Crow looped a tress of hair behind one ear. Another tear twisted through the lines on his face. 'I was furious with him. I wanted to wrap my hands around his throat and squeeze the life from his body, but my staid mind favoured pity. I told him what I tell you now, Scott No Fingers: that I am just a man. I cannot control the spirits any more than I can control the sun or the moon. Only *Ptesan-Wi* can decide your fate.'

I shuddered, as if ghostly fingers had stroked the back of my neck. *Ota Kte* howled again, and I had a sudden sense of Mia's presence. I looked over my shoulder like a man who thinks he is being followed.

The old man must have sensed my anxiety. 'Not yet,' he said.

My shirt was pressed to my skin, damp with sweat. 'What happened?' I gasped. 'Did she get him?'

Dreaming Bear did not translate my question. He chose to answer it himself: 'He ran away, maybe thinking he'd find peace and love in San Francisco. He was wrong.'

'She got him?'

He nodded. 'My cousin, William Storm Heart, was taking part in the Alcatraz occupation at the time. He heard all about it. This was in 1970; two years after

Mia went to walk with Great Spirit. This man—his name was Johnny Hester—had moved to the Bay Area with a flower in his hair. You can imagine the scene: free love, Vietnam War protests, Jefferson Airplane playing on the radio. I guess he thought that making love, not war, would absolve him from his terrible sin. *Ptesan-Wi* thought otherwise.

'The San Francisco *Chronicle* has stopped reporting Golden Gate Bridge suicides, believing that the publicity perpetuates the problem …'

'The Werther effect,' I cut in. I had written an article on it for *GQ*. 'Copycat suicides influenced by the media.'

'That's right, Scott No Fingers,' Dreaming Bear said. I could tell he was impressed, but I was (and continue to be) more impressed by him. I admit to have been expecting benighted, agrestic minds, but Dreaming Bear is humorous, well-spoken, and well-read (I have since visited his home and was delighted to find all three rooms, including the bathroom, loaded with books. Dreaming Bear is addicted to knowledge).

'As I was saying, the *Chronicle* no longer reports on the suicides, but back in 1970, they did … and the more bizarre they were, the better. Johnny Hester and his gang fit into the bizarre category.'

The *freaky-deaky* category, I thought.

'The story ran for three weeks,' Dreaming Bear said. 'My cousin mailed the cuttings—I still have them somewhere. Anyway, long story short: Johnny moves to San Fran in 1968, gets in with the hippie-chicks and the whole expanded consciousness deal. Every time he takes LSD, what do you think he sees? Not a pink elephant, but a …'

'White buffalo,' I finished.

'Ten out of ten, Scott No Fingers. You're a smart kid.'

I looked at my disfigured hands and shook my head; not smart at all.

'According to his hippie friends, Johnny claimed the white buffalo appeared closer to him every time he dropped acid, and believed that when it got close enough, he'd be able to climb onto its back and ride the rainbow. He started to name the drug White Buffalo instead of LSD or acid, and I guess it caught on because his friends started to call it White Buffalo, too. Many of them claimed to see this beautiful creature while they were tripping. Anyway, time moves along: Nixon becomes president, man lands on the moon, and The Beatles break up. Johnny Hester develops quite a following—they call themselves the Rainbow Riders. One night in October of 1970, they drive to the Golden Gate Bridge in their psychedelic school bus: fourteen groovy cats singing, 'I Feel Like I'm Fixing to Die Rag.' They park the bus, pop LSD for the last time, then join hands and ride the rainbow.'

'They jumped?' I asked, thinking about Shintaro and the Followers of the Voice: young, senseless sacrifice. 'All of them?'

Dreaming Bear nodded. 'Fourteen stoned lemmings wearing bandanas and bellbottom pants. There was one survivor. She broke nearly every bone in her body, but found enough strength to sell her story to the *Chronicle*. She was holding Johnny's hand as they fell. Apparently, he turned to her just before they jumped and uttered his final words: "White buffalo is here. She found me."'

Dreaming Bear held out his hands, as if to say: *there you have it*. Big Crow stirred and *Ota Kte* cried again. I got up and looked through a gap in the shutters. The dog was howling at a bird that had landed on the roof of the rental. The bird, not comfortable with the attention, took flight. *Ota Kte* gave its tail a couple of self-righteous swings, then returned to its patch under the yellow pine, and rolled in the dirt.

'What about me?' I asked, turning to Dreaming Bear and Big Crow. 'Why am I here?'

Big Crow moved in the shadows. His pale eyes flashed. 'Yes, now we come to you, Scott No Fingers: a man brave enough to listen to his heart, to follow its call, and begin his great journey. You know why you're here. You don't need me to tell you.'

I dropped onto the crate and stared at my drying tears. Big Crow was right. I knew why I was here. I knew what I had to do.

'White Buffalo Calf Woman is coming,' I said to them. 'She's coming home. She's coming for me.'

'Her spirit follows you like a shadow,' Big Crow said.

'I just want this to end.'

'She is always with you. Her beauty is in your dreams and her anger flows through your veins.'

'She's killing me.'

'Desire is killing you, Scott No Fingers. Only desire.'

'Mia is my desire.'

The old man sighed, still trembling, still weeping. Once again I imagined him showing Mia to the stars. *There is a beauty here on earth to challenge yours now.* And eighteen years later, offering her body to the wind, the sun, and the sky. I had, in that second, a sense of his pain (if mine was the colour of a sunset, his would burn your eyes).

'There will be a ceremony,' he said, 'just as there was two thousand years ago. We will prepare for her coming, and build a medicine-tipi twenty-four poles strong. Tell the proud Lakota nation to celebrate. Tell them that White Buffalo Calf Woman comes again.'

'Celebrate?' I said in a detached voice, thinking about my fate.

The glowing lines on Big Crow's face were pushed into smiles. 'We will celebrate end times, Scott No Fingers.'

'A new beginning,' Dreaming Bear added.

I looked at my right palm, at the place where my life-line reappeared.

'Two thousand years ago,' Big Crow continued, 'White Buffalo Calf Woman brought us a gift: the *chanunpa,* the sacred pipe. The Lakota still have this pipe; Arvol Looking Horse keeps it in Green Grass, Cheyenne River. This time, when she comes, we will have a gift for her.'

There was a brief but heavy silence. Big Crow's pale hand trembled from the shadows.

'You, Scott No Fingers,' he said. 'That gift will be you.'

The shack creaked and swayed. The old man settled into its darkness and said no more. All I could see of him was his bare feet—the floor between them studded with tears.

*   *   *

We drove back to Shining River in silence. I gulped two of the beers, despite the way the car pitched and bumped; my throat was so dry. The setting sun spread a red wing across the windscreen. The prairie burned in thick flashes of gold, with the pines and cottonwoods picked out like proud, standing men. I could see why the Oglala loved this land.

I expected Dreaming Bear to say something, but he respected my silence and I was grateful for it. He kept both hands on the wheel and concentrated on the sway of the land. My senses were rocked, my mind was hurting. I looked at the rolling world, and a cruel voice advised me to take it in while I could. So much beauty, so little time. I wiped away yet more tears and let the landscape drown my sad eyes.

We bounced onto the strip of dirt road that wound through the dilapidated shacks and trailers of the village. There was some excitement at the sight of Dreaming Bear driving a new car. An old lady towing a sewing machine on a cart waved emphatically. A circle of men stared, as if a car that operated under its own power was a wondrous thing (their hands and faces were smeared with oil where they had been working on their jalopies all afternoon). By the time we stopped outside the gates of the Wildlife Reserve, there was a stream of children trailing us, laughing and calling out, their faces turned brilliant colours in the vivid western light.

I handed Dreaming Bear the last beer. He popped the top, took a couple of loud swallows, and wiped his mouth with the back of his hand. He looked like a man in a commercial.

The children ran around the car, voicing their approval and running their hands along the bodywork. Dreaming Bear grinned. He flashed the main beams and the kids' bare backs shone in the light, pale as stones. They seemed to be as interested in me as they were in the car, or in the fact that Dreaming Bear was behind the wheel. Every time I looked at the passenger window I saw a different face. It was like make-believe. My life had become a playground for aesthetics, like a drawing board in an advertising agency.

'How are you feeling?' Dreaming Bear asked. I remembered the tear-bracelet around his wrist and felt a pang of hurt so deep it took my breath away.

'Like I'm in a dream,' I said.

'Sure. But you're gonna be okay?'

I shrugged. 'You tell me. What happened in the end ... just before you woke up?'

'Everybody got drunk and crazy,' he replied with a smile. 'We all got naked, ate peyote buttons, and had the best goddam powwow Pine Ridge has ever seen.'

I didn't feel like smiling but I couldn't help myself. Something in Dreaming Bear's voice just drew it out of me—drew it out of nowhere, like an alchemist spinning gold from some dull matter. I looked at him—I *really* looked at him ... at the cobweb lines that laughter had placed around his eyes, at the weight of kindness in his expression, the gentle shape of his eyes, and the curve of his upper lip that made it look as if he was always smiling. Dreaming Bear has the kind of face you just have to love.

'Where are you going now?' he asked. 'I guess you don't have anywhere to stay.'

I shrugged. 'Are there any motels near here?'

'On the rez? Shit, no. The nearest would be in Chadron, Nebraska. That's about an hour south of here. Or there's Hot Springs, back toward Rapid. There are lots of nice places to lay your head for the night ... once you cross the reservation border, that is.'

A little girl pressed her face against the passenger window. I wriggled my nose at her. She giggled and disappeared, leaving the shape of her lips on the glass.

'Maybe I'll sleep in the car,' I said. 'Or maybe I'll just keep driving … see how far I get.'

'I think you've been running long enough, Scott.'

'You think right. I've lost my best friend, I've lost too much sleep, and I've lost my way. All I can do is be brave and face my demons. *Hoka hey*, right?'

'*Hoka hey*. You learn quickly, Scott No Fingers.'

'Yeah … beneath this desperate exterior there's a genius banging his head against the wall.'

Dreaming Bear frowned. 'Are you always so hard on yourself?'

I shrugged again. The children began to drift away, their fascination redirected to one of their number who had fashioned a baseball bat from a length of board and was slapping small stones into the sky. They disappeared into the sunset, as if burning up.

'Listen,' I said. 'I could do with some company tonight. How do you fancy grabbing a crate of beer and a bucket of chicken? We'll check into a hotel, find a game on TV, and shoot the shit until we fall asleep. My treat. Sound good?'

'Hell, yeah,' Dreaming Bear said. 'But I can't; we have a pregnant cow on the ranch. She's full term and ready to pop. We have to be there for her. We can't lose this one.'

'You work here?'

'It's my little brother's baby. I'm his right-hand man.'

I nodded. 'Maybe some other time.'

'Sure.' He clapped me on the shoulder and got out of the car. I slid behind the wheel, having to adjust the seat so that I could reach the pedals. Dreaming Bear tapped on the window and made a winding-down gesture.

'You know, Scott,' he said. 'I may not be as wise as Luther Big Crow. I may not have the insight that he has, but I can see the cloud that surrounds you. It's dirty brown. It makes a sound like fingernails running down a chalkboard, and it's making you ugly. Do you know what I'm talking about?'

'I know,' I said. My throat was dry again.

'White Buffalo Calf Woman is coming,' Dreaming Bear said. He placed his hand on my forearm. I felt the strength in it, like the vibration you feel when you stand next to a generator. 'You can go to her in one of two ways: as you are, beaten and full of bad colour; or pure of heart and tall, like a warrior. It's up to you.'

I looked at him. 'Do you think I like feeling this way? Do you think I enjoy the burning, suffocating, crippling need to fix? And it *is* a need, not a desire, but a *need*, just like breathing, and you do it to feel normal … and then you do it again because feeling normal is so fucking depressing. No, Dreaming Bear … I don't enjoy it at all. And becoming a heroin addict isn't a conscious decision you make when you're younger, like wanting to go to college or join the army. It's like a huge snowball rolling down the mountain of your life, and if you don't have the heart to jump out of the way, it gathers you up and takes you down. And once you get rolling it's almost impossible to stop. In fact, you just get bigger and roll faster, and then you hit the bottom and smash into a million pieces. When that happens it's too late to go back up the mountain and try again: the ride's over, man. God bless and good night.'

The pressure of his hand increased. The hum increased, and I felt shame for having spoken to him with such impatience. I knew it was a masquerade of self-reproach and guilt, and Dreaming Bear knew it, too.

'Sorry. Listen, I just—'

'Do you want to be helped, Scott No Fingers?'

'I'm not sure I *can* be helped; my soul is withered.'

'Ask yourself … are you going to be beaten, or will you go to White Buffalo Calf Woman like a warrior? Not full of colour, but full of light …'

'Full of light.' The words tripped off my tongue with dreamy ease.

'I know a man who can help you.' Dreaming Bear's voice was as kind as the lines on his face. 'But you have to *want* to be helped.'

'I want it.' My voice was soft and tearful, but I touched his hand to try and convey the power of my suffering.

Dreaming Bear nodded. He squeezed my hand and I felt his faith—like spiritual shock therapy. He let go, but the faith remained. I looked at him with my jaw hanging. It was like being star-struck.

'Meet me tomorrow morning,' he said. 'You know Big Bat's in Pine Ridge Village?'

'No, but I'll find it.'

'You can't miss it, everybody goes there. You can buy me breakfast and I'll introduce you to a friend of mine—a medicine man. If you let him, he'll take away that brown cloud, and you'll walk like a warrior.'

'A medicine man,' I said, nodding slowly, as if medicine men were all part of the old Hennessey routine. 'Okay, no problem.' Although everything inside me was screaming that this wasn't real. *Sketches on a drawing board,* I thought: children playing in the road; three guys sitting on upturned orange crates, drinking beer and swatting flies; a dog nosing in the trash; the impression of the little girl's lips on the glass; the blood-light on the horizon. Not real, just ideas—some good, some not so good (the crushed beer cans in the footwell; the toxic grumbling of the car's engine). That's what drawing boards are for: keep the good, toss out the bad.

'I feel like I'm dreaming,' I said, running my hands down my face. 'I'm not sure if it's a nightmare or ...'

'You need sleep,' Dreaming Bear said. 'Find a motel. Have a long shower, then sleep. Everything will be clearer tomorrow.'

'I hope you're right.' I licked my lips and wiped a skin of sweat from the back of my neck. 'Thanks, Dreaming Bear.'

'There's goodness in your heart, Scott No Fingers,' he said, placing his hand on my arm again. I had known him for only three hours, but he was already one of the most amazing people to have come into my life.

'You can see that?' I asked. I wanted to get out of the car and hug him. It hadn't been a great day, but with one simple sentence he had made it better.

'Yeah,' he replied. 'I can see it.'

'What colour is it?'

'Does a smile have a colour, Scott No Fingers? Does the wind have a colour when it blows in just the right way and lifts your heart? Does friendship have a colour? Or love?'

I shook my head.

'Beauty doesn't need to be defined. It just *is*. Do you understand?'

'I think so,' I said, and thought: *ah, what the hell.* I got out of the car and threw my arms around the big guy. I needed that hug, I really did.

'Thanks, Dreaming Bear.'

'Okay, Scott No Fingers. Okay.'

I drove out of Shining River with tears in my eyes. I looked in the rearview mirror and saw Dreaming Bear, and all the children, standing in the road. They were waving, and I was elated. My fate was uncertain, *Ptesan-Wi* was pointing at me from some distant, unknown place, but at that moment my heart was lifted. There were tears in my eyes, but I was smiling.

I got southbound on Highway 18, heading for the Nebraska state line. I flicked on the radio. It was still tuned to KILI, the Lakota station that Dreaming Bear had been listening to. I turned it up and drummed along to the music, slapping the wheel as I cruised down to Chadron, where the transmission finally faded ... where the sounds of the Indians faded.

*   *   *

TCB: Cold Turkey #3

Very different from Turkeys #1 and #2, or at least the parts I can remember. Memories of the experience are sparse. The beginning is crystal and the end is all there—surreal yet solid. It's the middle section that's missing, when I was left alone in the shack with the medicine man. Certain aspects remain, but none of them are real: levitating to within six inches of the ceiling, for instance, or Sebby wheeling in and telling me that he didn't blame me at all, and that he loved me. These snapshots are lodged in my memory like shapes in the clouds. They look like things you can reach out and touch, but you know if you try that your hand will pass right through. They're mental vapour, that's all. They're steam.

The medicine man's name was Jimmy High Pipe. He was young, perhaps as young as me, although the sun had weathered his face so it was difficult to be sure. I had expected an old man in a breechcloth with feathers in his hair and charms around his neck—a preconception that was to prove fallacious; Jimmy High Pipe wore Nike basketball sneakers, Elvis-style sunglasses with chunky gold stems, and had a Walkman clipped to his belt.

'Hey, you know Elvis was one-quarter Sioux?' he asked, pumping my hand with might and main. 'Not a lot of people believe me when I tell them that, but it's true.'

Dreaming Bear rolled his eyes. I gave him a look: *Are you sure about this?* He read it and grinned in a way I didn't find reassuring.

'And these sunglasses ... see these shades I'm wearing?'

'Yes,' I said. 'Impressive.'

'Sure they are. You probably think they're replicas, but you'd be wrong. These are The King's actual sunglasses, man. Do you remember the scene in *This is Elvis* where he's riding in the back of a limousine with the Memphis Mafia? You know the scene I'm talking about, right?'

I had never seen *This is Elvis,* but I nodded anyway.

High Pipe grinned. 'These are the sunglasses Elvis is wearing in that scene. You better believe it, man. Look here ...' He took them off and showed me, pointing at the letters E and P stamped across the bridge. 'See that? EP: Elvis Presley, man. And here, look ...' There were three more letters set into the gold along each stem: TCB. 'How about that? You know what TCB stands for?'

'No, I—'

'Taking Care of Business, man. That was Elvis's motto. And that's what we're gonna do with you. We're gonna Take Care of Business. You better believe it, man.'

I bought them breakfast at Big Bat's Texaco before we Took Care of Business (Jimmy High Pipe ate like Elvis—you better believe it, man). I drank black coffee and listened with growing apprehension as High Pipe told us how The King should have been given an academy award for his 'deeply moving portrayal' of a half-Kiowa in the movie *Flaming Star*. Dreaming Bear sat in silence, but there was a look in his eyes that told me he was enjoying every minute of the show.

The Elvis experience continued on the drive to High Pipe's trailer just north of Wounded Knee, site of the infamous massacre of 1890. He took the cassette from his Walkman and played it in the car stereo. 'Guitar Man' shook the body-work at a relentless volume, enhanced by High Pipe singing along, sneering, '*Show 'em, son*,' and playing air-guitar. We were similarly treated with renditions of 'Jailhouse Rock,' 'Don't Be Cruel' and a live version of 'Suspicious Minds,' complete with karate moves. By the time we got to High Pipe's trailer, I was all shook up.

'Okay, man,' High Pipe said, still sneering. 'TCB, uh-huh?'

'Uh-huh.'

He nodded. 'Uh-huh-huh,' and entered his trailer.

'Jesus,' I whispered.

'Don't worry,' Dreaming Bear said. 'His healing is better than his Elvis imper-sonation.'

'I hope you're right.'

'You better believe it, man.'

I said goodbye to Dreaming Bear and gave him the keys to the rental (*Do you mind if I borrow it while you're with Jimmy? I promise to go easy, and wheels are always useful on the rez.*). I watched as he drove back towards Pine Ridge. I was in the trailer with Jimmy High Pipe for two days. The next time I saw the rental, the offside wing was missing and the door was a different colour.

Dreaming Bear may not have been right about 'going easy' with the rental, but he was right about Jimmy High Pipe. I don't know what he gave me—what he *did* to me—but I walked out of his trailer a cured man, and that ugly brown cloud was gone forever. This was five weeks ago. I haven't touched heroin since, and moreover, I haven't *wanted* to. There have been no cravings, no cramps, no diarrhoea, no fits of depression. I'm a new man. I am pure.

I stepped into a tiny room at the rear of the trailer, where Jimmy High Pipe waited. He had taken off the sunglasses and the Walkman was gone. His eyes were sandy brown—the same colour as his skin—and his look was penetrative, almost frightening.

'Take off your clothes,' he said. 'All of them. Lie here. Be comfortable.' He pointed at what I thought was a bed, but was actually a board resting unevenly on crates, draped with a comforter of fiery colours. I removed my clothes and lay on it, vulnerable in so many ways. High Pipe lowered his head, his arms straight at his sides. He whispered a string of syllables so quickly I wasn't sure if he was speaking English or Lakota. He was silent for a moment, then crossed to a long curtain, which he pulled back to reveal an arrangement of shelves stacked with jars and bottles. There were several plants jostling for space on the top shelf, all but bursting from their plastic pots. There were other items—several smooth stones, what looked like the jawbone of a small animal, a long black feather with a white tip. High Pipe took this, kissed it, and uttered something in Lakota. He came over and ran the white tip down my body, an excruciating line drawn from the hollow of my throat to the tip of my penis. He put the feather back on the shelf and came back with the smooth stones. He arranged these in an oval shape on my chest and said to me:

'Listen carefully, Scott No Fingers, and you will be cured of your addiction. Do you understand?'

'Yes,' I breathed.

'I am going to give you a medicine, and that medicine will heal you. Do you understand?'

'Yes.'

'But you have to *want* it to heal you. To do this you must welcome the medicine into your body as you would welcome a guest into your house. I want you to close your eyes and think this: Body, I am going to introduce you to something new. You may not like the taste of this new thing, and you may not care for the feel of it, but you must accept that it is here to do you good. Embrace it. Embrace the medicine, Scott No Fingers. It is your friend. Do you understand?'

'Yes.' My anxiety was causing my heart to thump and my chest to shudder, but the oval of stones was not disturbed. It was as if they were magnetised, drawn to something inside me. I had a feeling that if I tried to peel them off they would come away from my skin like leeches.

'Embrace the medicine, Scott No Fingers. Say it.'

'I embrace the medicine.'

'Welcome it into your body. Mean it.'

'I welcome it.'

'Mean it.'

I closed my eyes. 'I *welcome* it into my *body*.' And then I felt them on my lips—what I thought were High Pipe's fingers, long and hard and full of bitterness. My eyes snapped open. High Pipe was leaning over me but it was not his fingers in my mouth; I saw a tangle of yellow roots, felt them on my tongue. My mouth exploded with a taste like battery acid. I felt my cheeks draw in, my eyes bulged, and my tongue retreated to the back of my throat like a party favour rippling back in. Everything inside me protested (I'm not sure about a welcome; I was slamming doors and sending out the dogs). My throat convulsed and swelled in refusal. My thumbs snatched at the comforter. I could hear cloth tearing.

'Welcome it. Mean it.' High Pipe—his sandy, spooky eyes less than an inch from my own—pushed the last of those awful yellow roots between my lips and applied the slightest pressure beneath my jaw to close my mouth. 'Mean it,' he said again, and then—I swear to you—he disappeared. I didn't blink or look away as he left the room. I can't be *certain* about that; I was vulnerable and confused, but as I remember it—and this was before the hallucinations began—High Pipe was with me one second, and then he was gone.

I looked around the room, taking everything in—*snatching* it in, as if my brain were throwing a rapid shutter-effect over my optic nerve: images received and analysed as if viewed through a strobe. My heart kicked like a child. My thumbs were vicious mouths snapping at the comforter. *Welcome it.* This was the only thought that had balance, and I held onto it with imaginary hands. *Welcome it.* Sweat poured from my pale skin. My balls had shrivelled to the size of dried peas. *Welcome it.*

The heat came off me in heavy beats. I lay with my head back, staring at the ceiling as I prepared to welcome—to swallow. My breathing was pained and from-the-gut and the roar of my heartbeat filled the world, but I could hear—or *thought* I could—the smaller sounds: the crates creaking as I shifted my weight; the sinews in my legs rasping as my muscles were pulled taut; the click-clicking of saliva running through the ducts and channels beneath my tongue.

Welcome it.

The minutes dripped by with a wet, uncomfortable feel. My body temperature levelled, and then began to drop. A sense of calm worked through my tension like a mantra. It was bliss. I steadied myself to first chew into, and then swallow the medicine, recalling Jimmy High Pipe's words: *Embrace it … it is your friend.* I imagined my body to be a house, and the weird, twisting roots (they moved inside my mouth like tentacles) to be a guest. I opened my arms and welcomed it.

The taste was immediately sickening—a drool of offensive flavour, thick as blood. I felt the roots shivering as they burst between my teeth and I swallowed them in one fist-sized gulp. My body mounted its offensive. I wanted to vomit but managed to hold it down by clapping a hand over my mouth and thinking: *It is a friend. It may not taste like a friend or feel much like one, but it's here to do you good. So welcome it, throw your arms around it and ...*

High Pipe was with me again, like a vision. I reached out to him, appealing with my eyes. He ignored me and went back to the shelf.

'High Pipe,' I gagged, my legs kicking furiously. I thought then that I was going to die, that High Pipe had mixed up the plants and accidentally given me root of belladonna or something equally lethal. 'Wh-wh-what ha-have ... what ...?'

He came to my side carrying a jar of water and a severed eagle's wing, its feathers long and black. His sandy eyes held no expression. His mouth was so tightly closed that it had disappeared. He dipped the wing into the jar, then took it out and held it over my chest. Water ran from the feathers, following their lines in a way that made me think of Luther Big Crow's tears. The last thing I remember before the hallucinations started was the feel of the water dripping on my chest: individual drops, splashing in the centre of the oval.

And then ... shapes in the clouds: mental vapour.

'Wake up, Scott No Fingers.'

I opened my eyes. High Pipe stood above me, his face solemn. He was still holding the jar and the eagle's wing but his clothes were different. The quality of the light had changed. It had the feel of dusk or early morning.

'How long have I been ...?' My memory touched on fragments of hallucination, like a tune in your head you can't quite remember. I closed my eyes and swallowed. The battery acid taste was still thick on my tongue.

'You have been here twenty-one hours,' High Pipe told me. 'We are nearly finished. The worst is over.'

'Nearly finished?'

'You are cured, but you are not pure. The poison lives deep inside you. Most of it is out but the darkest part remains: the heart of the poison—the part that draws you back again and again ...'

'Addiction,' I said.

'The *seed* of addiction. But it is coming, Scott No Fingers. You will be pure.'

High Pipe dipped the eagle wing into the water. 'To purify,' he whispered, and the water ran from the feathers onto my chest. 'Water is the purest gift from *Wakan Tanka*. It is life. When White Buffalo Calf Woman came to the Lakota two thousand years ago, the chief of the tribe offered her water. From that day it has been used to purify.'

It came down in a crystal flow. I closed my eyes, letting its rhythm soothe me.

'Pure,' High Pipe said, and he repeated this every time he dipped the wing into the water and let it flow. I tried to visualise that hard seed of addiction inside me—not as something barbed and twisted, but smooth like a splinter … easily drawn. The feel of the water, coupled with High Pipe's breeze-like voice, had a lulling quality. I felt myself slipping away. The next time I opened my eyes the light had changed again. It was vivid, almost too clear. Fairies of dust whirled in the air. There was no sign of High Pipe. I drifted back into sleep, and again the light had changed when I opened my eyes: the small room burned in the last of the daylight, a deep red glare that threw kisses off the jars stacked on High Pipe's shelves, and turned the plants' exotic colours into evening shades of cherry and mauve. High Pipe was there, but only in silhouette: a towering Indian shape holding a dripping eagle's wing.

'Pure,' he said, and the water fell, calming.

I slipped away, a sense of peace lying on my naked body like dew. Just before I was given to my dreams, I grasped at a mental image of the *seed*: the darkest part of the poison and the cause of my pain. It followed me down like a light: a smooth, dark splinter coming free. I knew that the next time I woke it would all be over.

I heard birds singing. I felt the sun's hand on my face, and before my eyes were fully open I was aware of the lightness of my body, the freedom. It was like being rid of a pain that had been with me for so long I had gotten used to it. I thought of Mia saying: *The life-line reappearing would suggest starting over; not simply turning a new leaf, but becoming a new person—from the soul.*

'Welcome back, Scott No Fingers,' High Pipe said. He was standing in the doorway with the Walkman clipped to his belt, wearing his Elvis shades.

I sat up, aware that my body was cool and dry, and that the oval of stones had gone. I touched my chest and looked around the room. Everything was poetry, even the dirt on the window and the smell of the room's old heat.

'Are we finished?' I asked.

'You better believe it, man,' High Pipe replied with a handsome sneer, which made him look, if only for a second, just like Elvis Presley. 'TCB, honey … TCB.'

*   *   *

'Jesus, Dreaming Bear, what happened to the car?' I looked at the place where the wing used to be, now a dusty grey gap revealing the bulkhead and front strut. The door wasn't even close to the same colour. It was red. The car had been a slick, polished silver when I had picked it up from the rental company in Rapid. No dents, no scratches. Now it looked like one of those cars you see abandoned at roadsides with POLICE AWARE stickers in the windows.

'Yeah, sorry,' Dreaming Bear said. He had a wounded look in his eyes that made me believe he was sorry, although I was about to learn that his troubled expression had nothing to do with trashing the car. 'I let my brother borrow it. Not a good idea. Charlie says it wasn't his fault, but I could smell beer on his breath. I should have known better. We got the door at a junkyard in White Clay. It's not a great match, I know, but we'll have it sprayed before you return it to the rental company, and we'll grab a new fender from somewhere.'

I shook my head, dismissing it; my spirits were too high to be brought down by a beaten up car that didn't belong to me anyway. I decided—give it a couple of weeks—that I'd phone the rental company and tell them that the car had been stolen, then I'd drive it into the middle of the prairie and just walk away. That was if I was still drawing breath in a couple of weeks. The reality of the ceremony danced at the back of my mind like an indecipherable shape in the shadows. But even this couldn't dampen my new pure feeling. I was a bird. I was flying.

Dreaming Bear looked south, where the worn buildings of Wounded Knee Village baked in a liquid shimmer of May heat. His expression was broken, and it struck me how different he looked without his smile.

'Your offer ...' His voice cracked, trying for strength that wasn't there. 'The hotel, a bucket of chicken and a crate of beer ... does it still stand?'

'Absolutely,' I said. I turned and looked at High Pipe's rundown trailer, its door hanging open, Elvis blaring. 'I owe you one; that guy works miracles.'

'You don't owe me anything, Scott.'

'Yeah, I do. I'm clean. I can feel it right here ... *inside*. Do you have any idea how difficult it is to give up something you're addicted to?'

He shook his head.

'Trust me, I owe you one.'

Dreaming Bear shrugged, drawing lines in the dirt with his boot. I was about to ask where his smile had gone when it came to me like a punch in the stomach: the reason he hadn't been able to spend the night at a hotel before was because one of his buffalo on the ranch was close to calving. It must have happened while I was in the trailer with High Pipe. *We can't lose this one*, Dreaming Bear had said, but judging by the absence of his smile, they had.

'Not all my dreams come true,' he said. His mouth was a quivering line where he was trying to keep it from turning down at the edges. 'Just before you came I had a wonderful dream: one of our cows had given birth to a white buffalo calf—a symbol of possibility and triumph, and maybe the end of pain ... the end of all the shit we go through here on the rez. People came from miles around to see the white buffalo calf. They were lined up right to the highway, man. I woke up thinking, this is what will happen, everything's going to be okay. I got out of bed and ran down to the ranch, to our pregnant cow. She was sleeping. I touched her stomach and said a prayer. Charlie came over and I told him about my dream. Man, he was so excited he did a dance right there and then. We thought it was going to happen, we really thought ...'

Dreaming Bear kicked the ground. A gritty cloud flowered between us, smelling of heat and oil.

'Not all my dreams come true,' he said again.

I didn't know what to say, so I said nothing. There are times, I have learned, when all you want is silence.

'It happened yesterday afternoon,' he continued, looking at his boots. 'The cow was eight years old and in great health. Her eyes were alert and her temperature steady. Prime condition for calving. Charlie and I were on hand as she drew close, and we helped her deliver a forty pound calf—just on the light side of normal, but nothing to worry about. She wasn't white but that didn't matter; she was out in the world and responsive, and all of a sudden the future looked a little brighter. We haven't had much luck on the ranch over the years; the conditions aren't great and this makes for a stressful environment—for everybody, not just the animals. Anyway, a new calf was born—the first on the ranch for two years. We knew it was too early to celebrate, but we celebrated anyway. We thanked Great Spirit and Mother Earth. We even danced. It probably sounds like an overreaction to you: crazy Indians dancing and praying over the birth of a buffalo calf, but you have to appreciate what the buffalo means to Native Americans: pre-rez it was our livelihood, and to this day is regarded as holy: a symbol of unity and strength, of everything that was once great about this land. I guess we thought that, if the calf pulled through, it would mean that better days lay ahead. But it wasn't to be, Scott No Fingers: she developed respiratory problems last night, and died early this morning.'

I will never—even if I live through the ceremony and for fifty years after—understand Dreaming Bear's pain during this time, not through lack of sympathy, but because we are different people, *from* a different people. My world is made of rush hours, concrete streets, and the smell of industry. Emotional pain comes with the loss of love. Dreaming Bear's world is a simpler place, made of dirt roads, cramped shacks, poverty, and standing on a foundation of tradition and belief. For him, for his family and all of the Oglala, emotional pain comes when hope seems frail ... when that belief is tested.

'I don't know what to say,' I said to him. I looked at the shapes he had drawn in the dirt, then reached out and touched his arm. Our eyes met. His were bloodshot, his eyelashes thick with tears. 'I want to help. Whatever you need.'

'Your heart is big, Scott No Fingers. No doubt about it. And your face, now that the dirty cloud has been lifted ... it's the way you were meant to look.'

'I look different?'

Dreaming Bear nodded. 'There are no dark circles beneath your eyes, your lips are red and full, your skin is clear. And your shoulders ... look at the way you stand: straight as an arrow, man.'

'Like a warrior?'

The ghost of a smile was suggested by the way the lines on his face changed shape, though his lips did not move. 'You'll be a warrior at the ceremony, Scott No Fingers. You'll stand brave, and if White Buffalo Calf Woman brings end times to the rez, you'll be a hero, too.'

These words affected me, and deeply—as deep as the seed that Jimmy High Pipe had pulled from my soul. I stood perfectly still, my elevated spirits riding a wave of fear and fortune. Dreaming Bear's troubles were forgotten. I was embraced by a sense of destiny. Childhood images of heroes occurred to me, and here I was—a million miles from everything I knew—on the verge, perhaps, of being one.

The here and now swam back in a series of colourful shivers: Dreaming Bear's wounded eyes, the beaten up rental, the village to the south almost lost in the haze. I let it in—breathing it, wanting it.

'Sorry to hear about your calf,' I said, tasting the dust of reality. 'Things will get better. I know they will.'

'They can't get much worse,' Dreaming Bear responded. He kicked the ground again, lifting another gritty cloud into the air. 'Come on, *kola* ... let's blow this taco stand.'

*　　*　　*

I drove to Sioux Falls twenty-six days ago and bought a laptop computer, having decided to write a journal of my experiences on the rez. It never occurred to me to tell the whole story, not until I sat down and wondered where to begin. This was when the self-doubt and deliberation set in. We're nearly at the end now, and with all these words behind me I feel that I have made the right decision. The exercise hasn't exactly been therapeutic, but it has been fulfilling, like putting a child to bed. And I have found that, over the last couple of weeks, the writing has come more freely. I've found the groove, in other words—committed to the task, for better or worse.

Let me bring you up to date …

'When is she coming?'

'Can you feel her?'

'Will it be soon?'

'Is she close, *Nabokazunte Nichola?*'

I have become something of a celebrity on the rez. The people know who I am and why I am here. They call me *Nabokazunte Nichola:* No Fingers. They stop me wherever I go and they always ask the same questions. I always answer in the same way, with the same truth: I don't know when she's coming, but it will be soon. Yes, I feel that she'll be here very soon.

'I will pray for you, *Nabokazunte Nichola.*'

'The spirits are with you.'

'Be brave. Be true.'

They started to arrive at around the time I started writing this journal—in small numbers to begin with, maybe only twenty or thirty a day. But as word has spread that White Buffalo Calf Woman will soon return, the numbers have grown: the Pine Ridge Reservation has become a mecca for the Sioux and, in smaller drifts, other tribes: Pawnee, Shoshone, the Aroostook Band of Micmacs, Navajo, Cherokee, Hopi … they keep coming, drawn to whatever is going to happen here. Pine Ridge has gone from being America's dirty secret to its Native heartland.

The Bureau of Indian Affairs (the BIA is a governmental department concerned with American Indian issues) has been throwing its weight around, not entirely comfortable with what has become a mass gathering—a pilgrimage, if you will—of tribes whose history is steeped in violence. The Native American is, by and large, still regarded as little more than a savage, and the BIA is concerned that there could be a massive tribal war on the rez. To this end there is, alongside the locals and the travellers, an FBI presence, with the threat of military involvement at the first sign of unrest. This has caused some bitterness among the people of the rez and American Indian Movement hardliners, those who were in Pine Ridge in 1973 and remember Wounded Knee II when, during an AIM protest occupation of the village, FBI/BIA goon presence had turned what should have been a peaceful protest into bloodshed. The AIM—their politics somewhat left of centre—do not want a repeat of that (and neither do the BIA, in their defence) and feel resentful of the heavy outsider presence during such an important time, and one so essential to their beliefs and heritage—a resentment at least partially justified when said outsider presence has come armed with M-16s and tear gas.

Although the politics surrounding this exodus to Pine Ridge may be delicate, the travellers themselves—mainly Sioux from North and South Dakota—have shown no signs of aggression. The BIA and AIM continue to get the feel of each other like a couple of boxers during the first round of a fight, but meanwhile the Blackfoot Sioux have found companionship with the Wiciyela, the Hunkpapa are laughing and singing with the Sisseton-Wahpeton, and the Oglala and Cheyenne River Sioux have come together like old friends at a school reunion. Even tribes outside the Sioux, while more reserved in their celebrations, have settled in for the event with dignity, and all seem to be enjoying themselves. There is about the rez an undeniable and quite awesome sense of peace—a unity that vibrates through the land with rhythm and tranquillity. I asked Dreaming Bear about it and he said it was the *tiyospaye*.

'The *tiyospaye?*' I asked. 'What's that?'

He gave the question some thought. 'It's difficult to explain, because it's more of a feeling than a meaning ...'

'Like *déjà vu*,' I said.

Dreaming Bear nodded. 'Kind of like that, sure. Now, I don't speak French, but I think the words *déjà vu* translate to something like 'seen before' or 'already seen', but the translation doesn't mean anything until you *feel* it. It's the same with the *tiyospaye*. The nearest English words would be 'kinship' or 'extended family', but the feeling runs deeper. The *tiyospaye* isn't so much the family, but what the family *becomes* when it's together. It's the soul connection. It's the unbreakable bond, the love, the sense of contentment and accomplishment you feel when the same heart is beating in a hundred different bodies. That, Scott No Fingers ... that is the *tiyospaye*.'

And still they come, arriving in colourful droves, hundreds every day. This morning Dreaming Bear and I drove west across the Clay River bridge and saw them lined up on Highway 18—tribal flags rippling from car aerials, RVs coated in dust and miles, trailers painted with traditional colours. Tribal police and BIA volunteers are working to designate camping areas on the prairies. Everywhere you go, everywhere you look, they can be seen—in tents and tipis posted on the rolling green world around Pine Ridge Village, thinning as they spread towards Oglala, Wounded Knee, Manderson, Loneman ... up as far as the Badlands in the northwest corner of the rez. It's like a festival site: one big powwow, and the business in stores on the rez has escalated. The Wildlife Reserve and Buffalo Breeding Ranch took more visitors in a single day than it had in the whole of last year. Bessa Ecoffey, who runs the tiny store in Shining River selling food and crafts, has had to acquire the help of her mother and sisters, and has set up three new stalls in order to meet the demand. The reservation's only casino, Prairie Wind—a small, struggling affair—has been booming since the masses started to arrive. If nothing else, this ceremony has brought a much-needed flush of trade to the rez.

With the peace, the laughter, and the electric sense of anticipation in the air, the Pine Ridge Reservation—statistically America's poorest area—has suddenly become the place to be.

I watch them come, setting up their tents and their trailers. I see them kiss the earth and wait. They play games, greet each other, and dance. Fires burn into the night, and the beautiful songs of different tribes rise like burning ashes into the darkness. I watch and I listen, and sometimes I weep. White Buffalo Calf Woman is coming again. The belief in this is as heavy in the air as the sense of peace, as loud as the laughter and the songs by the firelight. She is coming, there is no doubt.

'When, *Nabokazunte Nichola?* When is she coming?'

'Will it be tomorrow? The day after?'

'Have you seen her yet?'

'Have you seen her?'

'Have you …?'

The only answer I have is that I just don't know—that, like them, all I can do is wait.

*   *   *

I have also taken up residence on Pine Ridge, in a canvas tipi on Luther Big Crow's land, not far from the spot in the shade where *Ota Kte* sleeps the days away. I share it with Dreaming Bear (to whom my affection grows by the day), although we are usually not without company; the good people at MasterCard have ensured that the tipi is crammed with cases of Budweiser. Needless to say, our home is extremely popular. One night there were at least forty of us sitting around a fire outside the tipi, singing Lakota songs and exchanging stories. Luther Big Crow sang the loudest, and he completed the evening by telling us the Legend of White Buffalo Calf Woman. He told it beautifully, smoking his Camel Lights as the stars spread above us. On another night—we were entertaining Jimmy High Pipe and Dreaming Bear's brother Charlie—I remembered something that Graham 'Chip' LaVerse had said to me at the bar in Youngstown: *All those crazy Oglala do is crash their damn cars, get drunk, and cry over their precious Black Hills.* When I asked about the Black Hills, they winced and shook their heads. A sensitive issue, no doubt—this defined by the measure of their remonstrance.

'That land is *ours.* Always has been, always will be.'

'It was stolen from us. That's all there is to it.'

'A sacred place, Scott No Fingers. Understand?'

They told me—all too colourfully, I might add—that the Black Hills is an area of sacred land along the western edge of South Dakota: 'The heart of our home, and the home of our heart.' It was taken from the Sioux when Congress passed the Black Hills act of 1877, disregarding the Fort Laramie Treaty they had signed nine years before. And why? Gold, of course; the Black Hills were alive with it. Prospectors knew this but they couldn't start drilling with the Indians standing in their path. And so, with a little unconstitutional contrivance, the land was pulled from under their feet. The prospectors came into possession of what would become one of the world's most abundant gold mines, leaving the Sioux divided among six unavailing reservations.

Charlie Dreaming Bear told me that the Lakota Sioux have since—and after far too many court cases—been recognised as the rightful owners of the Black Hills, and that the way this sacred land was taken from them was both immoral and dishonourable. In 1980 the Supreme Court awarded them compensation exceeding one hundred million dollars.

'We told them they can keep their damn money,' Charlie said, cracking another beer and gulping it down as if it were the last one in the tipi.

'Let me get this straight,' I said, looking at each of them in turn. 'You live here on the rez in overcrowded, rundown shacks, you have a poor healthcare system and little employment, and you were awarded ... how much was it?'

'One hundred and six million dollars,' Jimmy High Pipe said. 'Although that figure is probably closer to half a billion now, once you consider interest and other payments ...'

'Half a *billion!*' I sat thinking what could be done to improve the rez with a share of that money: the roads could be repaved, houses could be built with plumbing and electricity, businesses could be established, and jobs—real jobs—could be created. Not to mention boosting the healthcare system, the hospitals, building better schools. 'Half a billion,' I said again. 'And you turned it *down?*'

'The Black Hills were never for sale,' Charlie told me.

'Yeah, but—'

'But nothing, Scott No Fingers,' Dreaming Bear said, his voice deep and serious. 'You're missing the point. The Black Hills are sacred—a part of *us*, a part of our history. If we were to accept money for that land we would lose our identity as a nation. We would lose our pride. Some things are more important than money, *kola*.'

'They can keep their billions,' High Pipe said.

'We want the land,' Charlie added. 'It's ours, baby, and we want it back.'

The three Indians raised their beer cans, smiled at each other, and went on drinking.

I have learned so much about these beautiful, desperate people through such stories, told with heart and feeling and a pride that shines with every word. They told me about the ghost dances and how they led to the massacre at Wounded Knee. They told me about Crazy Horse, his morality and bravery, and about the mystery surrounding the disappearance of his body after he was stabbed at Fort Robinson. I have learned about other great Sioux leaders: Red Cloud and Sitting Bull—how the latter, alongside Crazy Horse's warriors, helped defeat Custer at Little Bighorn before travelling across Europe with Buffalo Bill's Wild West Show.

These stories are fascinating, but not nearly as entertaining, or imaginative, as the personal anecdotes they have shared (like High Pipe's earliest memory of being kissed by Elvis before a Vegas show, or Charlie Dreaming Bear going to Hollywood during the revival of the western in the late eighties, and how he would have landed a role in *Dances With Wolves* if he hadn't gotten into a fight with Kevin Costner during a poker game). I asked Dreaming Bear about his dreams, and how many had come true. He told me he had dreamt about several fatal car accidents on the rez, and how, after one vivid nightmare, he had warned his old friend Peter Whispering Low not to walk into White Clay to get his beer, that something terrible would happen if he did. 'That crazy old bastard didn't listen. They found his body at the side of the road three days later: hit and run.' He'd had his first 'premonition' when he was eight years old: November of 1963. 'I saw it all, man. I woke up and told my father that an important white man was going to be shot while riding in the back of a big black car. When I saw the Zapruder film twelve years later, it was like watching my dream again—as if someone had a camera in my head and had pushed the record button.' He had dreamt about plane crashes, the San Francisco quake of '89, the Oklahoma bombing, and the twister that had ripped through Oglala in June of last year.

When I asked Dreaming Bear if any of his *nice* dreams had come true, he looked at me and smiled.

'I dreamt *you* were coming, Scott No Fingers,' he said. 'Yeah ... that was a nice dream.'

I shared some stories, too: my life on the streets (edited version); my experiences at the Centre (but not *all* of my experiences, blessedly); the three and a half years I had spent with the Followers of the Voice (Director's Cut). I told them about Mia, and how I had loved her. I told them—spirit trembling—about the night that we had tried to offer her as a sacrifice.

'The memory lives in my mind like a virus. It's difficult to talk about ...'

'You don't have to,' High Pipe said.

'I think I want to.' I looked at my hands; I couldn't look into their eyes. 'It won't be easy. There's so much guilt ... so much pain.'

'Take your time,' Dreaming Bear said. 'We are not here to judge you.'

It is difficult to write about, even now. There is pain inside. I'm not talking about emotion, but real *pain*, like a blister. It's in my head and in my hands. My chest feels like it's been hammered with nails. I should be bleeding.

I can see her tied to the scarred trunk of an elm, the rope cutting into her thighs, her stomach, her breasts. I can see kerosene oozing from the rope and running down her body in oily ribbons. We stand in a tight circle around her, dressed in our black robes, some of us holding burning torches like frightened villagers in an old witch-hunt movie. She looks at us and prays in Lakota. George Lasky, who is standing beside me, asks if I think she is speaking in tongues. I tell him that it sounds like Red Indian. Shintaro splashes Mia's feet with more kerosene and drowns her Lakota prayer with his own voice. He is offering her to the Voice, and nobody tries to stop him. I want to—I know this act is brutal and wrong, but I stand still and silent and I watch, even though my heart is drumming and I feel nauseous and all I want to do is run away. Shintaro drops his torch at Mia's feet and she begins to burn. The flames climb her naked legs. She stops praying and starts smiling. I have time to wonder why she isn't crying or screaming, and then everything is turned to hell.

It was so much easier when I couldn't remember—when the Centre had removed years and episodes from my life like photos from a scrapbook. I used to think that place was good for nothing, but now I'm not so sure. This pain is bright red, and it *burns*. What good does it do to remember something that hurts so much? The therapists may rave about it, but none of them have seen the things that I have.

I was able to tell Dreaming Bear and the others everything, because their companionship made it sufferable. I can write only fragments of it now: words like broken glass. I hear a tiny shattering sound every time I strike a key.

Let's see if I can ride the pain ...

It happened quickly: Mia burning, breaking away from the tree as the rope binding her frayed to ashes. She went for Shintaro like a force of nature. I can see his face now, a bloodless shape expressing shock, like the afterimage of a bright light. He screamed as Mia's fire consumed him, falling to her feet. His ponytail fizzed and blazed like a fuse.

She turned to the rest of us, smiling and burning. She seemed to *generate* fire, pulling it from the sky and throwing it at the followers as they stood locked to the spot. Within ten seconds our number was halved. I turned and saw something that struck me as wildly comical, although I may have been experiencing the first suggestion of delirium: Bobbi Sugar breaking from the circle and running—*trying* to run: a stiff, shambling effort on her prosthetic legs. One of them popped loose and she fell. But she didn't stay down. She wanted to get away—she *had* to get away—so she picked up her plastic leg, tucked it under her arm, and started to hop. That was when I realised that running might not be such a bad idea.

I turned back once and looked at Mia: a beautiful Lakota girl standing in a circle of burning trees and burning bodies. They writhed around her, smoking, throwing up sparks and screams. I stumbled and she looked at me. The flames had died on her body and she stood clean and naked in the firelight. Our eyes met and I saw something ancient and wonderful: a power that I would never comprehend. It was like starlight in a bottle, or lightning in the palm of your hand. She pointed at me and smiled.

Twenty-eight of us walked Mia into the woods, but only four of us came out. We assembled at Shintaro's house, half-crazy with the things we had seen, unable to believe that we had gotten away.

'But you didn't get away,' Dreaming Bear said. 'Mia Floats Softly followed you—her dark and angry spirit—over the years, over the miles. She followed you.'

One night, when Dreaming Bear and I had the company of Luther Big Crow, I asked the old man if I would know when White Buffalo Calf Woman was coming for me, if there would be a sign, something to prepare me.

His sightless eyes washed over me, the same colour as the smoke drifting from the tip of his cigarette. 'You'll know when she's coming, Scott No Fingers,' he said (Dreaming Bear translated. The English seemed to carry the same broken sounds as the Lakota). 'Believe me ... you will know.'

God, I was so scared. I *am* so scared.

'What's going to happen to me, Big Crow?'

'Only *Ptesan-Wi* can decide your fate.'

'What if I run ... keep running?'

'She will find you.'

'Is there anything I can do?'

'You have done all you can. Now ... just wait.'

The blue glow from the laptop bathes my crippled hands. My thumbs blur, hammering at the keys. Dreaming Bear sleeps beside me, dreaming of the future, perhaps. His long hair is loose, spilling over his face, whispering as he breathes. The night is full of song. I can hear drums, laughter ... carried on the wind with a vague quality, like the memory of a sound. I know that if I step outside I will see their fires flickering to all distant points: a thousand bright eyes watching. I wonder if these people will see me die.

When is she coming, Nabokazunte Nichola? *When?*

Will it be soon?

I wonder if they'll sing, if they'll cry.

Be brave. Be true.

I wonder if these people will see me die.

*   *   *

The Legend of White Buffalo Calf Woman
As told by Luther Big Crow

Long ago, during the hot months of summer, the seven sacred council fires of the Lakota Sioux made camp together. As dawn broke, the chief of the Without-Bows, Standing Hollow Horn, sent two of his best hunters out for game. They set out full of hope, but the country was dry and they found nothing. Then, in the distance, they saw something white coming towards them. To begin with it was so small they could make out no detail, but as they came together they could see that it was a beautiful young girl dressed all in white, more beautiful than any living creature they had seen. And it seemed to the hunters that she was not walking on the ground as humans do, but float-ing as a butterfly. This told the hunters that the girl was wakan: *holy. Her long black hair shimmered in the sunlight, hanging loose except for one thin braid tied back with buffalo fur. Her eyes were full of power and they shone like the stars she had seen. This beautiful stranger floating on the air was* Ptesan-Wi: *White Buffalo Calf Woman.*

Her beauty and power immediately affected the hunters. They trembled like the branches of a tree in winter. One of them was so taken that he dropped to his knees and began to pray. The other hunter was different; there was darkness in his heart—a desire that angered Ptesan-Wi. He reached out to touch her in a bad way. Such was her anger that a burning cloud came down and consumed the bad man. It was the colour of his desire and it burned him. All that was left when the cloud had gone was a small pile of charred bones.

The other hunter finished his prayer and stood before White Buffalo Calf Woman. She told him to return to his people with a message: 'Tell your people that I will come to them in four days. I will bring something holy—a message from the buffalo nation. Tell them to prepare for my arrival. A medicine-tipi of twenty-four poles must be built and made holy for my coming.'

And so the young hunter returned to the camp of the Lakota nation. He gathered all the people in a circle and told them what had happened, and what White Buffalo Calf Woman said they must do. The elders said it must be so, and all the people worked together to build the medicine-tipi.

Four days later, as she had promised, Ptesan-Wi came to the people of the Lakota nation. Once again she appeared to float like a butterfly. Her white buckskin dress was made brilliant in the sunlight. She carried a bundle in her arms. As she entered their circle she sang a sacred song, and she floated over to the chief and opened the bundle before him. In it was the chanunpa: the sacred pipe. She showed it to the Lakota, taking the stem with her right hand and the bowl with her left. The pipe has been held this way ever since.

She told the people: 'This holy pipe is a gift from the buffalo nation, and with it you will walk as a living prayer. You stand upon the earth with the stem pointing like a finger at the sky, and your body becomes a soul-bridge between the Sacred Beneath and the Sacred Above. This is Wakan Tanka's wish: now everything is one—all living things, the trees and the grasses, the sky and the earth. Everything is part of the same family, held together by the holy pipe.

'The stone bowl of the pipe represents two great things: the flesh and blood of the native man, and the buffalo. The buffalo is a symbol of the universe and its four directions. He has four legs, each one standing for an age of creation. Wakan Tanka gave the buffalo to this land when the world was new, to keep the waters in their place so that the land could grow strong, like a great and wise tree. The buffalo loses a single hair with each circle of the seasons. He will lose a leg with the passing of every age. The waters will flood the earth when the sacred circle ends—when all the hair and the four legs of the buffalo are gone.

'The wooden stem of the holy pipe represents all that grows on Mother Earth. The twelve feathers that hang from it are from the wings of Wanblee Galeshka: the sacred *spotted eagle, messenger of* Wakan Tanka *and the wisest of birds. It signifies the connection of all living things with the universe.*

'Here on the bowl you can see seven circles. These represent the seven sacred ceremonies to be practised with the pipe, and the seven sacred campfires of the Lakota.'

White Buffalo Calf Woman then taught the people the seven sacred ceremonies. These were: the sweat lodge ceremony, the naming ceremony, the healing ceremony, the adoption ceremony, the marriage ceremony, the vision quest, and finally the sun dance ceremony. After this she taught them the songs and the traditional ways, and said that for as long as they performed these ceremonies they would remain the guardians of the land. She said that, while the Lakota respected the land, they would live forever.

Ptesan-Wi then turned to leave, but not before promising that she would return—'I shall see you again.' They saw her float away into the gold and deep red of the setting sun. After a short while she stopped and rolled over four times. On the first roll her young female body turned into that of a black buffalo, the second into a brown buffalo, the third into a red buffalo. The fourth and final time she rolled over she turned into a white buffalo calf, and as such she ran until she became lost in the fire-colour of the horizon.

There is no living creature more sacred than the white buffalo. To the Native American the birth of such a wonderful animal is a sign of end times. After Ptesan-Wi *had left the Lakota nation, vast herds of buffalo appeared on the plains. And so it was that we survived, the buffalo giving us meat and clothes. No part of the great animal was wasted. From the heart to the horns, it was life to us.*

And now we wait again—as a nation, as the guardians of Mother Earth, we wait and we hope for end times.

We wait for the return of White Buffalo Calf Woman.

*   *   *

I have asked Joseph Dreaming Bear to conclude this account, in the event that I am not around to do so. I trust him; he has read what I have written several times, and he understands that, although I have done things of which I am ashamed, there are times when life leads you down some hard roads. It grabs you by the hand and all you can do is follow. To suggest that every man is in charge of his own destiny is, I'm afraid, a romance. You never know when the rain will fall or the sun will shine. You just never know, *kola*. All you can do is roll with it, and hope to smile.

*   *   *

I believe that Mia Floats Softly was the Second Coming. Her life ended before her divine work was completed, but her sacred spirit lives. It charges across the rotten apple of the land, and it is furious.

'What are you thinking about, *kola?*' Dreaming Bear asked me earlier. His eyes were heavy with sleep and the firelight outside the tipi threw shadows across his face. It looked like he had been carved from wood.

'What Big Crow said to me,' I replied. 'How he believes Mia is the Second Coming. And I was thinking about the Legend of White Buffalo Calf Woman ... the hunter with desire in his heart, and how he had wanted to touch her ...'

'A pile of charred bones.' Dreaming Bear said.

It charges across the rotten apple of the land, and it is furious.

'I don't understand,' I whispered.

Dreaming Bear lay back, covering his eyes with one large hand. 'What don't you understand?'

'How something so beautiful, so pure, can be so full of anger.'

'As Icarus found out, the sun may be beautiful, but she will burn your wings if you fly too high.'

I stepped outside, letting the night air soothe me. The sound of drums rose and fell on the wind, the voices of the tribes like exotic birdsong. I stood there, one man in the heart of the buffalo nation. I closed my eyes and heard Dreaming Bear preparing for sleep, reciting the Lakota prayer he said every night. Now I said it with him, every word full of meaning, finding rhythm as the night music played:

> *Wakan Tanka,* Great Mystery,
> teach me how to trust
> my heart,
> my mind,
> my intuition,
> my inner knowing,
> the senses of my body,
> the blessings of my spirit.
>
> Teach me to trust these things
> so that I may enter my Sacred Space
> and love beyond my fear,
> and thus Walk in Beauty
> with the passing of each glorious sun.

The darkness was brought to life around me by the flicker-flashes of the camp-fires. I turned in a full circle, sensing the world and everything in it as a circle where everything returns to its natural point. When I looked at Luther Big Crow's hut—where Mia was born ... where it all began—I saw nothing but its crude shape and a single candle stuttering behind the broken shutters of one window. This triggered the memory: Mia's fairy tale house in the woods, the wind chimes floating like angels, the candlelight flickering in the windows ...

Standing before me, her dangerous smile.

Now I've got you. Now you're mine.

The raindrops running down her body like tears.

*   *   *

Her voice woke me. My eyes snapped open and I expected to see her floating above me, or feel her body next to mine. I held myself on the verge of a scream, searching the shadows cast by the low-burning fire. Mia was not there, except she was; I could feel her, and can feel her still as I sit writing this entry. She is out there. The time has come.

I rolled over, shaking Dreaming Bear awake.

'Dreaming Bear, wake up. She's here. It's time.'

He opened one eye. 'What ... now?'

I looked out into the night, hearing the thunder of drums, the thunder of my heart.

'Yeah,' I said to him. 'Right now.'

5

When it comes time to die, be not like those whose hearts are filled with the fear of death, so when their time comes they weep and pray for a little more time to live their lives over again in a different way. Sing your death song, and die like a hero going home.

—Chief Aupumut, Mohican

He appeared in my dream as a vibrant body of light, a *feeling*, and although he had no shape I knew he was a man and that he was coming to us. I knew his name and I knew his purpose. There was about this light a suggestion of character, a glimpse of the color of his heart. But what I felt most strongly was his connection with *Ptesan-Wi*. This stranger—faceless in my dream—was *meant* to come, and his purpose was to bring us a miracle. It would trail him as the shadow trails the running fawn.

Not all my dreams come true, but this one has. I have witnessed the miracle and I want to tell you about it. About her. She wears the purest white and she is more beauty than you have the mind to imagine, *kola*. When she moves her feet do not touch the ground. She casts no shadow.

Here, then, I will do my best to honor my friend and tell you about the night that *Ptesan-Wi* came again to our people. You will learn about the birth of a new star and the rebirth of a proud nation, so that you may hear the song of its people and feel the brightness of its color.

My name is Joseph Dreaming Bear, and I want to tell you about a miracle.

*   *   *

"Can you feel her?" Scott No Fingers said to me. There was about him a fear I could almost smell. Certainly its light was cold and when he touched my arm I could feel his animal-trembling. It was too dark in the tipi to see his expression; I had just woken and my eyes needed time to adjust, but I didn't need to see him to know that his lips would be trembling and his skin would be pale despite the sunshine he had seen since coming to the rez.

I wrapped my hand around his. "Be brave," I said.

"Can you *feel* her?"

I could. It was like the heartbeat of someone you hold close.

"Can you *hear* her?" he asked.

Drums ... the charge of a thousand buffalo.

"Be brave, *kola*," I said again. I stood and walked outside, leaving Scott inside the tipi, his animal-trembling a sad white shape in its dimness. I could see eyes of light opening across the plains: torches being lighted, car headlights staring blindly, fires being rekindled. I could hear the excitement building. The people knew that the time had come. They had been lured from their dreams, from their tents. They had heard the buffalo charging. *Ptesan-Wi* was here.

I saw the first shooting star then. It swept a blazing arc across the darkness, leaving a trail that shimmered in the air like smoke. Another burning star followed it, then another. Even as I watched, the night seemed to relinquish its hold on the planets. They broke loose in amazing clusters, shooting from east to west in dizzying displays. I was held to the ground as the tree is held. It was like one of my dreams.

"Are the stars dancing?" a dusty voice asked from somewhere in the darkness.

I looked and was just able to discern Luther Big Crow's stooped shape in the fire's dying light. He seemed to have his head turned skyward, and I wondered if the shooting stars left their trails in the gray world of his blindness.

"It's beautiful," I said.

He nodded. "The heavens moved like this when Mia was born. It is a sign of *Wakan Tanka's* great pride. She is here, Dreaming Bear. Yes, she has returned to us, and when you see her you will truly see beauty."

More lights flickered into life around us. The voices of the tribes—the Oglala and those visiting our home—became a chorus, growing louder as they left their shacks and tents and made their way to where we had posted the medicine-tipi.

"It is time," Luther Big Crow said.

Scott came out of the tipi, clasping his hands to his chest like a mime artist performing heartbreak. He looked at the night and his body seemed to surrender to its wonder. When he had seen enough—or too much—his eyes met mine. I saw the stars and the firelight reflected there. It brought his face to life.

"Are you ready?" I asked him.

He let out a heavy breath and pulled his shoulders square. I realized he was clutching his chest to keep his hands from trembling.

"*Hoka hey,*" he said, his voice as feeble as Big Crow's.

I could not look at him. The racing stars filled my eyes, like excited children.

"Let's go, *kola,*" I said.

*   *   *

We walked the quarter-mile to the medicine-tipi, following the trail of stars to the west. The going was hard and slow because of Big Crow's years. He needed to stop and rest every few minutes, dragging in whispery breaths and leaning on me, muttering dry prayers. The darkness slowed us further. Scott No Fingers and I had our night-eyes and the burning torches of the people around us offered some illumination, but we still had to pick our way with care. The prairie is a wild land marked with dips and rises and we tried to find a route that was kind to Big Crow. Both Scott and I offered to support him as we walked, but he said that he must walk alone.

"I may be slow, but I'm proud with it," he groaned. "And there's no hurry, they're not going to start without us."

The activity of the stars had been reduced to occasional strips of light by the time we saw the circle of burning torches. Big Crow stopped and raised his head. He reached out with one hand, not for support, but to gain a sense of what lay ahead. His pale eyes made darting movements, as if he could see everything. The crowd that had gathered around the medicine-tipi was impressive. It appeared to swell and surge like the sea, and the torches gave the darkness a warm tinge. Tribal flags waved in flickering colors, like a rainbow broken into squares. I could see children playing, women of different tribes holding hands, and men dancing in full native attire. Others were praying, some on their knees, and some with their arms thrown wide.

They sang with one voice: rhythmic and beautiful. And behind this—in perfect time—was the heartbeat of the land ... the charging of the buffalo.

"We have waited for this moment for two thousand years," Big Crow said. "How I envy your eyes on this great night, Dreaming Bear, to see White Buffalo Calf Woman. Still, my heart is more alive than it has ever been."

We approached the crowd—it was easily ten thousand strong—and a respectful hush descended. The dancing and singing ceased, and all faces were turned toward us. We walked in a direct line toward the medicine-tipi. Big Crow inched along, guided only by the vibration in the land. Beside him, Scott walked with his head high, and I could see the fine threads of his tears. I told him he looked like a warrior. He smiled bravely, but his fear was a bright cloud hanging over him, like the bronzed, smoky air hanging over the crowd. They parted as we approached, creating a wide pathway to the large, colorful tipi, in the center of which stood an *owanka wakan*—a sacred altar. The *chanunpa* had been placed on top of this, brought down from Green Grass on the Cheyenne River Reservation by its keeper, Arvol Looking Horse. He stood to one side of the *owanka wakan*, waiting ... just as everyone was waiting.

We slowly crossed the last few yards, and the only sounds to be heard were Big Crow's broken breaths, and the thunder-buffalo sound of the world's heartbeat. It was like a great machine warming, or like power gathering momentum.

The last shooting star blazed across the night.

The people's torches offered great warmth to the scene. From the sky our circle would look like a huge eye set in the dark face of the land.

We finally reached the medicine-tipi. Arvol Looking Horse embraced Big Crow and guided him to the *owanka wakan*, where he dropped to his knees and whispered a prayer. I followed him, stooping on one knee on the red earth. My prayer was softly spoken: words of thanks to *Wakan Tanka*, and a blessing for Scott No Fingers, who was walking brave despite his fear. We turned to the gathering. So many faces, merging with the shimmering torchlight as the circle arced away from us. I could see fear, and happiness, and expectation. But most of all, I could see love. Many were praying, while others wept with emotion. I saw AIM leader Stephen Pourier kiss his baby granddaughter, who was pointing at the stars as if it were the first time she had seen them. On the other side of the circle, a red man with a pale face dipped sweet grass into water and sprinkled it over his half-naked body, purifying himself for the event. A woman close to him was praying on her knees. Her braided hair was tied with a strip of bleached animal's fur, in the style of *Ptesan-Wi*.

I was so adrift in the sea of faces that I did not feel Scott pulling my shirtsleeve—not until it became more urgent, causing me to lose balance and stumble into him. I looked at his pale face, beaded with perspiration and tears.

"She's close," he said. "I can feel her." He patted the left side of his chest. "Right here."

It occurred to me that I could feel her, too—and in the same place. I looked at Big Crow and Looking Horse, about to tell them that *Ptesan-Wi* was close, but I didn't need to. They already knew; both were holding their hearts.

As I looked around the colorful circle, I could see that *everybody* was clutching the left side of his or her chest, feeling *Ptesan-Wi*: ten thousand hearts beating with something new, something holy. A murmur of excitement rippled through the shape. Many of them cried out, unable to contain their emotion. Two thousand years of waiting, from a time when the red man ran only with the land—long before Columbus, when the world was beautiful because it was simple.

Two thousand years.

Scott No Fingers stepped forward. "She's here," he said.

The people gathered at the western rim of the circle started to fall away to the left and right, creating a wide pathway as they had when we came in. A collective sigh was lifted on the air as the first of them caught sight of White Buffalo Calf Woman. My eyes are good, but I could not see her; there were too many people moving aside or falling to their knees, and the torchlight created tricks of shadow and light, making it difficult to determine what was real.

I asked Scott if he could see her. He drummed the left side of his chest and shook his head. The sigh of the crowd swelled and the circle started to change shape, breaking apart and reforming as people moved to get a better view. The respectful hush was replaced by an enthusiasm of sound—steady drumbeats and tribal song and prayer: the voice of a nation calling out.

Arvol Looking Horse pointed. His lips were trembling and there were tears of pride in his eyes. "There," he said. "*Ptesan-Wi.* It's really her."

"Mia," Scott said, still holding his heart. I could tell that he was fighting to stand brave.

Luther Big Crow's weathered face became bright. His tears ran into his smile and he opened his arms.

"Does she still float softly, Dreaming Bear?" he asked, and his voice seemed strong now. Indeed, he was standing straighter than he had for many years.

"She does," I told him, placing a hand on his shoulder. I felt warm tears seeping from my eyes. *Be brave, kola,* I thought, and then wiped away the tears and looked at White Buffalo Calf Woman.

She floated down the pathway that had been made for her. It may have been that her white buckskin dress shimmered and flowed, but it appeared, as in the legend, that her feet did not touch the ground.

I felt Scott's hand on my arm but couldn't look at him. Everything inside me was centered on the beautiful woman floating toward us. She was infused with light—a luminance that made her shimmer, even in the haze and trickery of the torchlight. She entered the circle and the pathway closed behind her. The drumbeats grew louder: an extension of my heartbeat. The tribal songs filled the night and once again I thought about our circle and how it would look if seen from above. There was a subtle adaptation—where it had shifted on the eastern lip for a clearer view, where it had broken and come together again in the west—so that now it was more like a heart-shape ... a heart of fire beating in the body of Mother Earth.

"She's so beautiful," Scott whispered. The color of his fear had paled to the rose-pink of wonder, and his bravery ran through this in powerful veins of red.

"My daughter," Luther Big Crow said.

"Our daughter," Looking Horse added.

She came closer, and I could see that she was indeed floating. Her white dress made the movement of wings. This was Mia Floats Softly as I remembered her as a young man, who taught me how to read and write, who told me to believe in the land and be proud of my home—words I have always remembered, so that even when I finished university and was given the opportunity to find success elsewhere in the country, I chose to return to Pine Ridge, to my home and my people. This was her, but with a prominent difference: her face, while still beautiful, was angled with harshness, and darkness lay under her skin like a strange flush. It was as if she had absorbed the badness she had witnessed as her buffalo shadow crossed the rotten apple of the land. She had become diseased with what she had been trying to destroy. It was in her eyes and the shape of her mouth. It looked like cancer.

This was White Buffalo Calf Woman, a tired but wonderful spirit. This was Mia Floats Softly, all of her anger at the world. This was *Ptesan-Wi*: goodness and wrath combined.

She stopped floating less than ten yards from where we were standing. Her feet swayed to the ground, like a feather when the wind dies. She held up one hand and the drums, the songs, and the prayers were silenced. I noticed that our circle—our heart-shape—had become smaller as the crowd drew in close to the sacred woman.

Our eyes met. It was like sun on a mirror, and I felt a glow of warmth that radiated to the tips of my fingers. This was the power of *Ptesan-Wi*. She looked at Arvol Looking Horse and I heard him sigh as he felt the same rush of energy. She smiled at him, acknowledging his role as keeper of the *chanunpa*, and thanking him. Her gaze moved to Scott No Fingers and stayed with him for a long time. He grabbed my arm and I felt his emotion, powerful and frantic, like a caged eagle. Finally, her gaze shifted to Luther Big Crow, who stood with his arms thrown wide and a gauzy veil of hair hanging over his face. He was blind, but he knew that White Buffalo Calf Woman was looking at him. His chest swelled with pride. It appeared that *he* was floating now.

Her voice was clear and gentle. It filled our heart-shape like running water.

"Come to me, Luther Big Crow," she said.

He nodded, pulling the fan of hair from his face. His tears fell freely as he walked toward her, and he seemed a stronger man than the one who had staggered the quarter-mile here in the dark, breathing hard and muttering prayers to keep going. Now he was more like the proud father who had shown his baby daughter to the stars, and had told her the stories and taught her the lessons that had touched her sacred heart. He went to her with his arms wide, and for many minutes they embraced. He pressed his face against her shoulder and wept the tears of a man who has made the circle of life, and is proud because that circle burns brightly. *Ptesan-Wi* held him in her arms and spoke words only he could hear.

They separated, and Big Crow seemed stronger still. I could see that some of the harshness—the darkness—had gone from *Ptesan-Wi's* face.

"This is Luther Big Crow," she began in her running water voice. "He is a shining light for the Oglala, and a proud father. His heart is as big as this land and it knows only goodness. Those of you with bad thoughts, those of you with darkness coiled inside you like a poisonous snake should look at Luther Big Crow and strive to be like him. Over the last two thousand years I have moved through this world as many things, with many faces, fighting to extinguish the long flames that are burning the beauty of this world. There is much evil. There is much desire. But there are also good people like Luther Big Crow. You must celebrate him and those like him, for it is they, not I, who will one day save this planet."

Voices of agreement cried out around the heart-shape, mine included. I simultaneously punched the air and burst into fresh tears. The drums started again, and the prayers, and the singing. Scott No Fingers was applauding loudly, and Arvol Looking Horse was shuffling in a joyous rabbit-dance.

White Buffalo Calf Woman held up her hand and silence fell again. She took Big Crow's face in her hands, using her thumbs to brush the fine strands of hair behind his ears. She spoke to him, but we all heard her words:

"*Wakan Tanka* took your eyes, Big Crow, to spare you from the sight of the world's deterioration. I look around me now and I see red faces, white faces, black faces, and brown faces: the colors of the buffalo. I see tribes and nations coming together, singing together, and laughing. It is the way *Wakan Tanka* meant it to be, and it is beautiful. A man with a heart as big as yours deserves to see such beauty, Luther Big Crow. This is why I have asked *Wakan Tanka* to bless your eyes with vision once again, and this is why he has said yes."

Big Crow's face fell with wonder and his body shook as White Buffalo Calf Woman leaned close to him and kissed his eyes. The drums started again, and I remembered what Big Crow said to me as we walked out here: *How I envy your eyes on this great night, Dreaming Bear, to see White Buffalo Calf Woman.* Her kiss ended. Her hands fell from his face and he staggered, blinking like a man waking from a long sleep. I could see that they were no longer white and sightless, but deep brown and young again.

"What can you see?" *Ptesan-Wi* asked him.

He shook his head, not breathing, looking at the heart-shape, at the medicine-tipi, looking at Scott No Fingers, at me ... at everything and everyone. Just *looking.* At last he turned—still like a man waking from sleep, not sure if what he is seeing is real or the last fragments of a dream—and looked at *Ptesan-Wi*. He reached out and touched her hair, her face.

"I see ..." he began, blinking huge tears from eyes that could suddenly see everything. "I see the world in the shape of a heart, and at its center there is life and beauty, my daughter, and my mother. I see enough that, if *Wakan Tanka* were to take my eyes again now, I would not complain. I have seen more beauty in ten seconds than most will see in a lifetime. I can go to Great Spirit as a complete man, and walk with him smiling."

Luther Big Crow embraced *Ptesan-Wi* again before returning to the medicine-tipi. He threw his arms around me and squeezed hard (he *was* stronger now), telling me with laughter in his voice that it was good to see me again. He gave Looking Horse a similar hug and whispered words I could not hear. He lowered himself before the *owanka wakan,* the *chanunpa,* and said a loud prayer of thanks. Scott No Fingers helped him up. They shook hands and Big Crow told him, as I have so many times, to be brave.

Silence again. We all turned to *Ptesan-Wi.*

She was looking at Scott.

"*Nabokazunte Nichola,*" she said, using the Lakota, knowing he would understand. And then in English: "Come to me."

He did not move for a long moment. We all waited. The heart-shape was a silent ring of faces, as if all the people knew his story, his struggle, and understood his fear. I looked at him, not surprised to see that some of the warrior had slipped from his stance. He appeared younger than his years.

"You have to go to her, Scott No Fingers," I said.

"I'm so scared," he told me. He even sounded younger than his years.

"I know, but you have come this far. You have to finish your journey."

"I've brought her to you. Isn't that enough?"

"No. Finish your journey, Scott."

"So scared," he said again.

"Go to her as a warrior. Go to her pure, and fear nothing."

He nodded and made the first important step, finding his warrior stance. He took a deep breath, then turned and looked at me. *I'll miss you, little friend,* I thought, and as if he had read my mind he came back and threw his arms around me, just like he did on the day we met. I held him close, feeling his animal-trembling and the storm of his heartbeat. I did not want to let go, but I knew he had a higher purpose. Tears of sadness trickled from my eyes and splashed on his shoulder. He must have felt my trembling, too, because his hold on me got tighter. We let go and looked at each other. I didn't try to hide my tears; I wanted him to see that he was loved.

"Goodbye, Dreaming Bear," he said.

"Goodbye, *kola.*"

He smiled and turned away from me. That was the last time I looked into his eyes.

With the dark trails of my tears on his shoulder, he walked to White Buffalo Calf Woman.

"Hello, Mia," I heard him say.

*   *   *

You can see *Nabokazunte Nichola* most clearly during the summer months, particularly in June when he sits with Na-gah. As summer leans toward fall he will drop lower in the heavens, close to Great Bear. His brightness will dwindle in the months of fall, and by late October he will disappear.

But in June, his glory month, his brightness can take your breath away. I have known him to penetrate cloud and to burn even as the sun rises in the east. There have been nights when I have sat on the roof of my old station wagon and looked at him for hours at a time, telling him what has been happening here on the rez, and sharing my dreams.

But mostly I am silent.

He is a great star, and his story—like Na-gah's—will be told on the Great Plains for many years to come. And the faces of the children will glow when they are told how White Buffalo Calf Woman kissed him, filling the world with the purest light, and turning him into a symbol of hope and bravery ... a star that shines on the road of life, and teaches us to finish our journey.

*   *   *

"This is Scott Hennessey," *Ptesan-Wi* said to the gathering. "He is a man whose good heart has been corrupted by desire. He is a man who has turned to darkness so that he may have that desire fulfilled. Even so, as we all know the child inside us, so his heart knows goodness."

They looked at each other, their lips only inches away.

"And his heart," she said, with the smile that Scott described as dangerous playing at the edges of her mouth. "His heart knows how to love."

She started to walk around him in sunwise circles, and he turned on the spot, so that their gaze was never broken.

"His journey has been long and hard, and he has made it bravely. It is because of him that I have been able to return to you. He listened to my call. He faced his fears and brought me here. I have asked *Wakan Tanka* if we should forgive his acts of darkness, and spare him."

She stopped walking and everything became still, even the crowd. It was like a wild tribal painting—a mural of fantastic depth and color. The flags were languid and the shadows were long and still, as if they had been carved into the land.

"Spare him," I whispered. "He is a good man. Let him live."

Ptesan-Wi glanced at me—little more than a blink, but enough to feel her heat (I had an image of the hunter with darkness in his heart, who had reached to touch her and been reduced to bones and ashes). I gasped and looked away, with new appreciation of Scott's courage.

She returned her gaze to the warrior. Their lips moved together, less than an inch apart.

"*Wakan Tanka* told me that his lesson is too precious to let fade. He told me that *Nabokazunte Nichola* will shine until the end of time. When we know that our hearts have been darkened by desire; when we need strength; when we seek the bravery to finish our journey, we should remember *Nabokazunte Nichola*. He will shine throughout the heavens of the world, in both hemispheres. We should look at him and remember his precious lesson, and let it direct us from the way of darkness and desire, and onto the road of life.

"And we shall be brave.

"And we shall be pure."

Sound returned to the world, not from the crowd, but from the land—from *her*: a vibration, a beating of hearts and drums: the charge of a thousand buffalo. The *tiyospaye* stirred and looked at the ground, and could see that it was moving. Tiny crumbs of red earth were trembling across the surface. Thin cracks and splinters appeared. I closed my eyes and felt Mother Earth's heartbeat. My body shook with each palpitation, and once again I imagined our shape as it would appear from the sky: a burning heart, booming with life.

White Buffalo Calf Woman spoke again:

"When I came to this sacred land two thousand years ago I brought the *chanunpa* with me: the sacred pipe—a symbol of the red man, of his connection with Great Spirit and Mother Earth. Now I bring a second gift: a star called *Nabokazunte Nichola*. As you have learned from the *chanunpa*, so you must learn from this star … and let it take you forward."

With these words she leaned close to Scott No Fingers and kissed him. He had no time to respond. Their lips touched and the world was filled with incredible light. Everything was lost. I could not move. I could not speak. The only sound was the earth's heartbeat.

This is how it feels to die, I thought. *And this is how it feels to be born.* Gradually, the intense light began to wane and the shape of the world returned. I saw the torches first, flickering through the *tiyospaye* like fireflies. I turned around and was able to discern the outline of the medicine-tipi and, moments later, the silhouettes of those closest to me. Arvol Looking Horse and Big Crow were holding each other—proud or afraid, probably both.

The world slowly regained its color, and I could see that everything was the same. *Ptesan-Wi's* kiss was like an explosion that had done no damage.

Except … everything was *not* the same: *Ptesan-Wi* was alone; Scott No Fingers was gone.

"Your new star," she said, and pointed to the heavens. "Your gift from the buffalo nation."

We looked, and there he was: a blazing speck of light in the northern sky. He was at Na-gah's side, in fine company. Together, they looked like the eyes of the universe.

The heart-shape erupted—its long silence broken by cheers and singing, by prayers and drums. I looked at our new star with tears in my eyes and a smile on my face. He was eternal, he was proud.

He was *Nabokazunte Nichola,* and he was beautiful.

*   *   *

White Buffalo Calf Woman stayed with us until daybreak. She talked to the elders of the tribe, to the tribal chairmen and AIM leaders. She told them to *believe,* that when they were feeling dispirited they should remember the new star, and finish their journey.

"Spiritual unity and harmony will return to our people," she said. "And we will flourish, as all new life flourishes."

Nabokazunte Nichola was still shining when she took her leave. I noticed that the harshness had left her face, and once again she was pure and beautiful, having done what she had to … having crossed the rotten apple of the land and returned home. Many people were crying, but they were happy. They made their heart-shape around her, and she floated at its center, white dress streaming, like a lily in the wind.

"*Toksha ake wacinyanktin ktelo,*" she said to the people, to the tribes and nations that had come together to witness this miracle. This means: *I shall see you again.* Then she followed the legend by rolling over on the ground four times.

After one roll she became a black buffalo; the second roll turned her fur brown; after a third she became red; and then, when she had rolled four times, she became the most sacred of all animals: a white buffalo calf.

She stamped the ground, raising its heartbeat, and turned in a circle, regarding the heart-shape. She threw back her mighty head and grunted once in triumph before leaving us again, charging to the west in a cloud of red dust. A pathway was made for her and she ran down it at great speed. We watched until she had disappeared ... until the cloud of dust had dissolved into the horizon and the buffalo-thunder sound had gone from the land.

Even then we did not return to our shacks and tents. We danced and sang as the sun came up and *Nabokazunte Nichola* shone.

One nation.

One love.

It was powwow time.

*   *   *

Two years have passed since that night. It has taken me this long to decide whether or not I should do what Scott No Fingers asked me to and conclude his journal. I didn't think I would; I'm not as good with words as I used to be, and it's not my story, after all. But something important has happened on the rez, something that has *made* it my story.

I want to tell you about it.

*   *   *

"Let's hustle, Charlie. She's gonna blow, man."

I had managed to engage the pregnant cow into the headcatch on my own, which wasn't easy; she was in great discomfort having been in the preparatory stage for more than four hours. The fetus had come around to the upright position, the water sac had ruptured, and contractions were hard and frequent. I couldn't wait any longer. I flicked on the floodlights around the catch and started to move her in. She balked and kicked, I pushed and jostled, and finally she was engaged. I pulled the rope to shut the catch, and positioned the panels around her. This gave her room to lie down and do her thing, and me room to work in. Just as I was beginning to think I would have to assist the delivery on my own, I heard Charlie's truck pull into the yard. I ran out of the calving barn and told him that we were in the Go-Zone.

"This is not a drill, Charlie—move that fat Indian ass!"

He ran as fast as I had ever seen him run, his beer belly swinging and his red face crossed with panic and shame. Not that he had anything to be ashamed of; Charlie has been a rock over the last two years, and the ranch's success is down to him. Things have been good lately—ever since White Buffalo Calf Woman came, in fact. The money that the visitors brought to the ranch before and after the ceremony has allowed us to upgrade our equipment. We bought a headcatch for restraining cows during calving, and built a four-stall calving barn with all the trimmings: insulation, heating, drainage, hot and cold water, and good lighting. Charlie's idea—an expensive one, but it paid off: last year our buffalo gave us three newborns. We kept two for breeding and sold the other. We also invested in a second-day pen, which is an intermediary between the barn and the field, and allows for bonding between the mother and calf. A steady run of visitors has provided the money to buy fresh straw for the barns, to keep them clean and disease-free. We have also bought new pulling chains and handles, disinfectants, lubricants, and a better quality feed.

We've increased the price of admission and put in a gift shop.

Our ranch has produced seven healthy calves this year. We've only had one stillborn due to a traumatic birth (a breech we couldn't reposition). And last week we were gifted with a special birth: a miracle.

"C'mon, Charlie ... we're at DEFCON-1. Let's go, let's go!"

"I'm coming," my little brother panted, his tongue hanging out like a thirsty old hound. "Hold your goddam horses, *ciye.*"

We raced into the barn and saw the cow lying down. Her cervix was fully dilated and the membranous tissue from the expelled water sac was hanging from her vulva. I dropped the pulling chains and handles into a bucket of disinfected water and pulled on my OB gloves. Charlie washed his hands, pulled on his gloves, and went to the cow. He stroked her hindquarters and applied lubricant from a squeeze bottle.

"Calf's in the birth canal," he said, as if I needed to be told. "Man, she's ready to pop."

"I thought I was going to have to take care of this on my own," I said, crouching next to him.

"I haven't missed a birth yet, Joey," Charlie said with a grin. "And I don't intend to. Besides, I have a good feeling about this one ..."

I did, too, but I didn't want to say anything. I didn't want to jinx it.

The cow was making voluntary contractions now, trying to push out the calf. She snorted with pain, one of her front legs pawing at the air as if she were reaching for something to hold on to. I could feel her great body trembling with the effort.

"Okay, sweetie," I said. "You're doing real good. C'mon, now ..."

Charlie applied more lubricant and I mopped the sweat from her hindquarters, using soothing strokes. She grunted loudly, her body jerking, and then we caught our first glimpse of the miracle.

"Am I seeing things?" I gasped. "Pinch me, Charlie."

Sneaking through the membranes of the water sac were the forelegs and nose of a white calf. My heart stopped—I swear it actually stopped running for a moment—and I shook my head like a man who has black spots swimming in his field of vision. I was seeing things, I was sure of it, but then Charlie said:

"She's white. Play that funky music, *ciye*, she's *white!*"

The cow groaned and snorted, shifting to allow for the easiest delivery. More of the forelegs and now the head of the white calf were out in the world, its tiny eyes closed. I gasped, caught my breath and fought back tears. I think Charlie was doing the same.

"C'mon, girl," he said. "You can do it ..."

I uttered a small laugh and looked at Charlie. He looked at me, his eyes misted with disbelief and love. We high-fived, so excited, but we knew it was too early to celebrate.

"C'mon, girl ..."

"Okay, sweetie. You're okay ..."

The cow pushed, groaning, froth bursting from her mouth and nostrils. Now came the difficult part—trying to push the shoulders and chest of the calf through the pelvic girdle (death or injury can occur if the newborn is too large for the pelvic area). We were set to deal with any difficulties should they arise.

And they did arise.

The cow kicked and grunted. We had to tie down one of her legs to keep her from doing damage to herself or the calf. Her body heaved as she pushed, but she couldn't work the shoulders free.

"Get the chains, Joey," Charlie said.

It is better to let the cow deliver without assistance, if possible, but that wasn't going to happen this time; the calf would die if we didn't step in. I took the pulling chains from the bucket and looped them over those tiny, protruding forelegs, sliding them three inches above the ankle joints. I attached the handles and began to 'walk out' the shoulders, gently pulling one leg at a time. The cow's rear end shifted with discomfort and she began to make an odd throaty sound. Steam plumed from her nostrils, her head shook in the catch, and her leg snapped angrily at the rope.

"Okay, girl. Okay, baby," Charlie soothed, squeezing more lubricant around the cow's swollen vulva. "That's it, baby ... that's my girl."

Adrenaline surged through my body. I was sweating—heart slamming. My hands trembled as I clutched the chains, but I had to keep the work delicate. It was like trying to thread a needle while riding a rollercoaster.

"Tell me she's coming," I said to Charlie.

"She's coming," he said. "Slowly but surely. Keep it up, *ciye*."

With great patience, inch by inch, I pulled the calf from between its mother's legs. It lay on the straw, still and wet. Not breathing.

"Not this one," Charlie said. "Please, God ... *please.*"

I took off the chains as Charlie wiped mucus from its nose and mouth. One of its dark eyes opened lazily, as if it were tired and giving up on life so soon. Its mother grunted with exhaustion but fought with the catch, trying to turn so that she could smell and lick her newborn. She sensed that something was wrong. I picked up a piece of straw and tickled the inside of the calf's nostrils, trying to get it to snort and clear its airway. It blinked twice, but did not start breathing.

"Legs," Charlie said.

I nodded, stood, and grabbed the calf by the rear legs, holding it upside-down to get the mucus and fluid from its lungs. Charlie rubbed its chest vigorously.

"We're not going to lose this one," he said. He was close to tears. "You hear me, *ciye?* We're *not* going to lose her."

"I know that," I said, and thought: *Help us, Great Spirit.* Charlie continued to rub its chest and a string of clear liquid ran from one nostril. We gently set down the calf. It was still not breathing.

The mother groaned, shifting in the stall and snatching at the rope. I shook my head, on the verge of despair. The white buffalo calf looked at me. Its eye closed slowly. It was dying.

"*Hey!*" Charlie snapped, seeing that my spirit was fading. "She's not lost, Joey. Get the hose, get it quick, and remember what I told you about the fat lady."

"I don't hear her singing," I said, racing for the hose we use to wash the stalls. I took out my knife, flipped the blade, and cut off a two-foot length. I tossed it to Charlie. He pushed one end of the hose into the calf's left nostril and the other end into his mouth. I crouched next to him, using my large hand to cover the calf's open nostril and mouth.

Charlie began to breathe for the calf: one respiration every five seconds.

"Breathe," I whispered. "You can do it, sweetheart."

Charlie's face glowed as he worked. His shoulders rose and fell.

"Don't break my heart," he said.

Another slow respiration. I prayed to all the Gods. I prayed to *Ptesan-Wi* and *Nabokazunte Nichola*.

"This time ..." Charlie breathed again, and my prayers were answered: the white buffalo calf spluttered. Eyes blinking, suddenly alive, it started to breathe.

I clenched my fists triumphantly as Charlie pulled out the hose. "That's my girl," he said, and kissed the calf. "Joey—the headcatch, man."

"Yeah ... right." Feeling dazed, drunk with emotion, I staggered to the front of the stall and threw the gate. The cow immediately turned and nosed her newborn. Her long tongue drooped out and lapped the sticky white fur.

Charlie was holding out his hand. I shook it, both of us smiling nervously. He reeled me in and we hugged in a clumsy, brotherly way.

"I need a beer, *ciye*," he said.

But I found I couldn't say anything.

*   *   *

We were not in the clear. The first hours are critical—the celebration would have to wait. We were optimistic, however; we hadn't pulled the calf from the threshold of death only to have it die on us three hours later. We had the facilities on hand to ensure that mother and calf were safe and comfortable.

So far—after the initial scare—there have been no problems. The white buffalo calf (we have called her Hope) is six days old and growing quickly. She feeds well, plays with the other calves, and her eyes are incredibly bright: a healthy sign. I find it easy to stop what I am doing and watch her run, the bright sun shimmering on her fantastic white fur. Charlie has called her a gift for the ranch, and she is that, but I think he knows, as we all know, that she is much more. She is a gift for Shining River, for the Pine Ridge Reservation, and for all the Lakota Sioux.

She is life. She is Hope.

She is end times.

Trust me, *kola* ... great things are going to happen here.

*   *   *

Nicholas Black Elk once wrote that the Power of the World works in circles—that even life forms a circle from childhood to childhood. *Ptesan-Wi* called this the Sacred Hoop. It is the road of life. We go round, we start again.

This is how the circle turns: Hope has been born on the rez—a beautiful life created, yet another life has been lost: Luther Big Crow passed away last night. It wasn't cancer that took him, despite his love of cigarettes. It wasn't heart disease or the diabetes that had plagued him for nearly fifty years. It was old age. His clock stopped ticking, and the years didn't matter anymore. In a place where the average life expectancy for males is forty-eight years old, Big Crow defied all odds by hitting eighty-two. He passed peacefully, and painlessly, and with the promise of better days on the rez. I had told him about Hope, and he listened with a child's fascination.

"She is a sign," he managed, needing to concentrate to get every word out. "She is a blessing, bringing hearts together ... a unity of spirit and love."

I stayed with him, holding his dry, frail hand as *Wakan Tanka* freed his wonderful soul. His clear eyes faded to dusty marbles, and a perfect smile touched the lines on his face as he went away.

I kissed his forehead, spoke a Lakota prayer to ease the passage of his spirit to the Great Beyond, and stepped outside to give my tears to the land.

It was a beautiful night. The air was clear and comforting, and a powerful harvest moon shimmered in the dark sky. I found *Nabokazunte Nichola* in the north, a fleck of silver fire with my tears on his shoulder. I reflected on how our life was better with his light shining upon us.

I wiped my eyes and whispered another prayer. *Ota Kte* dragged his way over with his head hanging, knowing that his old master had gone to walk with Great Spirit. I got on my knees and scratched behind one ear as he likes. He gazed at me gratefully, but his eyes were full of sadness.

"Everything's going to be okay," I said to him, but maybe—I think now—I was talking to myself. "Everything's going to be fine."

Ota Kte nuzzled into my chest, resting one paw in my palm in a kind of handshake. I smiled and looked at *Nabokazunte Nichola* once again. I thought about Scott No Fingers, who had been brave and finished his journey ... who had come to Pine Ridge as a broken man, but had left as a warrior.

"I love you, *kola*," I said.

I went back inside, and sat in Big Crow's favorite chair. It looks out on the prairies to the west. When the sun goes down this view is staggering, a golden-red that makes you think there is no color more beautiful and no better place to be. It was too dark to see anything now, but I could wait.

I would sit there … let the circle do its thing. And maybe I would sleep for a while. Maybe I would dream.

Yeah … let the circle turn.

And dream, *kola.* Just dream.

The End

978-0-595-43786-
0-595-43786-9

Printed in the United Kingdom
by Lightning Source UK Ltd.
122763UK00001B/235-315/A